AFTER SILENCE

DOUBLEDAY

NEW YORK LONDON
TORONTO SYDNEY
AUCKLAND

AFTER SILENCE

JONATHAN
CARROLL

PUBLISHED BY DOUBLEDAY
a division of Bantam Doubleday Dell Publishing Group, Inc.
666 Fifth Avenue, New York, New York 10103

DOUBLEDAY and the portrayal of an anchor with a dolphin
are trademarks of Doubleday, a division of
Bantam Doubleday Dell Publishing Group, Inc.

BOOK DESIGN BY CLAIRE NAYLON VACCARO

Library of Congress Cataloging-in-Publication Data
Carroll, Jonathan, 1949–
After silence / Jonathan Carroll.
p. cm.
I. Title.
PS3553.A7646A69 1993   92-12698
813'.54—dc20   CIP

ISBN 0-385-41974-0

FOR
KAROLINE ZACH
GABRIELE FLOSSMANN
KATHLEEN WETS
GERT AHRER
REAL GUARDIAN ANGELS

Many thanks to

MONICA SULLIVAN DAWSON, RN

*who was essential
in helping to bring this book
to the finish line*

"Everything in the world gives us back our own features;
night itself is never dark enough
to keep us from being reflected in it."

E. M. CIORAN, *A Short History of Decay*

PART ONE

A ROSE IN THE THROAT

"With you I am the woman everyone thinks I am."
—*James Salter*

How much does a life weigh? Is it the product of our positive or worthwhile acts, divided by the bad? Or is it only the human body itself, put on a scale—a two-hundred-pound life?

I hold a gun to my son's head. He weighs about one hundred and thirty pounds, the gun no more than two. Another way of thinking about it: My son Lincoln's life weighs only so much as this pistol in my hand. Or the bullet that will kill him? And after the shot will there be no weight?

He is smiling. I am terrified. I'll pull the trigger and he will die, yet he's smiling as if this fatal metal against his head is the finger of a loved one.

Who am I? How can I do this to my own son? Listen—

Mileage meant cloud ears. If it had been a good day, full of long fares and chatty customers, my father often treated me to a meal at Lee's, the Chinese restaurant across the street from our house. Two dollars for the works, including a dish of cloud ear mushrooms on rice. Mom and Dad hated the place and would never go because everything there tasted "like grease pudding." But he was nice enough to trade me the two bucks for a hug and a kiss. I got the best of both deals because I loved hugging my father. Both of my parents were great hug givers, as opposed to many parents who accept them as either their due or a necessary evil of living with children.

I was lucky. My father taught me generosity, how to live with a calm person when you are not, and ventriloquism. He delighted in the art of throwing his voice, of putting words in someone else's mouth.

My mother was just like her maiden name, Ida Dax. Short, up front, no nonsense. To her dismay, my father nicknamed her "Daisy" on one of their first dates and refused to call her anything else. He said both she and her name reminded him of Daisy Duck. You can imagine what he had to do to win her offended, practical young heart after that. But he did, because in spite of her seriousness, she loved to laugh and Stanley Fischer liked nothing more than to make her laugh. Unfortunately, my father was also a man destined to be a mediocre-to-rotten businessman. By the time I became fully aware of him, he had bombed at a large number of jobs, so both he and my mother were satisfied that he'd become the town's only (and thereby "successful") taxi owner. Mama, although shorter-tempered and less forgiving than Dad, was luckily not one who cared very much about wealth or material things. As long as bills were paid, there was suffi- cient food and clothing for the family, and a little was left over for each of our "vices" (my eating Chinese food, their buying a televi- sion set or going to movies every weekend), then life was okay. I cannot remember her ever badgering him for ending up where he did. In retrospect I don't think she was proud of him, but she loved him and considered herself wise for having chosen a man she liked talking to, one who smiled with genuine delight on seeing her every night when he came home.

My childhood memories are rather vague, but that's probably because I was safe and content much of the time. I remember sitting in Lee's Restaurant and looking out the window at our house. I remember playing catch with a Wiffle ball with Dad. When the white ball floated through the air toward me, he made it talk. "Outta my Way! Here comes the Wiffler!"

My father always had time to play, my mother bought only the best colored pencils and paper when she understood how important drawing was to me. They loved me and wanted me to be whole. What more can we ask from another human being?

When my brother Saul was born, I was already twelve years old and more on my parents' side of the fence than his. As a result, he grew up with two parents and an intermediary, rather than a full-fledged brother who gave him noogies or made his life happily miserable. By the time I went to college, Saul was only six and beginning elementary school. It was not until a decade later when he was a teenager and I was working in New York that we developed any kind of relationship.

A writer friend recently published an autobiographical novel that was badly reviewed. She told me, "I'm not angry because it flopped: I'm angry because I used up my childhood on that book."

The idea is amusing, but I find it hard to believe anyone could "use up" their childhood on anything, no matter how old we get. Like some kind of personal Mount Olympus, our youth is where the only gods we ever created live. It is where our imagination and belief were strongest, where we were innocent before turning gullible, then cynical. Whether we remember in detail or only small bits, it is inexhaustible.

Luckily for my father, we lived in a town full of hills. Commuters getting off the train in the evening would take a look at the two-hundred-step staircase up to the town center and plod tiredly over to Dad's black four-door Ford. He knew many of the people by name and, leaning over the top of the car, would greet these rumpled men with a thump on the roof and a "Come on, Frank. Last thing you need now is to climb those stairs."

I often rode with him and was assigned the job of jumping out when we'd arrived and opening the back door for the customer. Sometimes they'd tip me a dime or a quarter, but more than the tip, I enjoyed being there to hear what was said during the ride to their homes. These were successful people, owners of big houses with river views, two cars, sometimes even a tennis court or a swimming pool. I knew their kids from school, but generally they were a snobby, aloof bunch. In contrast, their parents, because they were either tired and in the mood for comfortable small talk or just plain adrift in their well-appointed lives, talked to my father about many surprising things. He was a good listener and at times unusually perceptive. All the way across these years I think, by their remembered silences and nodding heads, that he might have helped some of them with what he said.

Once while home on vacation from college, I was with him when he took a woman named Sally O'Hara from the station. She had a notorious husband who slept with just about any woman in town with a pulse. Unfortunately, Mrs. O'Hara was one of those people who would tell anyone within hearing distance about their problems. That day was no different, but she also said something that stuck in my mind and later shaped my success.

"Stanley, I've decided what I need most in life is a detective of the soul."

My father, who was used to backseat philosophers, knew how to play the straight man.

"Tell me about it, Sally. Maybe I'll get Max here to go into the business."

"It's simple. All you've got to do is track down the people who know the *big* answers, Max. Find the man who can tell us why we're here. There's gotta be someone out there who can. Or the person who can tell me why my husband would rather spend the evening with Barbara Bertrand than me."

I was already doing cartoons for the college newspaper, often using a geometric form I'd created named "Paper Clip" to make zingy comments and complaints about life on campus. They were mildly successful and funny, and the editors allowed me to draw whatever I wanted. But when I returned from that vacation, I gradually began to turn "Paper Clip" into a whole new world.

Before, it had simply been a geometric figure standing in the middle of a drawing with perhaps an object or two nearby that related to the caption. Now that strange character continued on one side of the frame while a new one, a man, appeared on the other. In between them was a large drawing, very realistically rendered. It looked like they were both staring at this "photograph" and commenting on it. The first cartoon with this new format was of the figures looking at a very large hand applying mascara to the lashes of a giant eye. The caption read, "Why do women always open their mouths when they're putting on mascara?" We don't know which one of them is saying it, and there is no response.

I refined as I went along. The photograph part of the cartoon grew more and more realistic, but also more obscure. Sometimes it took a while for the viewer to even comprehend what was shown there. For example, a cigarette butt stuck into a partially eaten doughnut, but I'd gone in so close that seconds went by before you'd figured out what they were. Apparently that became part of the fun of the new "Paper Clip"—people would first decipher the snapshot, then go on to the caption.

Sometimes the two figures would be placed on the same side of the picture, sometimes behind it with only their heads showing, sometimes moving in or out of the frame. They dangled from strings like grade school angels, or sat in seats with their backs to us and looked at the photograph as if it were a movie. They rowed by the picture, jogged across the top and bottom, shot arrows at each other across its face. But always the same format—the two dissimilar figures, the ever more realistic but mysterious photo "between" them.

I thought of Mrs. O'Hara and her "detective of the soul" often because after drawing the new strip some months, I realized what I was trying to do was address some of the cosmic, albeit small, questions she'd wanted her detective to answer. Not that *I* had solutions, but it was clear from the reactions and letters I was receiving that my work was on target more often than not.

.   .   .   .   .

That is who I am. Yes, "Paper Clip" took me right into adulthood, slight celebrity status, and a comfortable life. As a cartoonist, you learn to cut to the bone of language. If three words say it better or funnier than four, great, use three. It would be easy to indulge myself here and ramble on about my various years, but there is really only one important time and that began the day I met Lily and Lincoln Aaron. So I will stop now and fast-forward the story of my life twice: Once to my thirty-eighth year then to my forty-fifth.

Picture a man walking toward the door of the Los Angeles County Museum. He has thick black hair cut short, wears trendy eyeglasses with blue frames, is dressed in weekend clothes—khaki pants, old gray sweater, expensive running shoes. Comfortable and colorless, it is his uniform when he works at home. You think you might have seen him before. You have, because there have been some magazine articles about him. But it is his work that has made him known, not his face or personality. He thinks he has the face of a high school science teacher or a knowledgeable stereo salesman.

It was three weeks after his, *my* thirty-eighth birthday. I had a great job, some money, no girlfriend but that didn't bother me so much. In retrospect it was a time in my life when I was calm and on top of things. I would like to have been married and had children to take to the museum, I would like to have had "Paper Clip" syndicated in more newspapers than it was. But it was certainly possible for both to happen. In retrospect it was a time when the only things I desired from life were not only possible but quite probable.

I saw the Aarons almost as soon as I entered the building. Because her back was to me, my first impression was that the two were brother and sister. Both short, both in jeans and T-shirts. Maybe five foot two or three, Lily was taller than the boy but not by much. Her hair was swept up in a girl's ponytail. They were arguing. She was louder than she knew because her voice, very feminine and adult, carried clear across the lobby to where I was.

"No. First the museum, then lunch."

"But I'm *hungry.*"

"That's too bad. You had your chance before."

Although she turned then and I saw she was attractive, I already had an unpleasant image of her: one of those pretentious, superficial women who drag their kids around to "cul-chah" and force their noses into it like a puppy's into its own shit. I turned away and walked into the exhibition.

I have a nasty, sometimes gothic imagination. Perhaps those are a couple of the requirements needed to be a cartoonist. Whatever, that imagination carried a picture of bitch mother and hungry child around the museum with me that afternoon. I couldn't shake the whine in the boy's voice or the woman's closed eyes when she loudly told him tough luck. Why not just buy him a hot dog, let him wolf it down in five minutes as kids invariably do, and then go to the show? I was no expert, but had had a few girlfriends with children and I'd gotten along pretty well with them. In several cases, better than with their mamas. In my experience, you played a kid like a fish once you have it hooked. Let it run with the line a ways, then reel it slowly back in. You know you've got control; the trick is to finesse the fish into thinking it does.

I had been looking forward to this show for a long time. The title was "Xanadu" and the subject was visionary cities. There were works by artists, architects, designers . . . There were even some by cartoonists like Dave McKean, Massimo Iosa Ghini, and me. I'd been invited to the opening a couple of nights before, but at openings you don't get to look at the work. People push you out into a crowd of beaming piranhas and oglers trying to play it cool but also show off their new dresses, or cut or deal, or sidle up to a movie star. I liked to amble, take notes, and not talk to anyone.

"Hey, Max Fischer! 'Paper Clip,' right?"

Blank-faced, I turned toward the voice. A young couple stood there smiling.

"Hi. How are you?"

"Fine. I don't want to bother you, Max. Only wanted to tell you how much we love your strip. Read every one of them. And we saw your piece here. Terrific! Right, honey?" He looked at his wife, who nodded vigorously.

"Well, thank you very much. That's kind of you."

"It's nothing. Thanks for all you've given *us!*" Both gave shy waves and walked off.

How nice. I stood there watching them disappear into the crowd. "Paper Clip" came so easily that part of me was always vaguely ashamed at my good fortune. Other people worked so hard at what they did but received so little in return. Not to mention those born damned, afflicted, handicapped. Why had my bread fallen butter side up so many years?

Thinking about this when I should've been smiling over the compliment, I came out of my haze on hearing a child's voice say, "You know what really scares me, Mom? Thin statues."

I took a pen out of my pocket and wrote "thin statues" on the palm of my hand, knowing I'd have to use the phrase somewhere in the strip in the future. What would his mom reply to it?

"I know exactly what you mean."

That was enough to make me turn around. Bitch mother and her hungry boy. She saw I was looking at them and directed her next sentence at me.

"Thin statues and thin people. Never trust a thin person. They're either vain or on the run."

"I never thought of it that way."

She scratched her head. "Because this isn't a thin *society*. We put such a premium on it because we've been told to, but then we turn around and enjoy our fat: fat homes, fat meals, fat wardrobes. What kind of car do you buy when you're rich? Rolls-Royce. A small house? Nope. No matter how little money you have, the point is to buy as big as you can afford. Why's that? Because deep in our hearts, we love fat. People come into the restaurant where I work and pretend to like nouvelle cuisine, but they don't. You can see when they look at the bill that they feel cheated having to pay so much for such small servings. That's all nouvelle cuisine is anyway—a clever new way of cheating a customer out of their money's worth. Give 'em a couple of spears of asparagus, artistically arranged, and you can charge more than if you gave them five. Jesus Christ, I talk too much.

"I'm Lily Aaron, and this is my son Lincoln."

"Max Fischer."

As we were shaking hands, the man who'd complimented me a few minutes before returned, holding a catalogue of the show.

"I'm sorry to bother you again, but would you mind signing this? I should've asked before, but I felt kind of funny invading your privacy. Is it okay?" Assuming Lily Aaron was with me, he looked from one to the other, as if asking both of us for permission.

Now, bitch mother or not, there is nothing nicer than being publicly recognized right in front of a pretty woman.

"Sure it's okay. What's your name?"

"Newell Kujbishev."

Listen to our silence after he said that.

"Excuse me?"

"Newell Kujbishev."

I looked helplessly at Lily. She smiled and grew a look on her face that said, "Get out of this one gracefully, big boy."

"I'm afraid you'll have to spell that, Newell."

He did while I slowly took his dictation. Then we shook hands and he walked away. "There goes a man who should be required to wear a name tag at all times."

"Your work is in this show?"

"Yes. I draw the comic strip 'Paper Clip.' "

"I don't know it."

"That's okay."

"Have you heard of the restaurant Crowds and Power on Fairfax?"

"I'm afraid not."

She nodded. "Then we're even. That's where I work."

"Oh."

"Mom, are we going in or what?"

"Yes, sweetie, right now. But would you show us your piece,

Max? I'd like to start that way. Okay, Lincoln? You don't mind, do you?"

The boy shrugged but then, as we moved from the spot, tore off and disappeared around a corner. This didn't seem to faze his mother. He reemerged a couple of minutes later to announce he had found my picture and would lead us there. It was an endearing gesture, pure jealous child. He didn't know what to make of me or his mother's interest, so he'd steal my thunder by finding my work and, in announcing its place in the museum, make it his own. We followed him, chatting as we went.

"Lincoln loves to draw, but mostly battles. Catapults flinging boiling oil, warriors. Every picture has hundreds of arrows flying about. I only wish they weren't always so aggressive. That's why we came today: I'm hoping he'll be inspired by this and start drawing Xanadus, instead of soldiers with cannonball holes in their stomachs."

"But kids like violence. It comes with their territory, don't you think? Isn't it better if he works it out by drawing, rather than if he were to conk someone?"

She shook her head. "Nonsense. That's only the easy way out. Reality is, my kid likes to draw pictures of people getting shot. All the rest is psycho-fluff."

Stung, I averted my eyes. It took a split second to realize she had stopped. "Listen, don't have thin skin. Life's too short and interesting. Don't think what I said was an insult. It wasn't. I'll tell you when I'm insulting you. I'm also wrong a lot and you're allowed to tell me that. A fair trade. I guess that's your picture?"

Before I could catch all these balls she was throwing at me, we came across her son, arms crossed and stern-faced, standing in front of my drawing. His back was to it.

"What do you think, Lincoln?"

"Pretty good. You're sure you did it, you're telling the truth? Swear to God?"

He wore a crisp white T-shirt. Without asking permission from either him or his mother, I took out a black marking pen, pulled him to me, and began drawing on the front of his shirt. He gave a small peep of protest, which I ignored, and I kept going. His mother remained silent.

"What's your favorite part of my picture?"

"I don't know. I can't *see* it from here!" He twisted and fidgeted but not too much. It was plain he loved what was going on. Under my hands he felt like a puppy getting its tummy scratched.

"Doesn't matter. Use your memory. Can't you remember things?" I kept drawing. The pungent smell of felt-tip ink was everywhere.

"Yes, I can remember! Better than you, probably! I like the part where those big buildings are shaking hands."

"Okay, I'm putting that in right now." I stopped a moment and turned to Lily. "Are you angry?"

"Not a bit."

So I let fly. Dancing clocks, birds in top hats, buildings shaking hands. It took a few minutes to complete but both of us had such fun (Lincoln squirming and giggling, me drawing fast) that it seemed no time at all. Sure I was showing off, but come on, it's allowed when you're making a child laugh.

When I was finished, Lincoln pulled the shirt off and held it up in front to see what I'd done. His smile was as wide as a plate. "You're crazy!"

"Think so?"

"Ma, did you *see* this?"

"It's great. Now you've got to take good care of it because Max is famous. You've probably got the only shirt like that in the world."

He looked up at me with big eyes. "Is that true? The only one?"

"I've never decorated a shirt before, so yeah, it's true."

"Cool!"

There were features on both their faces that gave away the fact they were related: thin well-formed noses, long mouths that went straight across with no lift or curl at either corner. When they weren't smiling, although both smiled often, you couldn't read what they were thinking by their expressions.

Lincoln was nine but small for his age and it bothered him. "Were you small when you were my nine, Max?"

"I don't remember, but I'll tell you this—the toughest guy in my town was short and nobody messed with him. *Nobody.* Bobby Hanley."

"What would he do if you did?"

"Pull your ear off." I turned to Lily. "That's true. I once saw Bobby Hanley, who really was the toughest kid in town, almost pull someone's ear off at a basketball game."

"He sounds like a peach."

Lily wore a man's white dress shirt and a long blue linen skirt that came to the top of her ankles. Intricate, beautifully woven leather sandals and toenails that were painted red.

"How come you do your toes but not your fingers?"

"Toenails are funny; painted fingernails are sexy. I don't want anyone getting the wrong idea."

She was full of opinions, and she was glad to tell them to you at the drop of a hat. At first I thought she was pompous and/or a tad screwy because some of her beliefs were unrepentantly black and white, others absurd. All television was bad. Travel was confusing rather than broadening. Gorbachev was a sneak. She believed one should spray house plants with water whenever it rained because they "knew" it was raining outside and longed to be there. She was reading a famous composer's biography but, as with all biographies, preferred reading it last volume to first because it gave her a better picture of the artist.

"It's like that in life—first you meet a person as they are now, then only after you're *interested* in them do you want to know more about their past or their childhood. True?"

Seeing an exhibit with a new person is like doing your homework and listening to the radio at the same time. You want to look, but you also want to make an impression. And remember the child who likes you but is suspicious at the same time. The only work

Lincoln liked was a loony 3-D city street by Red Grooms. The rest of the time the boy kept wandering away for long stretches, or asking his mother if they could leave now.

Contrary to the first impression, I liked the way Lily Aaron handled her son. She paid real attention to the boy, listened carefully to what he said, spoke to him with no condescension in her voice. If one were to hear only that voice, it would sound like she was talking with a friend, someone she cared for but in no way felt superior to.

She was great, but was she married? Committed? I hinted left, right, and center. I prompted unsubtly but none of it got me the answer I sought: Yes, I am married. No, I'm alone now.

"And what does your husband do?" We were sitting in front of a bank of video screens watching Lincoln walk back and forth from one to the other, checking the different action on each. The same film ran on all the screens, only at different speeds: construction workers putting up a skyscraper.

Lily turned and served me a look that had a lot of topspin on it. "You asked that question like you're committing a crime. You're allowed to ask. I'm not married anymore. Lincoln's father hasn't been around for a long time. Rick. Rick Aaron. Rick the Prick." Having said that, she smiled cheerfully. "When it comes to that man, I have no dignity. Only old words apply to him—'rake' or 'scoundrel.' 'Shithead' does very nicely too."

I laughed. She did too.

"I think we have to leave soon, Max. I can tell when Lincoln is getting grouchy."

"Would you like to have lunch together?"

"That's a thought. Wait a minute." She got up and went over to the boy. Squatting next to him, she spoke in a low whispery voice. He stood still, looking straight ahead at the television monitors. Sometimes life narrows to one laser-thin word: yes or no. I watched closely. What if he said no? She was so pretty—

"Okay. But only if we go to Crowds!"

She looked over her shoulder at me and raised an eyebrow.

"That's where I work. He loves to eat there because everyone is his friend. Do you mind?"

Outside I walked with them to their car, an old but beautifully kept Volkswagen Bug. I'd just noticed the black leather seats when inside rose a figure that took up the entire back seat.

"Is that a dog or a Bulgarian?"

"That's Cobb. He's a greyhound."

Lily unlocked the door and the giant dog slowly leaned his thin head out. His face was graying and he had the calm faded brown eyes of an old boy. He looked at me philosophically and then stuck his long tongue out for no apparent reason.

"He likes you. That's his way of blowing you a kiss."

"Really? Can I pet him?"

"No. He doesn't like to be touched. Only Lincoln gets away with it. But if he likes you he blows you kisses, like that last one."

"Oh." Can you be interested in a woman while thinking she's nuts at the same time? I guess so.

The dog yawned and his tongue came out even further. It looked like a thick pink belt unraveling.

"How old is he?"

"About ten. He used to be a champion racer, but when greyhounds get too old to run it's not uncommon for their owners to put them down because they're too expensive to care for. That's how we got Cobb. They were going to kill him. Kill him or use him for blood."

"Excuse me?"

"Greyhounds have the richest, best blood of any dog. Veterinarians prefer to use it for transfusions into other dogs, so some people breed them just to take their blood out."

"Is that true?" I looked at the old giant and felt instant pity.

Lily leaned forward and, puckering her lips a few inches from Cobb's black nose, kissed the air between them. The dog looked solemnly at her. "That is the sad truth. You know now how to get to the restaurant?"

"Yes. I'll meet you there." I patted the roof of her car as she slid in. Behind me there was a loud squeal of brakes, then the brute metal crunch of a car accident. I'd barely turned to see where it was when Lily banged the door back open into my side.

"Look out! Where is it?"

"There. Nobody's hurt. Just looks like it's a fender bender."

"You don't know. Lincoln, stay here. Do not move!" She leapt out of the VW and raced across the parking lot.

"But nothing happened." I said out loud to myself.

Lincoln spoke from inside the car. "I know. She always does this. Whenever someone's hurt or there's an accident, she goes and helps. You can't stop her. She always does it."

"Okay, then I guess I'd better go see if I can help too. You stay here, Lincoln. We'll be right back."

"Don't worry. I've done this a million times. She's always helping *somebody* out." He put his small arm around the dog, who, at that moment, looked like a Supreme Court justice.

Across the parking lot a small group of people had gathered around a black Jaguar XKE convertible and a small pickup truck that were bashed together. The driver of the XKE, a thirtyish pregnant woman, was glaring daggers at the truck driver, a young Oriental man in a straw hat. The back of his pickup was filled with gardening tools. From her frown and his "I'm sorry" smile, it was clear the accident had been his fault. Lily stood next to the woman and looked at her worriedly.

"Are you sure you're okay? Sure you don't want me to call an ambulance?"

"No, thank you. Maybe a cop, though. Look at my car, will you? Damnit! That's going to be at least five thousand dollars to fix. I don't even know if it'll drive now."

The Oriental man said something in his own language, and to our surprise, Lily answered him back in it. The pregnant woman and

I looked at each other while the man spoke again, in obvious relief, to Lily.

"He says he's fully insured, or at least I'm pretty sure that's what he's saying. He keeps repeating you shouldn't worry."

"What language is he speaking?"

"Vietnamese."

"Wow, you can speak that?"

"The rudiments. The basics, but I can make out his gist."

Lily took over the whole scene. She got both causer and effected to calm down and go through the necessary steps so that when the police did arrive, there would be nothing for them to do. Both the woman and the Vietnamese fellow were so grateful for her help that they couldn't stop thanking her. She had nicely and efficiently taken the venom out of their situation and helped when she had no stake in the matter. How often does someone like that happen along?

"Well, Max, now I'm really hungry. How about you?"

"That was very nice to do for them."

"You know, it was. But I'm angry at myself for knowing it. I'd love to reach a point in life where I do things like that for others but don't even know I'm doing them, much less know it's a nice gesture. *That's* progress. Wouldn't it be great?

"Do you read mystery novels?"

"Mysteries? I don't know, sometimes." I was beginning to learn her abrupt topic shifts weren't so abrupt—they invariably arced back on themselves but you had to get used to the strange angles at which they turned.

She went on. "I don't. Too misleading. People buy them for the twists and turns and whodunits, but not me. Life is complicated enough—figure *it* out. You don't need mystery novels or crossword puzzles to keep you busy. Also, those stories imply people are confused because there's no Good or Bad. Nonsense—we can recognize the difference. Most of the time we know damn well what's good and bad, right and wrong. We just choose not to act on it. What I did back there *was* right—but only what anyone should do in that sort of situation. That's why I deserve no credit."

"Okay, but it *was* kind."

She shook her head. "I don't like living in a world where 'correct' is so rare that it becomes 'kind.' "

There is a terrific story in my family that needs telling here. My grandmother was a dangerously bad driver. Particularly because she drove so slowly, no one wanted to ride in an automobile with her when she was at the wheel. Once my grandfather was in the hospital for a minor operation. On the day of his release, his wife went to get him in their car. Still wearing pajamas and bathrobe, he was helped into the back seat. Grandma set off for home at her customary crawl. Usually so vocal about her driving, Grandpa lay in back absolutely silent. She thought it was because he was still suffering from the operation. But his silence was disconcerting. Once in a while, without looking in the rearview, she would ask him if he was all right. "Yes, but speed it up a little, willya?" "All right, dear." Then she continued at her fifteen miles an hour. Halfway home she stopped at a red light. It changed and a few minutes later she again asked if he was okay. No answer. She asked again. No answer. Concerned, she looked in the mirror. No Grandpa. Horrified he'd fallen out, she stopped the car in the middle of the street to look for him. No Grandpa. Since she was close to home, she drove there to call the cops to find her poor ill husband. Guess who was sitting on the porch at home waiting for her. Guess who'd gotten out at that red light, hailed a cab in his pajamas . . .

Lily had a great sense of humor but I don't think she ever really got the funny in that story because she drove like my grandmother.

Following her to the restaurant that first day, I got the feeling something was seriously wrong with her car. Like the hand brake was full on, or the engine had fallen out and she was pushing with her feet. Little things like that. She called it cautious driving, I called it coronary driving. It had to be against the law to drive as slowly as this woman did. I couldn't believe she wasn't pulling my leg. But she wasn't—this was her, and from that day on there was no way I could convince her to speed it up. When I drove the car, she was perfectly content at whatever speed I chose. But when Lady Lily herself was at the wheel, you went back to the days of the bullock cart. Only she held a gearshift knob instead of reins.

On the ride over, Cobb stared out their rear window at me. He resembled one of those giant stone heads on Easter Island. Once in a while Lincoln turned and gave a small wave, but until we reached the place it was mostly the old dog and me eyeballing each other through crosstown L.A. traffic.

I didn't know them, but I liked both very much already. Lily was smart and talked too much. I imagined waking with her, the greyhound taking up half the bed. Lincoln would come in sleepily and sit on a corner warmed by sun falling across blue blankets. What did she look like in the morning? What did they think of me? Would I see them again after today, or would something happen to spoil it and make it go away? I was a romantic and believed in instant recognition, instant affinity. Why *couldn't* this happen? I'd had luck before and therefore faith that it wasn't a one-time thing.

From the outside, Crowds and Power was so low-key and cool that I first mistook it for a warehouse. Then a parking attendant hurried over to Lily's car and I knew this must be the place. A warehouse manned by parking attendants. It was blue-gray cinder block, and only when you looked closely did you see the small salmon-colored neon sign saying the name of the restaurant. I have nothing against subtle or cool, but in L.A. they try so hard to cool you right into oblivion that it is often both noisome and silly at the same time.

"Here we are, Max. What do you think?"

"It's hard to tell it's a restaurant. No big, uh, fanfare or any-thing."

"Well, you should have seen it last month! No face is better than what we had. Wait'll you meet Ibrahim. Come on."

The parking attendant jogged back to us and I saw he was Oriental. Lily said something in what sounded like the same language she'd used earlier at the museum. The two of them smiled.

"Max, this is Ky."

"Hi, Ky."

"Hello, Paper Clip. Hello, Max Fish-ah."

"You know me?"

"Ky knows everyone famous in L.A. That's his way of studying to be an American. Right, Ky?"

"This is right. I do not understand your cartoon but you are famous, so it must be very good. Congratulations." He bowed deeply and took my car without another word.

"What's with him?" We walked toward the restaurant.

"Just what I said. Ky's Vietnamese and wants the green card here. He thinks America will like him more if he memorizes its famous people."

"That's the oddest thing I've heard today."

"Not so odd. What's more important in America than being famous? Famous is best, notorious is second best. Come on."

The moment she opened the door, the voice spat out like a zap of static electricity, sharp and crackling with speed and random inflections.

"You think you're a skyscraper, Ibrahim. You think you got a World Trade Center imagination. Forget it. You've got one floor, ace. A molehill. You've got a strong antenna, Ib, but all the stations're coming in jammed. What *you've* got is enthusiasm and money; they can only buy you *material.* Popcorn and oil, but no heat to cook it up. Gays are supposed to have *taste,* man. Arabs have money, gays have taste! Thank God you've got me."

The speaker was short, dark, and handsome. He might've been an actor in an ethnic movie about Brooklyn neighborhoods or Italian immigrants. But because he was so short and spoke so fast he also sounded like a stand-up comic who told cruel funny stories about his family and himself. He was scolding another dark man, much taller and rounder, with an unmistakably Arab face. This bigger one wore a wonderful expression—a combination of love and shame and enjoyment in one. He listened carefully. By the look in his eye some of what was said registered, but mostly he was just happy to be near his haranguer.

"Oh, Gus, put a cap on it," Lily said, and walked straight up to them. The little guy swiveled on his heel like he'd been challenged to a gunfight. The Arab stood where he was but his face glowed even more happily.

"Hollow, Lily! It is your day off. Why are you here?"

"Hi, Ibrahim. I brought a friend to see the place. Max Fischer, this is my boss, Ibrahim Safid, and his partner, Gus Duveen."

Ibrahim threw both arms up over his head. "Hollow, Mox!"

Gus scowled and said disgustedly, *"Max,* not Mox. How are we ever going to get the fucking camel out of you? How're you doing, Max? Hi, Lil, Finky Linky."

Lincoln stepped forward and took Gus's hand. "We went to the museum and saw a car accident."

"Probably a *happening* in the museum and some art school geek got a goddamned *grant* to do it."

Lincoln looked puzzled. "Whaaaat?"

"Forget it. Lily, guess what. Ibrahim wants to re-dec-o-rate." He turned to me. "My partner is passionate about two things—me and this restaurant. Once he knew he had me, he started wooing this place into becoming famous. He gives it whatever it wants—face lifts, hair transplants, tummy tucks . . . In the last two years it has had three entirely different decors, but now we have reached the end.

"I promise you, Ibrahim, if you change this restaurant again I'm leaving. I will not share a bathroom mirror any longer with a man who has no faith in his own judgments. I don't care if you can afford it." Narrowing his eyes, Gus gave his lover a look that would have made Medusa look away.

"Stop it, Ignaz. Fight when you're at home."

Later, Lily told me she called them Ignaz and Krazy Kat because they were both so much like the characters in the famous comic strip: Duveen never stopped throwing "bricks," while Ibrahim never stopped looking at him with love or, when he was really mad at the other, absolute affection.

Luckily there weren't many people in the restaurant, so Gus's blast wasn't heard by many. Those who did looked up and calmly down. I got the feeling they'd heard it before but paid it no mind.

"Who's cooking today, Ibrahim?"

"Foof."

"Oh good! You can eat anything, Max. Foof is cooking."

"Foof? Great. Who's Foof?"

"Ky's girlfriend. They met at the Immigration Bureau and have been living together ever since. She alternates cooking with Mabdean."

"Mabdean?"

"Mabdean Kessack. He's from Cameroon."

"Very good at vegetables. But he does not like meat, so it is a bad idea to order it on a day he is in the kitchen," said Ibrahim, hirer and boss of meat-hating Mabdean.

Mabdean lived with Alberta Band, one of two waitresses at Crowds and Power. The other being her sister Sullivan, who, in *her* off-hours, performed with the infamous theater group Swift Swigger. Want more? These Band women were the daughters of none other than Vincent Band, the revolutionary/suspected murderer/bank robber extraordinaire of the 1960s, who is serving out his life sentences in San Quentin prison but may be due for parole any day now. According to the Bands, Father would eat the world alive if and when he ever got out.

We finally ate lunch, but what did we have? What was said at the table? Did I speak? The restaurant was a fire storm of energy, tempers, goings-on. Customers knew each other, food came when you weren't expecting it. Foof the cook appeared wearing a chef's hat and a T-shirt saying "Butthole Surfers." It pictured two circus clowns giving the finger.

Generally speaking, people either loved this restaurant or never came back after one invariably raucous meal there. The food was delicious, the rest depended on one's sense of theater or, too often, theater of the absurd.

Ibrahim Safid came to L.A. years before as an exchange student from Saru, one of those small Middle Eastern countries that have a hundred times more oil than citizens. He came to study economics with the intention of returning home one day and injecting some Western know-how into a land rich in natural resources and old wisdom but not much twentieth century. Instead, he became addicted to everything California and stayed. His father was rich and indulgent, so when his only son said he wanted to live in America and open a men's clothing store, Dad supplied the money. The store did well but Ibrahim grew bored and sold it. About this time he met Gus, who was working as a waiter at a swank restaurant in Beverly Hills. After they'd been together some time they decided to open their own place.

From the beginning it had been called Crowds and Power, and whatever else you might say about the restaurant, the food was good. Ibrahim had a knack for hiring cooks. He was also a neophiliac. *Neo,* not necro: things constantly had to be new. Paint the place, change the furniture, the cuisine. The most dreaded word off his lips was "redecorate" and the people who worked there heard it very often. Not that he was looking to improve or refine either. It didn't matter to him if the avocado soup was perfect, the walls a wonderful blue, or that the strange high-tech cutlery made people smile and heft the pieces in their hands like delighted children with new toys. Out with the old. Out! Out! Out! What was exasperating was that the man was often right. Los Angelenos love change. The more Ibrahim changed the style, the look, the dishes at Crowds and Power, the more people came. Lily contended her boss knew what he was doing, no matter how flutterbrained his decisions appeared. Gus insisted his lover had only been lucky. One day he'd change everything again and suddenly they'd be empty "as a nun's cunt" and it would stay that way because even the best customers finally grow tired of never knowing what the hell they're coming to. Krazy Kat Ibrahim listened to Gus and smiled full of love but continued to do it his way.

Lily managed to manage the place. I got the feeling it was because she had the ability to stand back from this melee at the right moments. She wasn't a particularly patient woman, but in her job she knew how to wait till all the information was in before making a judgment.

Everyone there liked and appreciated her, even the misanthropic Gus. You could see in the way people looked at her or asked her opinion that she was special to them, a valued spirit and arbiter who could see all sides and was generally fair with her assessments.

All this in one day. After lunch I walked out into the trombone blast of heat and light and was momentarily stunned. But was it because of what I'd walked into or out of? I had her address and telephone number written in nervous script on the inside of a pack of matches from the restaurant.

When Ky brought my car around, Cobb the greyhound was sitting next to him in the passenger's seat.

"Does he always do that?"

"No! He's very good dog, but sometimes there is a car he likes and he just do it."

"Don't people mind?"

"Yes! Many hate it. Then Ibrahim give them a free meal."

I climbed in and looked at the old boy, who had yet to move, although Ky had opened the door on the other side and was calling for him to come out.

"I have to go home now—if that's okay with you?"

He didn't look at me. I was about to pat his head but remembered Lily saying he didn't like to be touched. After some more time he yawned enormously and slowly stepped down and out.

I drove home with good new smells in the car—greyhound, hope, excitement.

.   .   .   .   .

My friend Mary Poe is the hardest-hearted human being I know. She is a private investigator who specializes in divorce cases. She's also a great fan of "Paper Clip" and on more than one occasion has told me stories from her working life that I've been able to use in the strip. That night while I was working and still basking in the events of the day, she called.

"Max? I've got one for you. I don't know if you can use it but it's funny as hell anyway. This cop I know told me they got a call from a woman who just moved into some ritzy new apartment up off Sunset. Said she was coming out of her place and heard someone calling for help. But the weird thing was, this 'help' was real quiet, you know? Not like HELLLLP! But 'help,' in small letters. So they shoot a squad car over and the woman shows them the apartment. Sure enough, they put their ears to the door and hear it too—a little quiet 'helllp.'

"Bang! They break down the door and charge in. The caller follows them in to see what's up. Nothing in the living room. Nothing in the kitchen. Bingo! Guess what's in the bedroom. A totally naked woman tied down on a brass bed. S&M time, right? Even better, down on the floor next to her is a guy in a Batman suit and he's not moving. Looks like he's maybe dead.

"The skinny is, it turns out these two lovebirds are married. The only thing that gets them hot is for him to tie her down, then get dressed in his Batman costume, climb up on the dresser next to the bed, and jump down on her, screaming 'BAAAATMAAAAN!' Only this time Mr. Romantic missed and cracked his skull on one of the bedposts. He's been lying on the floor more than an hour and wifey's scared he's dead, but embarrassed about being where *she* is, so all she's been doing is calling, 'Help,' but real quietly, hoping only the right kind of person will hear and come."

"Was Batman dead?"

"Nope, only a concussion."

"I like it, Mary, but it ain't for the strip. Listen, something else. Do you know a restaurant named Crowds and Power?"

"No."

"Do you owe me a favor?"

"No, Max. You owe me two."

"Oh. How about making it three?"

She sighed. "I'll get a pen and paper."

"No need. I only want you to find out about that restaurant."

"Anyone in particular there?"

"Just a kind of general look-see."

"How come?"

I considered lying to her but what was the point? "I met some-one who works there and I want to know—"

"Very romantic, Max. You meet a woman and immediately want them investigated. What's her name?"

"Lily— No, look, you're right. It's terrible. Forget it. Forget I asked."

"Hey, don't get me wrong—it's not such a bad idea these days. Isn't love wonderful now? You meet someone and get excited, but you can't sleep together because they might have AIDS, and you can't marry them because every other marriage breaks up, and who's supposed to give who flowers now that we're all liberated? . . . Tell me if you do want me to look into it. I always like it when you owe me favors."

"I will. How's Frank?"

"Frank's Frank. He's wrestling this weekend. You wanna go?"

Mary's husband was none other than Frank Cornish, better known as "Tackhead," onetime world wrestling champion. One of Mary's favorite pastimes was going to his matches, sitting ringside and booing him. I'd gone along a few times and spent most of the evenings pulling her back into her seat. One memorable night Tackhead leaned over the ropes, pointed a menacing finger at his wife, and growled, "Dance on my dick, Rat Queen!" At home they watched Preston Sturges films, read science fiction novels, and she bossed him around. Not that he paid any attention. I never fathomed the dynamics of their marriage although we spent a good deal of time together. They fought constantly and openly, and even when they were at peace, it was like the loaded pause between lightning and its slow husband, thunder. Any second now . . .

I had an idea. "Can I have two tickets?"

"Two? Ah-hah, you want to bring Ms. Restaurant?"

"Why not? You can't get more romantic than heavyweight wrestling for a first date."

"It's clever, Max. She'll either be impressed or run screaming. Let's hope she doesn't turn out to be another Norah."

"Amen to that."

My last girlfriend, Norah Silver, was a brilliant, nervous woman who worked as an illustrator for medical textbooks. She loved to travel and we went many places I never would have gone without her. She had surprising stories—she'd gotten close to Mecca; an old boyfriend's pet python got loose in her car and hid somewhere in the dashboard for five days. She was funny and had kept the most endearing child's sense of wonder. Both of which helped her over a natural pessimism about things and the belief life was only a series of atoms and events bumping randomly into each other. I got used to her dark moods and it appeared she got used to my unintended aloofness. For a time, for a few months, we felt the light of the world had fallen on us as a couple and we were readying ourselves for a life together. Or so *I* thought.

Then one night she admitted she'd started seeing a man who flew airplanes. That was how she described him the first time. "He flies airplanes." As if his profession was enough to justify her betrayal. We were in bed, ten minutes beyond love in that drifting no-man's-land where truth has a tendency to float up like mist off the sweat and pleasant emptiness of the act.

Why is sex so often both the beginning and the end of a relationship? What is there about it that gives it such range and versatility? Whether Norah was afraid of getting further involved with me, or her Airplane Man had irresistible qualities I didn't, I honestly couldn't fathom her action, decision, choice . . . whatever it was.

Mary Poe was sure she knew the cause. "She fucked the other guy to see how you'd react. Simple as that. Max, I've known you most of my life and love you, but you act like getting married is the same as lining a plane up to land on an aircraft carrier. Not until everything's perfect can you start going in. But that boat's on water and it's rocking back and forth, man! You can't keep dillydallying, or adjusting your flaps and waiting for the perfect moment before you start down. You've got to do what you can, then go in hoping God and vision will do the rest."

"I believe in sticking to something once you've begun."

"Maybe Norah didn't think you'd begun yet."

"Baloney! There's loyalty and there's trust. We all know what they mean."

Mary put her hand on my head and slid it slowly down to my hot cheek. "I agree, sweetie. It depresses the hell out of me every day in my job. Seeing these greedy people sneaking around, grabbing for as much as they can, but when they get their hands caught in the cookie jar, they start screaming like six-year-olds, 'It wasn't me! I didn't do anything! Wa-wa!' That's what I like about Frank—he's dumb, but he's good and I can trust him. The only other women he sees throw tomatoes at him."

My relationship with Norah spiraled down into two dogs barking at each other through a chain-link fence. It was hopeless. The last time we slept together was the best it had been in months. We talked about that, sadly, until her telephone rang. She grabbed the receiver before the answering machine took it. Listening, she said, "I'll call you back," then chuckled when she heard the other's answer. I got dressed and left. A month later I received a postcard from the Robin Hood Museum in Nottingham, England. On the back was a quote written in her flawless script: "She would've been a good woman

. . . if there had been somebody there to shoot her every minute of her life."

Before I had a chance to invite Lily Aaron to the wrestling matches, she invited me to a birthday party, Lincoln's tenth, to be held at his mother's restaurant. When I asked what sort of present he would like, she said, "A monster. Buy Lincoln any kind of monster and he'll be a happy man."

This was one man I most definitely wanted to be happy, so I set out to find the *ne plus ultra* monster in the city of Los Angeles. I began by going to toy stores and saw attempts that were dumb or only disgusting, but nothing that would bring any genuine delight or surprise to a ten-year-old. A friend tipped me to a place downtown that sold only Japanese robots and monsters. I went and was momentarily tempted to buy a six-foot-tall blowup Godzilla, but that was taking a chance—what if the birthday boy already had a six-foot-tall blowup Godzilla? I could imagine the scene at the restaurant: right in the middle of opening his presents he'd either have to pretend to be pleased or, more like a kid, tell me he already had one. Disaster! This was a strategic purchase, an important moment in the birth of my rapport with his mother. I needed to do it right.

In a pet store I looked hard and excitedly at a gigantic unmoving iguana, but there was already a gigantic Aaron dog to consider and what if the two didn't mix? Sighing, I left the monster and went searching for one with neither heartbeat nor appetite. For an afternoon I tried sketching the world's greatest cartoon ogre, six feet high too and enchased with dripping, oozy gore. But children like to do their own drawings. Besides, what if my idea of horrible was only ho-hum to this boy? Another potential calamity.

It gave me a good excuse to call Lily. Exaggerating here and there to make my search sound both strenuous and goofy, I quickly had her laughing. Although her speaking voice was mid-range, her laugh was high and tinkly.

"Don't be crazy! Just go get him a mask or one of those Beetle-juice figures and he'll be happy."

"I don't want him happy. I want him overwhelmed."

"I like a man with big plans. You were a hit at the restaurant the other day. I've brought people there who think it's a loony bin. But I think you liked it. Anyway, they liked you. Even Gus. I caught him looking at 'Paper Clip' the next day and he's not the kind of man who reads comic strips. Good luck with your monster. I don't know who'll be more excited to see it, Lincoln or me."

Beware the Ide(a)s of Max. It came while I was drawing and struck me as being wonderful but also something that could backfire easily and cause trouble. So I chose to sacrifice surprise for sure success and called Lily again to sound her out. She liked it as much as I did and said if I could pull it off, her son would be thrilled.

Full speed ahead!

I called the pet store that sold the iguana and, after some explaining, was told to call an animal handler who specialized in training creatures for the movies. This handler heard me out, then quoted a price so outrageous that I could easily have bought a small circus for the same amount.

"You've been living with your snakes too long, bud. I think they bit your brain."

He was still cursing when I hung up on him and his price. I called other pet stores and got more numbers and names to contact. Finally the name Willy Snakespeare was mentioned and that's where I found what I was looking for.

California is full of people from the dark side of the moon. Whether it is the climate or the fact it is as far west as you can bring your madness before falling into the ocean, there are species of human cuckoos in the state like no others. Willy Snakespeare was a man who reputedly did nothing but talk and live with two boa constrictors named Laverne and Surly. I was told I could find him on Hollywood Boulevard every day somewhere in the vicinity of the

Frederick's of Hollywood lingerie store. Where or how he lived I never found out in the two days I knew him. I simply drove to the street, parked, and went looking for a man with a beard and snakes draped over his shoulders. It didn't take long. He was at an outdoor newsstand looking at a computer magazine. Only one snake accompanied him, but the way its head hung, it looked like it was reading over his shoulder.

"Are you Willy?"

"I'm Willy. If you want to take a picture, it'll cost you two dollars."

"What if I wanted to hire you and your snakes for an afternoon? How much?"

"Depends on what for. Right off the bat, I'll tell you I don't do no sexy stuff. Don't let the snakes do it neither. 'Cause snakes *know,* you know."

"Know what?"

"Well, I'll tell you. Pigs know. Cats don't. Some dogs do. But snakes know most."

I wondered for a second if he was making some veiled biblical allusion, but there was such a crafty look in his eye that I got the feeling that, to this man, snakes "knew" something infinitely greater. I thought it best to leave that knowledge to him and his slim friends.

"No. I want to hire you to come with them to a boy's birthday party."

It's heartbreaking, the things we forget. Even experiencing them again later—the exact same things—often cannot remind us of their real truth, which is what they were like when we were children. Birthday parties are a good example. Sure, adults put on cute paper hats, scream, "Surprise!" and have a good goofy time. But that is only them being fake children. At a real kid's party, joy goes hand in tightly held hand with greed, true rage, exultation. Winning musical chairs or getting a smaller slice of cake, a dumb present from your most important guest, can lift or drop you off the edge of your small

earth. And most of all what we forget as adults is the dead seriousness of these details. To a child they are neither cute nor trivial, but
rather the crux of those essential days.

They had made the outside of Crowds and Power look like a
big birthday cake. No wonder Lincoln wanted to have his party
there! Ky stood outside wearing a Creature from the Black Lagoon
costume. That shook me.

"Ky, this isn't a costume party, is it?"

"Costume? No. Just me. I am the parking monster. You go like
that."

"Who did the decorating?" I gestured at the restaurant's
façade.

"We all. Last night we come out and do it."

That these many different characters had gathered in the middle
of the night to transform a building into a cake was the nicest thing
I'd heard in a long time.

"He's one lucky boy."

"We are a family. He is our son."

A car arrived and two children jumped out before it had
stopped. Watching them run into the building, I didn't notice the
driver until she was standing near me. It was Kathy Jerome, the
television news commentator.

"I have been hearing about this party for weeks. We couldn't go
on vacation till it was over."

We introduced ourselves and walked in together. It was funny
to hear this famously serious woman say, "Holy shiiiiiit!" when we
saw what had happened to the place. There were giant cobwebs
hanging from the ceiling, aluminum-foil lightning bolts too; what
appeared to be painted flats from horror movies against the walls.
Cobb the greyhound had a Superman cape tied around his shoulders. The Band sisters were dressed as Frankenstein and Dracula,
the sexiest-looking monsters in recent memory. It was all wonderful
and much too much. But I realized the crazy mix had been done for
a purpose—it was like a Spook House at an amusement park, but
one that small children could enter and not be frightened. The ex-

cess in every direction made it comic and tame, not nightmare country. Kids raced by, eating chocolate bats and marzipan rats. The real birthday cake—a monumental haunted house—stood on top of the bar and was one of several centers of attention. Games were held in one corner of the main room, run by Gus Duveen, who was dressed to look like the Wolf Man. Ibrahim dished out food and drinks wearing a high chef's hat and white outfit, his face painted the eerie tinfoil silver of the famous monster in the *Midnight* films.

What I liked most was that the many adults there were having as good a time as their children. The noise and joy were infectious. People danced with their kids to rock-and-roll music, respectable-looking fathers scuttled on all fours across the floor with little ones on their backs in races (all losers got to squirt dads in the face with seltzer bottles). A pizza large as a car tire was brought out to oohs and aahs and quickly set upon by young and old. It was a vegetarian pizza, and when cook Mabdean emerged from the kitchen, he was given a big round of applause.

"What do you think?"

"Oh, hi, Lily! I think it's a hell of a party. Everyone's having a ball."

"Yes, I think so too. Where're your snakes?"

"Coming! They have to have a little fanfare. Why aren't you in costume?"

"Lincoln asked me not to. He was afraid I'd come up with something better than him. That's okay, because I'm not big on dressing up. Come on, let's walk around."

Her company was a compliment. People knew her here, which meant they looked at me with eyes wondering who was I to rate this companion. She was cordial to the guests but not effusive. They were glad to see her; you could tell they wanted her to stay around and chat. But she played the room like a consummate diplomat—a little bit to everyone, a laugh that sounded genuine and perhaps was, then on to the next and "Hi! You made it. That's great!"

Lincoln kept coming over to ask about this and that. He was dressed as a sorcerer in red velvet cape and turban, gold rings and bracelets, elaborately worked leather sandals that swept up at the toes and looked like little gondolas. Today his mother stopped whatever she was doing to listen and advise. Normally she didn't do that. She believed her son should learn proper behavior, to lose some of his child's egotism and learn to wait until it was his turn. Once he made her bend over so he could whisper in her ear. She heard him out and turned to me.

"He wants to know if you got him a present."

"Ma! You didn't have to tellllllll!"

"That's okay. Course I got you a present! But it'll be here in a while. I had to order it and they said it wouldn't be ready till a little later."

That satisfied him and he took off with a girl who was wearing a T-shirt with a head coming out of the stomach, à la the Alien.

"How're you going to do it with the snakes?"

"Wait and see. It's been choreographed to the minute."

Beware the Ide(a)s of . . .

What was *supposed* to have happened was this: Although in his full-getup wrestling togs he looked bigger and meaner than a psychotic's nightmare, Tackhead Frank Cornish liked children very much. Never in a million years would he have wanted to scare them. But as his wife said, Frank is dumb and I'm sure he only wanted the kids at the party to get their money's worth. What we'd planned was for Tackhead to open the door of Crowds and Power and walk nonchalantly in with Willy Snakespeare's roommates, holding one in each hand. Willy fed them two days before, thus guaranteeing they'd be in a post-meal stupor. That was all. The famous wrestler comes in brandishing real live snakes and calls out in a nice friendly voice, "Where's the Birthday Boy?" Finding Lincoln, he hands him the comatose snakes and says, "These guys wanted to come to your party." All the kids get to pet the snakes and ogle Tackhead. It was meant to be a sweet showstopper. Just enough drama to amaze and delight for a few minutes. And when the air cleared, I'd be recognized as the giver and Lincoln would see me with new and loving eyes.

Frank is six foot six and weighs close to three hundred pounds. His shaved head looks like a blacksmith's anvil. Mary says he wears a size 15 shoe. I asked him to wear his wrestling costume because I thought it would look flashy and crazy.

When the door exploded open half an hour later and an outrageous, seismic roar instantly silenced every other noise in the place, I thought for one second: Oh boy, this is better than I hoped! But then again, *I* knew what was happening. Besides, I was an adult. In the doorway, silhouetted by the burn of California light around his enormous form, arms extended, snakes a-dangle, Frank didn't look much like a man, or even a human being. He looked like a shaved bear from Jupiter. A very furious bear. When he howled, "WHERE'S THAT BIRTHDAY BOY?!" and shook the poor snakes so they looked like black lightning bolts, people were already freaking out. If memory serves me right, a woman screamed first, not a child—the classic horror-film "AAAAAAUGH!"

Someone yelled, "Snakes!"

Someone yelled, "He's blocking the way!"

Someone yelled, "Ma-ma!"

Someone yelled, "No, wait! Wait, it's only—" That was me, but there was no holding anything back by then.

Realizing what he'd done, Frank crumpled in the door, but when you're that big, you don't crumple far. He was in the middle of saying something when a chair flew across the room and hit him on the chest. The only effect that had was to make him drop the snakes. Which started all new yelling: "They're on the floor!" "Look out!" "Get out!" "Snaaaaaaakes!"

I didn't know whether to go for the snakes or Frank. I chose Frank. Somewhere in the uproar, Willy Snakespeare shouted, "Leave 'em alone! They don't bite!"

For an instant I saw Lily down on her hands and knees, snake hunting. Thank God her face was lit with laughter. In the midst of that chaos she was laughing!

Others weren't. They were panicking. The birthday party had made many of them hyper, but this shotgun-blast entrance of a real roaring giant and writhing snakes helped push their gas pedals down to the floor, way past their speed limits.

So what could I, the accused, do? First, fight through the mob to the monster from Jupiter and get him the fuck out of there.

I was ten feet from him, arms already outstretched to intercept, when the pain hit. It burst up from the middle of my back and was unimaginable. I staggered, fell to my knees. It went away, returned twice as bad. I tried to wrap my arms around myself to protect from the agony inside, but no way. Part of me was trying to kill the other parts.

I didn't pass out, though there was only black crushing pain. No party, snakes, earth. Only pain and I couldn't breathe and there was no doubt I was dying. Just let me die and this pain'll stop. Let me die because nothing, nothing could be as bad as this.

If only I had been so lucky.

"What is that?"

"That is a kernel of rice, Mr. Fischer. Your stone was about half this big."

"How could something so small hurt so much?"

My question seemed to satisfy the doctor, as if I were a student who had asked the correct question in class. "The places it has to pass through are *very* small. Kidney stones are the most excruciating pain a man can experience. They're the equivalent of birth pains in women."

"Women bear children, we bear rice kernels. And you said I might get them again?"

"They do tend to recur. But you can fight them by drinking water and keeping yourself flushed."

He was a boring man who made himself more of a bore by repeating things constantly in a pontifical voice only his mother or another doctor could have loved.

As a parting gesture, he very dramatically placed the guilty rice on the bedside table and left. The kernel sat next to an art book opened to a poster that stated:

ADMIT NOTHING
BLAME EVERYONE
BE BITTER

I had kept it on that page for two days and would probably leave it there until I left the hospital, despite the fact that almost every visitor insisted the snake debacle hadn't been my fault. Gus said it was an asshole idea, but the result wasn't "really" my fault. Mary Poe split the blame between her husband, herself, and me. "I should've gone along. I *knew* I should have gone and kept an eye on him, but I was selfish. I admit, I wanted to finish my book."

What Lily and Lincoln thought mattered more than anything, and both of them were unanimous in their approval.

"There's this girl I hate, Brooke? I had to invite her 'cause I went to her stupid birthday party. But you know what's really cool? I know she peed in her pants when she saw the snake. Patrick Klinkoff told me."

"Why are you embarrassed, Max? No one was hurt and they have something to talk about. How many kids' parties can you say that about? In ten years they'll still be saying, 'Remember that crazy party where the snakes got loose?' I was scared too for a few minutes, but I loved it. I also haven't laughed so hard in ages. Snakes, wrestlers, monsters . . . Did you see what happened to the birthday cake? Oh God, it was fun!"

It's easy to love people who forgive us. Deep in my secret heart I also thought what had happened at the party was funny, but other parts of me that didn't like to fail and didn't like to be embarrassed felt Max Fischer should go live on the bottom of the ocean with the other creeping creatures. To top it off, falling down in the middle of a disaster I had created was no help. I have been healthy most of my adult life, but have also been haunted by the idea of suddenly collapsing because my body fails or shorts out like an electrical fuse.

Why had this longtime fear actually happened at that party? Were the gods creating the special effects, or had I only overdosed on trying to make a good impression?

No matter what you are there for, hospitals humble a person. Without saying a word they tell you you're older, more fragile, susceptible to things you never imagined possible. You can assume someone died in the bed you occupy. Your backless nightgown covered people who had no hope of ever leaving this final land of long corridors and the small hissing sounds of thick shoes and cart wheels. A day there is waiting for meals and test results. The only thing you can be sure of is there will be old magazines on the table at the end of the corridor. You try to remember where you were on the outside when you read that same magazine three months ago. It makes you inordinately happy to remember it was at a friend's house or the barbershop.

I had a kidney stone. It was excruciating but the doctors knew what to do with it. They shot some kind of rays into my side that broke the thing down and allowed it to pass. Afterward I couldn't get rid of the image of stones in my *body*. It was as if a part of me had slowly but secretly begun the process of dying and returning to primal substances. I was shown a picture on a screen and proudly told, "There it is, that's your stone." I looked because it was proof of me gone bad, defective, terminal. Some essential organ had created it, the way it might normally have cleaned my blood or processed food. How could I do this to me?

·

There are days or weeks in life where so much happens that it can take months, even years to sort out all that has taken place. Two weeks after I met the Aarons, booby-trapped their birthday party, and had a first serious meeting with my own mortality, I sat at home looking out the window at a bird feeder, not much interested in doing anything else. My mind was full of sighs and flimsy thoughts. The book I'd been reading with enthusiasm only days before lay untouched by the bed. For something to do, I cleaned the apart-

ment. Which only added to my dispiritedness because when I'd finished and was looking around, it reminded me of a picture in a
magazine. One of those anonymous, well-kept "homes" you glance
at uninterestedly and flip the page. No personality, no distinction.
Whoever lives there does things in the approved way, owns the right
objects, even develops kidney stones at the statistically correct time
of life. In the hospital, a girl was pointed out who was allegedly
dying of a mysterious unknown disease. People were in awe of this
tragic child. She drew doctors like suitors and made million-dollar
machines work as hard as they could just to keep her alive. I knew it
wasn't her but the disease that made her interesting, but still. Still.

Walking in from collecting the mail one morning, I heard the telephone ring. I wanted to ignore it because of what was in my hand,
but unlike other people, I cannot disregard a ringing phone. It
makes me both excited and uneasy for the same reason—what's
coming from the other end?

I was holding a child's drawing of a smiling man. The picture
included his whole head and neck. In the middle of the neck, looking as if it had been swallowed whole, was a big red rose. Written in
unmistakably adult script at the bottom of the page was: "We agree
we both have a rose in the throat for you." I receive a fair amount of
fan mail, but my first rushing hope was this had come from Lily and
Lincoln. Kid's artwork, grownup's handwriting. What did it mean,
"a rose in the throat"? The phone kept ringing. One thing at a time.

"Max? It's Pop. I've got bad news, son. Mom had a stroke last
night. She's in the hospital in a coma. You think you can come here
and be with us?"

I was on an airplane heading east three hours later. By late
evening I was holding my father's hand in a hospital room very
similar to the one I'd so recently left. Lying still and pale in bed, my
mother already looked dead. The stroke had done something to her
mouth and it gaped open oddly to one side.

It was the third time my father had told me the story of what had happened. I knew it was necessary for him to talk it out as much as he could, so I said nothing.

"We were watching TV. She said, 'Do you want a little snack, honey?' You know her, always wanting to feed you. Then she makes sure you eat every bit. I said no, I'm fine. Then she stuck her hand out like this, like she was pointing at something on TV. I even looked that way, but a second later she fell forward, right off the couch.

"Oh, man. Oh, Max. What am I going to do? If Mama doesn't get better, I don't know . . . I don't function . . . I can't do things right when she's not around. You know how I am, son." He looked at me desperately, as if waiting for me to explain him to himself: explain a way out of the final dilemma that was here now in the form of his too still wife.

"I think she's resting, Pop. She's in there sorting things out and seeing what she needs to do to come back to us. Mom wouldn't leave us in the lurch like this. Hey, listen, you know her—always sets lunch out for us before she'd go anywhere. She's not going to leave now without making sure we're taken care of!"

I meant it as a gentle reassuring joke, but the light in his eyes was suddenly bright and surer. "That's right! Ida never left things undone. She *is* in there, resting up for the next act. That's right. She'll wake up any minute now, yelling for us to take off our shoes."

Inescapable. At some point, life orders us to our parents' seat at the head of the table and suddenly we're responsible for "feeding" them after a lifetime of vice versa. It is a moving and genuinely disconcerting moment, one you can't fully bring into focus until later.

When the doctors spoke to us about Mother's condition and treatment, my father constantly watched my brother or me, as if only we understood and could translate what was being said. In the days we spent there, he never stopped asking, "What do *you* think, guys?" But what did we know that he hadn't already taught us? He was the one who had gone through the Depression and war, the loss of his parents, and nine *thousand* more days of life. Nevertheless, when Saul or I made a decision, he accepted it instantly. We never knew if he agreed, but I got the feeling the loss of his wife had entirely sapped his strength. Like someone who stumbles and starts to fall, *any* steadying arm is welcome. The fact it was his sons' made it easier to grab and hold on. Plus any decision made quickly and with a degree of certainty appeared to reassure him there was still some order and balance in his now teetering world.

He told us many things, both about Mother and about their relationship I'd never heard before. Some of these stories were intensely personal, others boring. What was disconcerting was that all three of us continually referred to her in the past tense. Even the tone of our nostalgia, or the way anecdotes were told, made it sound like the woman wasn't really there anymore; she was half ghost, or ectoplasm, rather than a living Ida Dax Fischer.

"Okay, so enough about your mother and me. What about you, Maxie? Have you got a nice girlfriend these days?"

"I think so, Pop. We only met recently, but so far I like her very much. You have to hear a story, though. She has a ten-year-old son and he had a birthday party the other day . . ." I went on to tell him about the party/snakes/Tackhead because he likes a good story and I thought this would make him laugh. To my disappointed surprise, he only half smiled and asked what had happened to the Aarons when I was done. I said they'd come to the hospital and appeared to have forgiven me, but who knew? Maybe I'd go home and never hear from them again.

"Do you think you'll get married one day?"

"I hope so, Pop. I like the idea of marriage but've never met a woman—"

"Listen to me. I wouldn't say this if your brother was in the room, but you know how I feel about the dragon *he's* married to. I got hitched young and was lucky. Saul got married young and Denise was the biggest mistake of his life. But now Mom's like she is and I feel like my head's cut off. So what does either get you? Know what I mean? If you're lucky, you end up feeling headless. If you're unlucky you got to get into bed for forty years with a monster from hell. I don't know if you can win, Max. Maybe you should stay single and play the field."

"I want to have children, Pop. I'd love to know what it's like to see kids in a sandbox and know they're yours. That must be a hell of a feeling."

"It ends up the same—kids grow up and leave, and you feel like your head's been cut off."

To our amazement and delight, Mother came out of the coma four days later and immediately asked for a screwpound. When asked what a "screwpound" was, she said a vodka and orange juice. With the exception of many of these eerie, funny "offnesses," she returned to full consciousness in decent shape. Her mouth remained crooked, as did many of the things she said, but nothing else was damaged and she was in good spirits.

"How much is the hospital costing?"

"I don't know, Ma, but don't worry about it. Saul and I will pay."

"Then get your father in here to take the other bed. It would be the first vacation we ever had."

My father walked on air. He had always treated her well and with the fullest respect and appreciation, but the return and recovery made her even more special in his eyes. He spoke of her in glowing, reverential terms. He spoke to her in almost a whisper, as if afraid any loud noise might scare her away, back to where she'd been or worse.

She chided him for his obsequiousness, but there was much love in her expression and she insisted on holding his hand whenever he was in the room.

Sitting there, I sketched them again and again. We talked, they held hands, Saul told stories about life in London and the company he worked for there. Although the four of us got together for family reunions once or twice a year, this was totally different. We were all breathing relief, love, and apprehension as one. It warmed the emotional temperature of that room fifty degrees. Mom had almost left us forever, I'd had kidney stones, my father had turned over familial power to us and spoken of marriage, family, and lifetime love as things that killed a person in the end. Perhaps he was right to whisper. Perhaps we all should have.

In my mother's room one afternoon while she slept, I remembered the drawing Lincoln had sent of the man with the flower in his neck. A rose in the throat. Wasn't that what was happening here? Choking on life's good things if they went down the wrong tube, the wrong way? Roses are meant to be seen and smelled, not swallowed. My father's love for Mother turned instantly lethal when he thought she was dying. This way, not that. It made such sense. But what did the Aarons mean in saying it? It was ten in the morning in L.A. There was a telephone in the room but I chose to use the public one out in the hall.

"Hello?"

"Lily? This is Max Fischer."

"Max! I've been waiting for you to call! How are you? How's your mom?"

"Okay. She was in a coma but she's out now and they think she'll be all right. Listen, apropos of nothing, I wanted to ask you something. Remember that drawing Lincoln sent me? The one of the man with the flower in his throat?"

"The rose. Sure I remember—I told him to draw it! Exactly to my specifications."

"Okay, but what does it mean?"

I could literally feel her smile through the telephone.

"Guess."

"Excuse me?"

"You have to guess."

"I've been guessing since I got it, but the only thing I could come up with was depressing."

"No, it's not depressing! That I guarantee you. You know how sometimes you're sitting somewhere and, very faintly, you hear music coming from the next room? You sit forward and cock your ears, trying to make out what it is? After a while you *do,* and you sit back like 'Okay, life can now continue.' That was me, Max. I figured out what music you are to me: you're a rose in my throat. Don't you love mixed metaphors?"

"But it's good?"

"Yes, definitely good. When are you coming back?"

I looked at the door to my mother's room and felt a slap of guilt. Now that she was better I wanted to leave and go back to my life, back to what might happen with Lily Aaron. "Soon, I hope. As soon as they say she'll definitely be all right."

"Let's go bicycle riding when you're here. The three of us."

"Great." I made a mental note to buy a bike the moment I set foot back in Los Angeles.

"Know what I've wanted to do for years? Ride a bicycle around Europe. Not with a backpack or anything. You have a car and you stay in hotels, eat good meals . . . but you have bikes too on top of the car and when you stop in a city or in the mountains, you only ride around or walk. No sightseeing from the car. Can you imagine how beautiful it would be to ride around the Alps?"

"Or Paris? That'd be a dream. Can I come?"

"I don't know. Come home and we'll check you out. Like a job interview—see if you're made of the right stuff."

Before he returned to London, Saul and I had dinner together. Although we have little in common, my brother and I get along very well. He loves business, women, traveling. When he's not working on a giant deal, he's either in bed with a beauty or getting on a plane to some exotic place. Our parents know only that he's successful and sends postcards or bizarre presents from the ends of the earth. His wife, Denise, is a stupid woman who used to be very beautiful before her stupidity and meanspiritedness wore the beauty away. They have no children and she's quite content to live well, spend money, and have an occasional affair when her self-confidence slips. Saul told me all this but says he doesn't care.

When my brother and I chat it's always comfortable because we like each other but wouldn't for the world wish ourselves in the other's shoes.

"What does this Lily look like?"

"Short, long dark fluffy hair. She looks sort of French."

"What's the last name again?"

"Aaron."

"Is she a Jew?"

"I don't know."

"And she's got a son?"

"Yes, he's nice."

"Are you sure you want to get involved with a woman who has a kid just entering puberty? Do you know how to skateboard? Are you ready for Little League?"

"Saul, my brother, fuck you. How many women have *you* been with who had children?"

"Different, very different. You're single. They always knew I was married. They were given that info before anything ever happened, bucko. I never gave any kid a chance to think of me as Papa. But 'cause you're single, the tighter you get with his mom, the more the boy will see you that way. Believe me."

"That may not be so bad either. Instant family. No diapers or teething. He'll probably even like the same videos I do. Didn't you ever want kids? I'm sure Denise wouldn't, but I could see you jiggling a nice little one on your knee."

"I could too, kind of, but then the idea of spending half a lifetime parenting exhausts me. Anyway, Denise would like kids if the only thing they did was serve the drinks and hors d'oeuvres. Other than that, she envisions children as little monsters who'd make her breasts sag and put runs in her silk stockings."

"Do you ever think of divorcing?"

"Seventeen times a day I think of it, Max. But know what stops me? This is going to sound funny coming from me, but we have a life together. That counts for something. I mean yeah, I have a million girlfriends and she's had her share too. Plus she drives me crazy, and I'm not at home enough to make her feel like she's got a full-time husband. But despite that, there is this life we've made together. We like to poke around in the Burlington Arcade, and go to Tottenham soccer games. Denise loves soccer. She's still the best lover I've ever had and . . . I don't know, man. Put all the good together and it counts for something. She can be dubious, but she's my wife *and* my history. She's the only one who knew what it was like 'way back when.' That means something." He talked on and I loved him very much both for what he said and for what he implied. Marriage, even in the most difficult "climate," can be as sturdy and sometimes as beautiful as cactus. Because now and then it surprises you without warning by blossoming into the most delicate, vibrant-colored flowers. "Who cares when a rose blooms, you know? A rose you expect to do what it does. But when a *cactus* flowers and it's gorgeous . . .

"Listen to what happened the other night. I was getting into bed and on my pillow was a slip of paper. It said 'sweet red splendid kissing mouth' in Denise's handwriting. So I called out to her, 'Hey, Den, this is really nice. Did you make it up?' 'No, Swinburne.' *'Swinburne?* You mean the poet? When'd you start reading poetry?' 'I didn't—it was inside the wrapper of one of those Baci candies. Isn't it sweet?' Christ, Max, did I love her more for writing it out and putting it on my pillow, or admitting right off she'd gotten it from a fucking candy wrapper!' "

A woman waiting alone in public has a determined, closed-door look on her face. To men it says, "Yes I'm waiting, but not for you, bub. Go away." To women it gives them the once-over, as if daring them to say something. When a woman is waiting for me I like to watch a moment, unseen, before making contact. Pretend I'm seeing her again for the first time with no prejudice or desire in my thoughts.

Lily was already through the gate, sitting in a blue plastic chair and giving "the look" when I arrived. Luckily I'd called Air France to make sure of the flight time and heard her plane would be arriving forty minutes ahead of schedule. A mad dash in the car down from

St.-Paul-de-Vence and no traffic had made me only a little late. Little enough to take one good look before saying hello.

Her hair was shorter and curlier. Something else was different, but what? I was so glad to see her, so flat-out grateful she'd gone along with my crazy, one-chance-in-a-million idea: Call a woman you hardly know. Ask her to drop her life for a week and fly to the South of France with the ticket you offer. If she wants to bring her son that's fine, but you'd prefer her alone. There is, *was,* a long pause on the other end of the phone, which naturally I take to be the beginning of "No." Instead she asks only one question—"Have you ever done this before with another woman?" And you know she is saying yes once you've said no, you never even thought of doing something so whimsical and hopefully romantic. Before she answers you know your whole life is about to change. God bless her.

Her lips were green. Her lips were *green.*

"Max! At last! What? What's wrong?"

"Lily, are you all right? Your lips are green!"

She gave a little "Oh!" and brought a hand halfway to her mouth. Then the "Oh!" turned into a smile, then a big laugh. "It's my stupid lipstick! That happened once before. It's this special stuff which when you put it on is green, then turns the red which most suits you. But that's right, the last time I put it on and it stayed green, I was nervous too. Oh, Max, isn't that dramatic? I fly all the way to Europe to show you nervous green lips."

Close enough to touch her, I did—hands to her shoulders, friendly, warm, intimate enough. "How're you doing, Lily? How was your flight?" Before she had a chance to say anything, I pulled her to me and gave her a long tight hug. She didn't do anything for a moment, then her hands moved tentatively up my back.

"I didn't know if you'd do that. Maybe that's why my lips were green. Maybe if I'd known you'd hug me right away, they'd have been red as pomegranates!"

Still holding her, I said into her hair, "You came. You goddamned *came!* It'll be great. I promise you we'll have a ball."

She pushed a little away and looked me sternly in the eye. "I

don't need France, Max. And I don't need a good time. I've got lots
to do at home. I came because of you. I came because you asked an
impossible thing that might end up meaning the world. Where are
we staying?"

"St.-Paul-de-Vence. It's about half an hour from here."

"That's where the Colombe d'Or is. Gus said I had to bamboo-
zle you into taking me there for dinner."

"Done. Who is Lincoln with?"

"Ibrahim and Gus till the weekend, then Foof and Ky. He's in
heaven—spoiled rotten for six days. Foof and Ky are taking him to a
Vietnamese wedding."

"You won't be worried about him?"

"Sure I'll be worried, but I gotta get used to it. He's ten now.
God, ten years old. Do you know what he said before I left? 'Are
you going to make love with him, Mom?' My son's now asking who
I'm having sex with."

I laughed. More because of her lips—since I last looked they
had turned a pale pink-red.

"You think that's funny?"

"I think your lips are funny. They've finally changed color."

She touched a finger to them and inspected it. "Don't you want
to hear what I said to Lincoln?"

"That's a dangerous question."

"You know you're dying to know. I told him yes, I'd be sleeping
with you after you've had an AIDS test. Lincoln's very paranoid
about me getting AIDS. He watches too much TV."

I put a hand on her elbow. "I already did. I had a test when I
was in the hospital."

"Me too. I did it there one day when we visited you."

Five steps ahead of me, she turned. I'd stayed planted, stopped
both by the revelation and by the coolness of her answer. Her jaw
dropped open comically and she shrugged. "Hey, you can't have a
romantic week without sex. I knew you'd get a test. You're that kind
of person. That's one of the reasons why I agreed to come. You're
interesting, but you're not nuts. I don't need any more nuts in my

life. Let's go. The only other time I was in France, I got hepatitis and had to go to the hospital."

People take it for granted that most famous beautiful places are ruined because of today's tourism, pollution, greed, land developers . . . but I disagree. If you know beforehand what to expect, they can still be splendid and fulfilling. What our cynical minds ignore is the fact that these spots are famous *because* of their beauty. Certainly some have been ruined over time, but many others are hearty and resilient and stubborn—they don't take kindly to change and resist quite nicely the cheap Day-Glo cosmetics of our age.

After we'd checked in at the hotel I did something I'd rarely done with a woman: as soon as we got to the room and were alone, I took Lily in my arms and brought her to bed. She was willing.

The first time with anyone is often only so-so, even if the relationship later develops into wonder. The newness and nervousness, the will-I/will-she-be-good? worries make it more of an experiment than an experience. But even considering that, Lily made love so ardently and interestingly our first time that when it was over, I looked at her and said, "Zowie." She was all opposites—hard and soft, fast and slow, tender then mean. She kept me off balance most of the time, which enhanced the whole experience incredibly. A kiss was suddenly a bite, then a lick, a nip, a long soft kiss. Her mouth pulled abruptly away, came back in for more, pulled away into a slow erotic smile. She made noise but it was quiet and low, noise meant only for us and no one else. I found myself watching her hands. They twisted and curled, became fists or lay helplessly open. They told the whole story. I was mad for those hands and kept putting my face on them or pulling them to me so I could feel their strength and warmth and smell everything on them. Both of us were on them and our smells were sweat and funk and Kouros cologne that had no chance against the other aromas.

Much later, when we were finished, she went into the bathroom and started the shower. I got up quickly and, going in there, reached around her and turned it off. She dropped her eyebrows and stuck out her bottom lip. "What are you doing?"

"Don't shower yet. I love the idea of your walking around out there with our smells on you. That's one of the best parts, don't you think? World's rarest perfume."

"Okay. That's interesting. Most men I know leap for the bath afterward. It's nice hearing you like the smells, Max. I do too, but I've been sort of brainwashed out of it over the years. You and another man are the only ones I've ever been with who were like that. I think most guys love pussy so long as it's used properly. Take it beyond that and a lot of them get *real* nervous."

"Who was the other man?"

"My ex-huzz, Rick."

"Rick the Prick?"

"The very same. You have a good memory."

"Will you tell me about him?"

"If you want. But it stings, so I can only do it in little bits."

One of those bits came while we were eating. Looking at a slice of cucumber, she wiggled it on her fork and smiled. "You want to hear a Rick Aaron story? I'll tell you one about cucumbers. It just came to me this minute. I haven't thought about it in years. After Rick and I had moved in together—this was in college—we decided it was time I met his parents. He'd warned me about them for months but I thought he was only being careful—you know, didn't want to build up my expectations. They lived a few hours from school, so one Sunday we drove over there, all dressed up, looking like Barbie and Ken dolls. I was supposed to ask his father about their garden first chance I got because Dad was gonzo about garden-ing. We arrived and I was introduced. The family gave me the big once-over, then it was time for Sunday dinner. They put me next to Mr. Aaron, and halfway through soup, I said sweetly, 'I hear you have a beautiful garden, Mr. Aaron. Can I see it after we eat?' "

"He says, 'Wellll, I don't know. Are you having your period?' I was twenty years old, Max. I'd never met this jerk before, but the first thing he asked was *that*. I was speechless. I looked across the table at Rick for help but my hero over there was staring into his soup. *But* the rest of his family were looking at me how-do-you-do and waiting for my answer! 'What does that have to do with your garden, Mr. Aaron?' 'Hah! Pretty darn obvious you don't know much about gardening! Only thing I can tell you is when a menstruating woman gets near cucumber plants it is *pure* death to the cukes. That's all there is to it.' "

The trees were moving yellow around us. There was a glass of milky-white Pernod on the table next to my black eyeglasses. Plates with crisp salad and soft cheeses. My wallet was full of those marvelously large hundred-franc notes they hand you by the bundle in a bank with a small pin in one corner to hold them together. Soon we'd go back to the room and bathe, then get ready for dinner. What would she wear? No matter what, I knew now what she was like beneath her clothes. I knew I would be there again soon and she seemed as eager as I about it. I believe both of us were so happy that first day that it could have been repeated again and again until it was time for us to leave France and we would still have been fully content.

It was the perfect land in which to begin our relationship, because the South of France is one long caress to the senses. Much of what you experience there can fuel a fundamental part of the spirit. For it is the earth, physical life, at its absolute best. That is what the beginning of love is too if you are lucky. I told Lily both "places" are where all the greatest ingredients in the world are found.

I could offer a handful of snapshots or switch on the slide show and bore you with pictures of how happy we were, how much fun we had, but rather than that, there are only two other scenes I must describe.

She loved open-air markets and we often came across them as we drove around that beautiful countryside. Our rented car was soon filled with perfume essences, old linen dresses, dried Provençal herbs and lavender. I loved standing beside Lily watching her sort

through boxes of old French magazines, or rub olive oil on the back
of her hand so she could better distinguish the quality. She taught
me a great deal about food that week and I was both grateful and
eager to learn. She laughed when I told her how her enthusiasm was
so invigorating and different from the attitudes of the women I'd
recently dated (excepting Norah Silver), who rarely took off their
sunglasses to even look at a menu.

" 'Say nothing, act casual,' huh? I'm not very California in that
way, am I? I don't even own a pair of sunglasses."

What was the name of the town? I can see it so well in my
mind's eye. The fast brown river running next to it. The restaurant
on the water where we ate. A historical plaque announcing that
someone like Petrarch had lived there. A big market was being held
when we drove in, so we stopped to eat and browse. The river, the
market, and the main road all ran parallel to each other. Lily and I
separated because she wanted to look at the food, while I discovered
a box of old cartoon books that had me rubbing my hands together.
We agreed to meet at the car in an hour, big kiss, see you later.
Another thing I liked about her—it was no big deal to go your
separate ways a while. More often than not, she was the one who
suggested it when we were someplace but had our eyes on different
directions.

I was so engrossed in the books, the sound of impact and the
howl of the poor animal didn't penetrate my skull for moments.
People started calling to each other and running in the same direction. My French is basic, but I heard 'chien' and "accident." Besides,
the screams were hideous and unmistakable. It was clear what had
happened. I only hoped it was a dog and nothing else.

"Oh pauvre—"

"Il n'est pas mort!"

"Qui est la dame?"

"Sais pas."

There was a crowd huddled in a semicircle over whatever was
on the ground. I came up behind and through their movement saw a
blast of shiny blood, entrails, and the beautiful gleaming black coat

of a young dog. Its rear quarters were crushed across the pavement. Next to it on the ground was Lily. She was shouting in French for something, loud enough to be heard over the screeching death wails of the puppy. She said later she was asking for string, wire—anything she could use to choke. I pushed through and squatted down next to her. The dog moaned and snapped its jaws in a mad shudder and snarl. It kept trying to twist around to its burst rear. Black fur. White frothing mouth. Red. Half its young blood was over my love.

"Max, get rope or string. No, give me your belt!"

I knew what she wanted, why. I slid the belt out but said, "I'll do it, Lily. Get back—it can still bite. It's crazy."

When the dog turned away again, I whipped the belt around its neck and choked it with all my might. What little life was left, it took only seconds. The noises were soft and very short.

"Hard, Max. Hard as you can! Kill it fast. Please kill it now."

Besides the grimness of the scene, what I found remarkable about it, and what kept coming back to me long after it was over, was how she reacted to what had happened. I remembered how she had run to help the pregnant woman in the parking lot the first day we met. She was unquestionably one of those rare good people whose first impulse is to help whenever it's needed, but this was different. Helping is one thing, putting a crazed, dangerous animal out of its misery is another. Pragmatic yet moral, self-sacrificing, a firm good mother, funny, *and* a flame in bed . . . This was it. Lily Aaron was God's gift to me. I knew I must do everything in my power to win her.

There was another scene that happened in France, though the other is a story rather than a scene. A story I told her at the beginning of our flight back to Los Angeles. But on second thought, I will not tell it till later. Let this part end with death and hope. The real possibility of joy. See us looking out a small round airplane window together at the world below. A world that would have been ours, if not for the child.

PART TWO

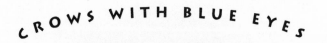

CROWS WITH BLUE EYES

"Why should we import rags and relics into the new hour?"
—*Emerson*

"Mary told me about a couple that went to Thailand for a vacation. They were walking down the street in some town and saw a baby puppy just lying there. It was adorable but had been abandoned and they knew if they didn't save it, it would die. So they took it and somehow snuck it back home with them. Back to America.

"It grew up and was a real cutie—affectionate and sweet. It liked to sit on their laps when they were watching TV. But they also had a cat that the dog hated and was always after. One day the cat disappeared and next thing they knew the man found little bones or something near the dog's bed."

"Get out! The dog *ate* the cat? Fur and all?"

"Wait, it gets better. The dog ate the cat, fur and all, which made the owners a wee bit suspect. So they took the dog to the vet 'cause they were afraid it might start eating other things in the neighborhood. The vet took one look at it and said, 'This isn't a dog. I don't know *what* it is, but it is definitely *not* a dog.' "

"What was it? What'd they do?"

"Took it to a zoo. Know what it was? A *rat*. It was called something like a Giant Siamese Rat."

"THEY KEPT A RAT IN THE HOUSE?"

"A Giant Siamese Rat."

"What'd they do with it?"

"Put it to sleep."

Lincoln turned to his mother and asked, "That means they killed it?"

"Yes, sweetie. Hey, Max, is that story true?"

"According to Mary it is."

It was a winter Sunday. The three of us were sitting around the kitchen table still in our pajamas, each with his different section of the newspaper.

Two months after returning from France we moved in together. It was a difficult change for all of us, but Lincoln had it hardest. Lily and I chose to do this because of our hope and new love. There would be difficulties, but there was also the elation that accompanies the possibility of real and long-lasting satisfaction. So, like diplomats negotiating a nuclear test ban treaty, we felt the boy out as delicately as we could and then worked our behavior and our words in such a way that he felt he was involved in our decision.

Lincoln was used to having his mother to himself. I learned he was not a terribly egotistical kid but, like anyone, enjoyed being the center of another's universe. They had lived alone together ten years. He was her history, while she was his rock and his truth. She had had boyfriends over the years, two of them quite serious, but nothing ever serious enough to threaten the straight distance between their two points. Lincoln's father, Rick Aaron, was a rumor and a ghost to the boy. He seemed larger than life, ten feet tall, an adventurer, Zorro, et cetera, but he was more of an event to his son than a real human being.

Lily and Rick met at Kenyon College. He was a handsome math whiz with a sleek ponytail of long hair, a blue Jeep, and a notebook of poetry he'd written two hundred pages long. He did photography, calligraphy, he knew a world about ornithology. Lily was enthralled and disturbed by him in equal measures. Why was this Mega Man interested in Lily Margolin, language major? She was good-looking, had enough self-confidence to hold her own in conversation, and liked sex more than most of her friends. *Butttt* Rick Aaron was one of those rare people who part the waters wherever they go. Men disliked him, yet they wanted to be his friend. Women looked too long at him, sometimes their mouths hung open a bit. He had a reputation, but from what Lily could gather, his old girlfriends were proud of their time with him and few of them said bad things. What bad *was* said was good: he was too intense, too hungry, too self-absorbed. She liked those qualities. Besides, with everything he had going for him, didn't he have a right to be self-absorbed? It made Rick all the more compelling when he shone his thousand-candle-power attention her way. One night she even dreamed he was a lighthouse. A human lighthouse with enough brilliance and power to illumine every part of the night. The only odd thing about this dream, which naturally she took as a crucial sign from her deepest heart, was that Rick's head swiveled completely around on his neck. But at the time, she took that as further proof of him as a true lighthouse. To include everything one must cover all directions, swivel or not.

And he sure shone his light in *her* direction! She had had boy-friends. There was even one now at another college, but that guy, any other guys, stood no chance compared with this man. That was part of it—although he was only a sophomore, Lily thought of Rick as a man. What was wonderful was that at times he could be as silly and charming as a boy, but his strength and curiosity made him sure, calm, *adult*. They met in September, and that Christmas, Rick gave her a hand-tooled leather album of poems and photographs he had done especially for her. She'd saved up for months and bought him a special lens for his camera but then felt like a superficial twerp hold-ing that beautiful black leather book, letting pages slip down her thumb. A lens compared with poems?

The more attention he paid her, the more happy and nervous she became. She was waiting for the bomb to drop or at least some-one to hand her the bill for what this man and their relationship really cost. Most people think they deserve better than they've gotten. Trouble is, if we ever happen to get "it" we become terribly suspicious.

The bill arrived shortly after they moved in together and Lily had survived her cucumber episode with Mr. Aaron. One evening Rick announced he was leaving school for a while. Just like that he was dropping out for a semester and going to San Francisco to see what all the fuss was about there. Like a brain tumor or terminal disease that lies dormant for years in our body until the day it comes to life and begins to eat us away from the inside, Rick suddenly was afflicted with either wanderlust or irresponsibility. It depended on how you saw it and on where you stood in relation to him. Always the good boy, good student, good good, he abruptly decided to hit the road and see what he was missing. Just like that. Unfortunately he left behind (among other things) a young woman hopelessly tied to him and willing to put up with this romantic bullshit so she could remain in his life. She even asked if she could go with him. That was an astounding realization to make. Emotions like this really existed! She had actually met a man for whom she'd sacrifice everything. She would desert her old life too if he'd let her. But he wouldn't. Not that he was thinking of her well-being. Borrowing from bad cowboy-film dialogue, he actually said something along the lines of a man's got to do what a man's got to do and left Lily Margolin on the doorstep in Gambier, Ohio, watching his Jeep buzz off into the sunset.

We do many foolish things at the beginning of a relationship. Later we're apt to forgive ourselves because it was that first deep breath of big love, like high mountain air, that made us dizzy and consequently made us act so wrongly.

Lily waited for him. She should have wept and cursed his name for abandoning her, worn black clothes and looked poetically tragic for a few weeks. She jumped back into the interesting life of a college campus, but she had a streak of the Victorian in her. She once joked she would have been a good sea captain's wife—the idea of waiting long months and writing longer letters that had little chance of ever arriving was very appealing to her sensibilities. Besides, what better experience had ever happened to her? She had grown up comfy middle-class. A pleasant life, but nothing in it ever shone, no, *burned* the way her relationship with Rick did. She felt lit by him, wattage she could never have conceived of before knowing this man. Anyway, maybe that was what you were supposed to do with something as magical as this—cherish it when it was there, worship it when it was gone. Perhaps Rick was even testing her—testing her long-distance dedication to him. No matter what the reason, she would show both him and herself what kind of stuff she was made of.

She became a hermit. She went to class, she went home. She studied too much for tests and took obscure courses that would never do her a bit of good. It pleased her to discover and read authors whose work had not been checked out of the library for years. Wyndham Lewis. James Gould Cozzens. She was the first because she had love's time on her hands. One book she found and kept renewing, not because it was good (it was incomprehensible), but because of the title—*The Desire and Pursuit of the Whole*. What silly things won't we do for love? Others asked her out but she wouldn't go. Her refusal made her more alluring and mysterious. She was neither. She was simply in love with one man who had blown her up like a hot-air balloon and then, with no instruction, cut her ropes and sent her drifting off into space. The view up there was great but when you don't know what to do next it becomes frightening. What would she do if he didn't come back? Did the pain she had begun to feel ever go away? Was there any way to survive the loss of someone so important? She would willingly float above the world, aimless and lost for a while, but what happened *after* a while?

She didn't have to worry. Rick reappeared two months later in a tie-dyed shirt, an Indian vest, and a beard that didn't look very good on him. But she was so happy, he could have had a third eye implanted and she'd still have been ecstatic. Despite his new look, he was unimpressed with what he'd seen. That didn't mean he was home to stay, however. The son of a bitch said he'd returned to Ohio only to see her, because his next stop was Europe. He was home! He was leaving! But he'd come only to see her! She said his visit was like going through a whole amusement park of emotions. What could she do but love him and give her all in the little time they had together?

Part of that all was sex. Lily said she never screwed so much in her life. She used a diaphragm. A month after Rick left for Luxembourg, she realized her diaphragm hadn't worked. She went home to Cleveland to tell her parents she had been living with a man, was pregnant, was going to have the baby. And oh yes, the man wasn't around anymore. Joe and Frances Margolin were the kind of progressive parents who wore dashikis and gave money to various revolutionary causes. If their daughter wanted to have a child, right on.

But before she'd completed her third month, Lily miscarried. When Rick returned from Europe, she told him for the first time what had happened. He was so touched and astonished that she'd been willing to have their child, even in the face of not knowing whether he would ever return, Mr. Wonderful decided then and there to stay put. They were married and lived happily ever after for two more years until he graduated and headed out for the territories again. This time it began via a job with a fledgling California computer company in the days before Silicon Valley when that whole new industry consisted of only a bunch of brilliant experimenters and enthusiasts flying by the seat of their pants. Rick liked the whole setup. One year short of her degree they moved West to disaster.

Six months. That self-obsessed asshole lasted six months at his good new job before complaining it was restricting and he had to split. That was the word he used. Where was he splitting to this time? Israel. A kibbutz on the Syrian border. He'd been talking with a guy . . . She stopped him in mid-soliloquy and asked point-blank if he was planning to take her this time. His answer was the beginning of their end: "Lil, you have to decide for yourself about your own space. It's fine with me if you want to come." When she told me about that conversation, a hardness entered both her voice and her facial expression that was years old and not the slightest softened by time.

"Decide for myself? I was his *wife*, for Christ's sake! Just the way he said it made me realize where I stood with him even then. He honestly thought it was enough to be Bighearted Jake and let me tag along. But what if I wanted to do something else at that moment in our life? Did he care? N-O. Rick the Prick. I think that's when I named him that. Rick the Prick. 'You have to decide for yourself about your own space.' Can you imagine saying that to your wife?"

As gently as possible I asked, "Then why'd you go?"

"Because I loved him. I couldn't get enough of him."

Her parents, who had been giving liberally for years to Israel, thought it was a great idea and financed their trip. They lived on the kibbutz three months, both of them working in its cardboard factory until Rick had a fistfight with one of the managers and the Aarons were on the road again. They went to France, where Lily caught hepatitis and ended up in the hospital. The last straw was her husband coming to her bedside, aglow with excitement, saying he'd met a man in a cafe who was an editor in London. This guy read some of Rick's poetry and wanted to publish him. Would Lily mind if he flew up there for a few days and talked to the people?

"I was so excited for him, Max. There I was in a French hospital, feeling two steps from death but telling him to use my parents' money to fly to London. God, he was gone two weeks!"

Like a rock climber going up a sheer face, Lily's love for her husband had reached the point where there were absolutely no handholds left with which to move further. It was as if the surface she was climbing had gone from craggy granite at the low points to brushed aluminum now way up higher where any slip meant death. Unless you are mad, you look for other ways to get over this. On discovering there are none, you climb down. Lily climbed down. Or rather, the day she left the hospital she used the last of their money and bought a plane ticket home.

No great love ever really ends. We can shoot it with a gun or stick it in the back of the darkest closet of our hearts, but it's clever; it knows how to survive. It can find its way out and shock us by reappearing when we were so damn sure it was dead or at least safely hidden beneath piles of other things.

Rick reappeared. Shaven, contrite, he reminded her of a man who was entering the priesthood. Suffice it to say she fell for him again. She had read an interview with an aging actress who said she loved the wrinkles on her face because each one came from a different man in her life. Lily had no lines on her face but well understood what this woman was talking about. She felt scarred by her husband, felt he had caused her spirit to walk with a limp. But he also knew how to wake the dead in her because it had never really died—only hibernated. It took time but he succeeded. She got pregnant again. She was twenty-three.

A year after Lincoln was born, his father walked into a market in Windsor, Connecticut. He bought a pack of cigarettes, but before the cashier had his change, the handsome man with the long hair collapsed and died of heart failure.

When Lincoln grew old enough to understand and began asking questions about his father, Lily told him the story of their relationship. He could not understand how she could love someone so much but end up hating him. Neither could he understand how this wonderful man could treat his even more wonderful mother so badly. She answered as best she could, but like a psychiatrist who rephrases the same question again and again to get to the heart of the matter, the boy never stopped grilling her about the subject.

After I began to gain his trust, he put me on the hot seat and asked why I thought these things had happened between the two most important people in his life. I was reading every child psychology book I could find, but there were so many different and valid ways to respond to his questions that I was often at a real loss as to what to say. How many times did I come up with *the* perfect answer to Lincoln's questions, but too late? Too damned many. Also there was the difficulty of not saying what I really felt about Rick in front of his son. I thought the man was a selfish, unconscionable bastard. I couldn't say that to Lincoln. But I wanted him to trust me. I knew I would never be able to replace his father, but if I could become a trusted friend, that was good enough. I was realizing that to gain a child's trust you must be adept at being both adult and child at the same time. You must show who's boss but make them happy and at ease with that power. Lily did it beautifully. As a result, she'd single-handedly raised her son to be a secure, self-confident fellow who was generally fair and willing to listen to reason.

What I found most interesting was how much I enjoyed living with both of them. They were like two new exotic tastes or smells that startle you at first but make you want more a moment later. Lily sang in the bath, read herself to sleep every night, liked sex first thing in the morning followed by a big breakfast. When she argued or got angry she often became unfair and overemotional. She expected me to do things but wouldn't always say what they were until I'd exasperated her and she started to fume. It was hard calming her down. It was easy making her laugh. From the beginning I knew how much I liked and wanted her. It came as a genuine shock how quickly I grew to love her.

Lincoln was different. Actually living with a child for the first time, I was constantly stopped in my tracks by both his presence and his perception. People are forever commenting on the different ways men and women see the world and how astonishing it is that we get along nevertheless. That's certainly true, but even more implausible is how adults and children function together on the same plane. They are more comfortable in life, we are more informed about it. Both see the other's vision as unreal and often ridiculous.

"Max, I have to tell you this terrible dream I had last night. I was being chased down a street by guys with big bags of salt. They caught me and said they were going to put my fingers in it. And then they did!" He sat back, satisfied. Nothing could be worse than your hand in a bag of salt. His expression said anyone in their right mind understood how terrible it was and what an ordeal he'd undergone just making it through the night in one piece. An adult would feel foolish even telling this dream. Lincoln was shaken by it. In sharing, he was giving me the radical gifts of his fear and wonder. Things like this are not small. They are not cute or sweet or kids say the darndest things. I was expected not only to listen, but to understand. His standards were high. If I was going to live with him, share his mother and his life, I would be tested continually until he reached a conclusion. I had no say in it. There were no in-betweens. Triumph or failure. He would be the only judge.

But having him there was also delightful much of the time. I walked him to school most mornings. We talked about everything and he knew he was allowed to ask whatever questions he wanted, particularly man's stuff. As a result, I once found myself leaning on a mailbox doing a quick sketch of a vagina, which he took but immediately shoved into his back pocket. "Do you mind if I look at it later? I'm kind of embarrassed." While riding in the car one time he sniffed his armpit, sniffed it again and said, "I'm beginning to smell like a man." He wanted to know about my family, my old girlfriends, what I was like when I was young. He confided he wasn't popular at school because he was too bossy and impatient. I agreed he was bossy, but interesting too, which canceled out the other. Lily said he asked her for a picture of me to carry in his wallet, but not to tell. The three of us went to Disneyland, Marineland, the wrestling matches. There's a photo of Tackhead Frank Cornish holding an ecstatic Lincoln Aaron over his head as if about to throw the kid ten rows out into the audience. In the next shot, blown up to poster size and on the wall of his room, Lincoln's standing with his foot on the downed giant's chest, victorious. We ate hamburgers and played video games way past his bedtime. We shared reading stories with Lily.

One of the unexpected pluses was a constant flow of new ideas for "Paper Clip" from both of them. People often asked where I got ideas for the strip. Usually I'd mumble something brilliant like "They just come to me." But now I could honestly say, "From the people I live with." I used the salt dream in there. I used the way Lily jerked violently awake from sleep, no matter what the circumstances. And Lincoln's way of praying at night. My life became more involved and in ways more difficult, but also much fuller and more interesting. Interesting was the word. When you live with others you never really know what's coming next. New noise, movement, life.

The door opens after school or the phone rings and there they are with things to tell you that can turn a day upside down or its volume up a thousand wonderful decibels. Their presence alone changes the terrain.

Taken to an extreme that can be maddening, but that wasn't the case for me. Quite the opposite. It was only after we'd lived together some weeks that I realized that before the Aarons my life had become so predictable and dull, I could've driven its flat road blindfolded. Worse, whenever there *was* a slight bump or detour on it I became nervous and unhappy. How dare existence be different from yesterday! Obviously that sameness was neither healthy nor productive. Then came the moment I walked in their door and TOTAL TRANSFORMATION. Living with this woman and child forced me off my old path onto new ground. It was not easier to live, but richer. So much richer.

Lincoln was crazy about baseball. I had been too as a kid, so we had real empathy there. The difference between us was my obsession had centered on the gods of major league baseball—who played on what team, their batting averages—whereas Lincoln only liked to play. For him, going to an L.A. Dodgers game was fun, but nothing beat going to the park and having a catch or hitting pop-ups and grounders. He believed deeply in sports. Reputations made in an afternoon, adulation or total failure always near. The great thing about them, especially for kids, is they *are* immediate black and white: good if you win, bad if you lose.

He played on a little league team and practiced two afternoons a week in a schoolyard a few blocks from our house. What I'd do those days was finish work as quickly as possible, then clip Cobb onto his long leash and the two of us would walk over to watch our friend play. Once there, the dog sat next to me on the lowest bleacher looking like a sphinx with a nose. When he got tired, he'd climb slowly down and lie on his side in the sun. I relish the memory of those afternoons. In retrospect, they were when I felt most like a father to Lincoln. Being there for him, watching him play, walking home together afterward talking about how he'd performed made me feel a bond with him that was solid and true. We had baseball on our minds. Both of us listened and considered carefully what the other said.

Inevitably, one of his sworn enemies played on his team. Inevitably the kid was better than Lincoln. Andy Schneider. I can still see his small lips curling in utter disdain and dislike when he said Andy's last name, as if it were a rare disease *and* another name for "fart" all in one word.

When it happened I was thinking about what to cook for dinner. Cobb was stretched out on the ground watching a bee buzz his head. Lincoln was playing shortstop, pounding his glove in anticipation of whatever was about to come off the bat of Andy Schneider.

"Strike out, turd!"

Lincoln's voice? I looked up. If it was, I wasn't happy. He could hate Schneider, but razzing him that way was low-rent behavior and I'd tell him as soon as—

CRRRRRACK!

Andy hit the next pitch so hard that the sound of the ball making its second impact came only seconds after it left his bat. The second sound came when it struck Lincoln in the face. He dropped where he stood.

I leapt out of the stands and ran onto the field, empty of any thought other than to reach him. He lay in a heap, one arm covering half his head. Herb Score. The first other thing in my mind. When I was a boy, Herb Score was a famous pitcher for the Cleveland Indians who was hit in the face and almost killed by a line drive.

There was no blood. I bent down and gently moved Lincoln's arm so I could see.

"Mother of God!"

His right temple was already swelling. Apparently he'd been able to turn his head a moment before impact and thus avoid being hit square in the face. But his temple was blowing up so fast that it was already the size of a golf ball and a hideous purple blue. His eyes were closed. He didn't move.

From behind, I heard a boy's voice yelling, "What'd I do? Is he dead? What'd I do?"

The coach squatted down next to me and tried to speak but kept dropping his sentences halfway through.

"We called an ambulance. It's not that far to . . ."

"Do you know anything about medicine?"

"No. My father was a doctor but . . . Hey, listen, maybe there's a . . ."

We spoke to each other but never made eye contact. Both of us watched Lincoln for signs of life. There were none. I kept bending down and putting my head against his chest. I needed to know his heart was still beating. Somewhere inside that still body, work was on to keep him alive.

"Do you think we should do artificial . . . ? Look at the damned swelling!"

There was no blood. That scared me most. I kept thinking of all the angry exploded blood blocked up inside his small head. If it could only burst out somewhere in one horrid flood he'd be okay. He'd wake up screaming with pain but be okay. But there was no blood. Swelling and swelling, but no blood besides the lethal purple beneath the skin.

"Did I kill him? I didn't do anything! I only hit the ball!"

The worst moments. He is alive but hurt so badly and there's nothing on earth you know to do. Only watch and pray and clench your fists at how stupid and inept you are. Why didn't you ever go to a first-aid class? What if he dies and you did nothing but watch? What will his mother say? What will the rest of life be like? Everything in your head is terror. Everything in your heart is dread.

There was a mobile telephone in the ambulance but I was too busy watching the attendants work on Lincoln. I didn't think to call Lily until we'd already arrived at the hospital and they were wheeling him into the emergency ward. A doctor strode into the room and brusquely told me to leave.

"He's my son, Doctor."

"Good. I'll treat him like he's mine. Now please go. I'll tell you what I can in a few minutes."

At the reception desk I filled out the necessary papers and called Crowds and Power. Lily wasn't there but I told one of the waitresses what had happened and she said she would find her.

What do You want? A few years of my life? Let him live. What can I do to save him? Let him live. I felt ten years old. I wanted to get down on my hands and knees. Oh, God, please help him out of this and I'll be good forever. I swear to You. Just let this kid live and I'll do whatever You want. I'll go to church. I'll stop drawing. I'll leave Lily. Let him be all right. Oh, please.

The look on people's faces in a hospital emergency ward is both broken and yearning at once. Part of them is prepared for the worst, the other part shows the sneaking hopefulness of a dog you've hit but which sidles up to your leg to see if their coast is clear.

One man leaned against a wall chewing his finger like it was a spare rib. He looked only at that hand. A child in a beautifully ironed yellow dress tried to play peekaboo with a woman who rocked back and forth with closed eyes. The child hid her face behind an arm, then popped it up again, looking delighted. Peekaboo. She saw me looking and quickly hid at the woman's side.

"Stop it! Stop it, will you?" She grabbed the astonished girl by the arm and shook her hard. I wanted to go over and stop *her* but knew I'd caused enough damage. "Just stand here and sit still. *Please!* Will you just please stand *still,* for God's sake!"

The child's face was all shock and fear. Nothing that happened in this hospital, nothing that happened to the hurt person she was waiting for, would be worse than this scold from her guardian. They'd tell her, "Daddy is dead" or "Mommy's very sick," but it would touch her far less than the other's scared fury. *That* was the end of the world as far as she understood it. Standing still, she stuck her thumb in her mouth and looked at me with absolute hatred.

A hand touched my shoulder, and before I turned, a man's voice said, "Mr. Aaron?" For an instant I knew they'd mistaken me for someone else. Aaron? Then a weird unnatural rustle, like leaves before a storm, went across me when I realized they thought I was Rick Aaron.

Turning, I was about to correct them when it came to me they thought that because I'd brought the boy in and said I was his father.

The doctor's name was Casey. William Casey. Faced with the moment of truth, I looked at his name tag too long. William Casey.

"Mr. Aaron, everything is going to be all right. You've got one lucky boy. The ball hit him on the temple and knocked him out. We've got a large hematoma there and he's going to have a hell of a sore head for a while, but other than that he's okay. No fracture or serious concussion. He regained consciousness right after you left."

"*YES!*" I punched both fists straight up into the air and closed my eyes. "YES!"

"We'd like to keep him here for observation overnight, but that's only standard procedure. I'm sure nothing is wrong."

I shook and shook and shook Dr. Casey's hand until he gently pried himself loose and told me to sit down, take a breather.

"But his head will be all right? There'll be no aftereffects or—"

"Not from what I can see, and we checked him thoroughly. He's going to have a bad headache and won't be able to wear his baseball cap for a while. That's it. He's going to be okay."

"Thank you, Doctor. Thank you so very much—"

"Mr. Aaron, when I was a young doctor and *very* pleased with myself, a patient would say thank you and I'd accept it as my due. In twenty-five years of medicine I've learned to stop taking credit for only doing my best. I'm happy for you. Happy I could give you good news. I must go now."

I sat down and inadvertently looked directly into the eyes of the woman with the child. She smiled and gestured toward the other room. "They're okay?"

"Yes. Yes, a very bad hit on the head but he's going to be okay. It's my son." Tears came to my eyes. My son.

"I'm glad it worked out."

"Thank you. I hope . . . I hope yours is well too."

"It's my daughter in there. This one's mother. Know why we're here? Because that Miss Smartso daughter of mine got her fat tongue stuck in a Coca-Cola bottle! It's the truth. Don't ask me how. We're all sittin' around comfortable and happy at the girl's birthday party. Her mama's drinking a Coke and the next thing we know, she's wavin' her arms like she's drowning or something. But no, it's not that, it's she can't get her tongue out of the damned bottle. Can you believe it? We had to take a cab here because my car's broke and the cabdriver laughed at us the whole way down. What the hell, I was laughing too."

Whether it was because of the relief I felt, knowing Lincoln was going to be all right, or the way the woman was smiling at the end of her story, whatever, I smiled, then tee-heed, then cackled openly. She did too. Each time we looked at each other we laughed harder.

"How do you get your tongue stuck in a Coke bottle? The opening's so small!"

"Don't ask me. My daughter's always had special talents."

A doctor bustled by but stopped abruptly when she looked in and saw all of us laughing so hard. Even the finger chewer was going by then. How strange we must have looked. Who laughs in the emergency room? Were we ghouls or madmen? The little girl didn't understand why we were having such a good time but it was fine with her. She started skipping around the room singing, "Coca-Cola. Coca-Cola."

And that's what Lily saw when she flew around the corner with Ibrahim right behind: everyone laughing, skipping child, Party Time.

"Max! Where is he? What's going on?"

Between the laughter, the surprise at seeing her, and relief still rolling around in my stomach, I only waved and smiled, which was appalling behavior. She didn't know her son was out of danger. As far as she knew, he might have been dead.

"Max, for Christ's sake, where's *Lincoln?*"

I stood up, still smiling. "Lily, he's all right. You don't have to worry."

"What do you mean? Where is he?"

"In the other room. But the doctor was just here and said he's all right. He got hit and was knocked out—"

"Knocked out? They didn't tell me that. They only said he was hit. Knocked out? Oh Christ—"

I took her by both arms. "Lily, listen to me. He was hit on the head and knocked out. But he's all right. He'll have a big bruise there and his head'll hurt for some time, but they did all the tests and he's all right. He's *all right."*

"Why did you bring him here? Why didn't you call and tell me?"

"Wait, calm down. He got hit and was knocked out. We were afraid, so we brought him to the hospital. We had to: it could have been very bad."

"Jesus Christ, you shouldn't have brought him here." She broke off angrily and shook her head. "Did you have to fill out papers? What did they make you fill out?"

Ibrahim was standing right behind her. He shrugged as if he didn't understand what she was ranting about.

"What did you fill out, Max?"

"Papers, Lily. You have to give them general information. It's normal in a hospital, honey."

"Normal for who? What did you say on there? What kind of information did you give?"

She was very angry. I slid it off to the pressure of what had happened. I spoke as calmly as I could. "His name, how old he is, our address. And whether he's allergic to anything."

"What else?"

"Nothing. Just the standard form."

"Standard form, huh? Shit on the standard form."

"Lily, *calm down.* That's what you do in the hospital. You gotta give them certain information—"

She grabbed the front of my shirt and pulled me to her very roughly. "You don't give them *anything,* Max. Nothing ever." Her voice shrank down to a gravelly growl.

Ibrahim had his hands on her then, pulling her back, talking quietly, pulling her away from me. It was bizarre and very disturbing. She had every right to be capsized by her son's accident, but her facial expression, voice, what she was saying all had to do with something else. Something way far away from this situation. What she said next confirmed that.

"Do you think they take fingerprints?"

"Of Lincoln? No! He's a patient, not a prisoner."

She listened, then turned to hear what Ibrahim thought.

"Lily, come on, please. Don't get cuckoo now. They don't take fingerprints in the hospital!"

"We don't know for sure, but all right. Now I only want to get him out of here. When can we take him home?"

"Tomorrow. The doctor said they'll keep him here overnight for observation. He can go home tomorrow."

"Tomorrow? Where's this doctor? I have to talk to him. We're leaving here."

What she meant by "we" was she wanted her son out of there that instant. We found Dr. Casey, who first tried to calm her, but grew insistent and coldly professional on realizing this distraught woman wanted to take her child home *now.* He said it was unwise, then not a good idea, then dangerous. There had been cases where—

"I don't care, Doctor. We're leaving. I'm his mother and I want to take him home. If there are any problems we'll come back."

Nothing he said could dissuade her. Nothing, that is, until they'd ended their face-off and he'd lost and was leaving to go arrange the necessary papers to release Lincoln.

"You are very peculiar, Mrs. Aaron. I don't know why you're so set on this. It's certainly against the better interests of your son and what you're doing makes me extremely suspicious."

Because he was scanning his clipboard, he didn't see her face change. In seconds it went from Fuck you! aggressive to "uh-oh" to cringe. Before speaking again she looked at me. Behind the cringe was something awful at work—rats under her floor, a hidden knife in the palm of her hand.

"Dr. Casey, I'm so sorry. I just—I can't . . . It's how this happened . . . Yes, let him stay here. You're right, of course. I'm sorry."

Doctors know the tone of the confused and desperate. It is part of their human agenda. When he spoke again, Casey was all sympathy and quiet power. "I fully understand, Mrs. Aaron. But it really is the best thing to do. Let us keep him here tonight, and if you want, you can stay in the room with him. But it's best if he's here overnight."

"Right. Absolutely. I'm sorry."

"You needn't apologize. I'll tell the nurse you'll be staying with him."

I watched her throughout this weird exchange. What the hell was going on? Which Lily was real here? Which Lily was the truth? Like the doctor, I might have fallen for her line if I hadn't seen her face working, or the fear and loathing in her eyes, the wriggle and pull of her mouth fighting against itself. She was a good liar if you didn't watch closely.

How could this be her? The woman who was so helpful and generous to others, so good in emergencies, the first one to run and help strangers out of trouble. Part of it was the fact it was her trouble now, her son. But not all of it, not all.

"Lily?"

Her eyes stayed on the doctor as he strode down the corridor.

"Lily?"

"Hmmm?"

"What's the matter? What is the problem?"

She looked at me as if I'd slapped her face. "Big mistake, Max. You made a very big mistake. Very stupid."

"What? What did I do wrong?"

"I don't want to talk about it now." She walked away.

"Ibrahim, what is going on?" Besides being upset, I felt like such a fool: I lived with the woman, but now that our first crisis was here, I had to ask her boss why she was behaving so oddly.

"I don't know. She is very strange about the boy. It is more than protective. Gus thinks that she is—" He pointed to his head and gave the universal sign for loony.

"Have you seen her like this before?"

"Yes, but only when it is about Lincoln. She is a good woman, but with him she is a little crazy."

The shock of the accident, the confusion events like that can cause, emotion pulled and released like rubber bands . . . any of those were good reasons for her outbursts and contradictions. But none of them were satisfying because I had seen that terrible sneak in her eyes. There was no other way to say it. Sneaking. Lying. Not to be trusted.

"Ib, can you stay with her for a while? I'd like to go get a cup of coffee and cool out."

"Yes, sure, go. But, Max, don't be hard on her. Remember, before you, she had only this child."

"I know. I understand. It's only . . . Don't worry. I'll be back in a half hour."

I sat in the hospital coffee shop five minutes. Long enough to buy coffee, but once a cup was in front of me I knew what I really wanted was air, some space. I paid and left. There was a park a few blocks away and I gratefully went in. Late-afternoon people strolled around. Women with baby carriages, old couples in bright clothes, kids on skateboards and bicycles. A few feet from where I was sitting, a woman played on the grass with a young Boston terrier. They're sweet little dogs and this one was having the time of its life chasing after a bright green ball the woman had brought along. I concentrated on its funny play because I needed mental space from Lily and what had been happening that day. The dog dropped the ball and barked at the woman to throw it again. I never had a dog do that. The ones I'd known, you threw the ball, they fetched, then ran with it in the opposite direction.

This ball flew, the puppy scampered off, snatched it up while it was still rolling, ran back. This went on until the pigeons arrived. A large flock of them dropped down out of nowhere and landed nearby. It was unusual: fifty birds suddenly there, preening and fussing, flapping their wings. People looked and pointed. The dog was staggered by it. He stood a moment in shocked surprise. Then, classic canine, lowered his head into attack position and tiptoed toward them. There's nothing dogs like more than charging birds. Slink-slink-slink POUNCE. They rarely catch one but who cares? What must feel good is having all those scared lives leaping off the earth because of you.

Slink-slink-slink. The terrier got to within a few feet of the flock, stopped, poised to jump, one paw hanging in the air. I was ready for its triumphant spring when an odd thing happened. Almost as one, the birds turned. Lots of cooing and fluttering wings, but they moved in a grayish-pink wave at the same time. As if understanding he was outnumbered, or that something was wrong when so many things moved the same at the same time, the little dog slowly relaxed its body and, watching them closely, lay down on the ground. Maybe next time.

The world is full of mysterious connections, especially when we're going through strong times in our lives. The puppy's reaction to the birds made people laugh. Isn't that cute? It made me shudder. Frisky and sure of himself, he walked up to what he knew by all rights was his. Done it before and had great fun. This time, though, these fifty heads, one hundred wings, sudden same movement . . . All said Stop! It isn't the same, doggie. Don't even try.

It isn't the same, doggie. What was happening with Lily? Her behavior at the hospital stopped me hard. Birds are birds until they turn as one small army. Lily's familiar face gone bad, her words, this strange mistrust and paranoia that had surfaced for the first time since we'd been together. It stopped me. What was happening here?

I am not a trusting soul. I don't even trust myself. Often I have no idea what I'll do in certain situations. Who does? If one cannot say I trust myself, how can one say I trust you and genuinely mean or feel it? Because of that, people hurt but rarely wound me. When Norah Silver admitted she was sleeping with another man it was a brutal blow to my spirit, but was neither crippling nor unexpected. Somewhere in my soul is a two-foot-thick door with a giant sumo wrestler standing guard outside, not letting anyone in. It's the door to Command Center, Mission Control, the heart of the matter. Whatever your credentials, the sentry keeps you out. I am not sorry it is like this. My parents are trusting people who raised my brother and me to be that way too, but we aren't. Saul is a finagler in business, a libertine, and an all-around truth stretcher. He likes scoundrels because he is one himself. Between us, we have enough trust to fill another person three-quarters. It is one of the few things we agree on.

The night Lily spent at the hospital with Lincoln I went through our house like a burglar. I had never had any reason to question what she had told me about herself and her life, but I felt I did now. Snooping around your own home looking for clues about the person you love is perverse, but I felt totally detached doing it. I thought only that this is her place, this is where her life is, so this must be where *it* is—a sign, a lead, the key. I knew what I was looking for might be so obscure and indecipherable that even on finding it there was the distinct possibility I wouldn't recognize what I had. A photograph or a ticket stub, a letter from a friend with one unimportant sentence that, once deciphered, told all.

I began in Lincoln's room. Through his closet, through his dresser, his desk, toy trunk, books. Flip through the pages of each one, turn them upside down and shake. The clue could be there—a bookmark, something written on a piece of scratch paper. Under his bed, in all of his boxes, the obscure corners of his room where things could be hidden or taped. I kept a pad of paper nearby. Anything that said something to me I either noted or put in the middle of the floor to be considered later when I was sifting the information through my mind.

I found nothing, so operations were moved to our bedroom. Same approach there—over, under, around, through. I even checked my own belongings to make sure they hadn't been used as new hiding places. Lily kept a diary, which I read, but I found nothing other than small gripes and triumphs, philosophical musings. Events and ideas that meant something to the day but would be quickly forgotten if not recorded. A touching note, but one that did not deter me, was how many times she wrote about us and how much better life had become since we met. There was progressively more nothing as I worked through our home from room to room, object to object. What was I looking for? Often I held something in my hand and stared at it as if I were the first archaeologist to discover hiero-glyphics. You *know* they are of the greatest significance, there are stories and information, whole worlds here, but all of it is a million miles away from your understanding although only twelve inches away from your eyes.

Working for hours, I cut my hands and tore a fingernail reach-ing and pulling, twisting things apart. I stopped to make a sandwich and ate it looking at the small pile I'd assembled on the floor that might mean something. None of it meant anything. I knew it. I knew Lily was hiding something. The more I worked and thought about it, the more I was convinced her outburst was only the tip of one big iceberg of a lie. The proof *was* here, but I could not find it.

In the end, at three o'clock in the morning, when I had filled the pad with notes, checked and double-checked that everything was back exactly as I'd found it, finished cursing, finished double- and triple-checking . . . I had come up with exactly two things: There was absolutely no trace whatsoever of Rick Aaron. No letters, no diary entry, no old shirts shoved in a back drawer with his name tag sewn in, no photographs, nothing. How could that be? How could you love someone so much and, despite a bitter end, not keep some-thing of theirs to remind you of a time in your life when you thought of nothing but them? I knew couples who'd thrown each other's clothes out the window when they broke up, or gave the other's belongings to the Salvation Army, but *all* of these people kept something. Not Lily. To judge by what I had "excavated," the only proof of Rick Aaron or Lily's relationship with Lincoln's father was the stories she had told.

The second thing I found was a couple named Meier. Gregory and Anwen Meier. At the bottom of her underwear drawer was a small clipping from a dog magazine announcing Somerset Kennels, home of champion French bulldogs. Proprietors Anwen & Gregory Meier. An address and telephone number were given at the bottom. Lily loved dogs, so at first I thought she'd saved the paper because she was planning on buying one of these bulldogs when old Cobb passed away.

The next mention of these people came in a newspaper article I found slipped into one of her books. The article was old and yellowing, whereas the book was new—the copyright date only a year old. Mrs. Anwen Meier miraculously walked away from a collision on I-95 that totaled her automobile. Mrs. Meier was admittedly driving over the speed limit when she lost control of the vehicle. It left the road and crashed into the pillar of an overpass. Although suffering from mild shock, she was treated and later released from the hospital. In the margin of this article, Lily had written: "Anwen = 'very beautiful' in Welsh." So they were friends, old school pals? I thought the connection must be with Gregory. Why else would she look up the name of the other woman?

The third "piece" of the Meiers was another newspaper clipping, also yellowed. It appeared to be from the same paper, simply announced the couple were leaving Fowler and moving back to New Jersey, their home state. Gregory Meier is quoted as saying they had had a great four years here but felt it was time to go back home "to fulfill a lifelong dream for both of us, which is to raise pedigree dogs."

Lily had some other clippings and photographs but not many: a group shot of the gang at her restaurant, one of an older couple I assumed were her parents, a few of strangers (none fitting her description of Rick), but the Meiers won the contest with three items. Interesting.

I was embarrassed going to Mary again with my suspicions, so I asked around and found another good detective agency. As if sneaking into a porno movie, I hurried through their door and explained what I wanted to a sympathetic middle-aged man with fishing trophies on his wall: Anwen and Gregory Meier. Here's the address in New Jersey. Please find out everything you can about these people. It was a brief, comfortable conversation. But when it was over and I was driving to my next appointment, two things struck me. First, the detective, a Mr. Goff, hadn't once asked why I wanted to know about the Meiers. Who was I and where did I get off sniffing into their lives? What if I were someone bad, or dangerous, and compiling this information to use against them? Goff wasn't interested. Just the facts, bud. You want to know about their foibles and affairs, blemishes, hidden scars, what they eat for breakfast when they're alone together and feeling very in love? You pay and I'll find it.

I did not feel wrong doing this so much as stained. Sometimes it is right to look all around another's life; yet the act, however correct, lessens us. This notion led to the second thing that chilled me about the meeting with this detective: no matter what I discovered about Lily Aaron via the Meiers, I was breaking the trust between us by taking this course of action. Even if it turned out she was hiding something surprising, or dubious, I was the one to blame. Granted, I had already looked through our house for telltale signs, but that was only between us. We both lived there. Now I'd crossed the line—gone "out" to search, and that changed our world.

In the meantime Lincoln was home, energetic and apparently fit as a fiddle, despite a big ugly bump on his head. Lily allowed them to keep him in the hospital the necessary twenty-four hours, but was slipping the kid into his sneakers and jacket the moment he was cleared. We were told to keep close watch on his alertness, reflexes, and orientation. If anything was amiss, we were to get him the hell back fast. We kept him home from school three days, but by then he was so itchy to get back to his life, we let him, after telling his teachers to watch him too.

For the most part Lily returned to her old good self once she felt the crisis was past, although there were exceptions. For one, she didn't apologize, much less mention, her behavior at the hospital. Instead she acted as if nothing had happened. Even Lincoln's accident was like a years-old ink smudge on a white handkerchief: yes, if you looked hard you could see the faint shadow of a mark, but why look when its presence was all but invisible?

One Sunday the three of us drove down to Venice beach to people-watch and have dinner. The skateboarders, bag ladies, beach bunnies, Rastafarians on roller skates playing guitars, flat-out insanes, and other beings from the great beyond that congregate there were out in force and we walked among them as if they were the surreal topiary and great loony statues at Bomarzo or Disneyland.

In the past we'd spoken several times about having our palms or tarot cards read one day. Feeling this was as good a time as any, I suggested going to one of the many fortune tellers who'd set up card tables along Ocean Front Walk. Lily wasn't interested. I didn't push it, but Lincoln got excited and started in. She said no three times before permitting him, but insisted she choose the one, who turned out to be a hippie so stoned out and vacuous-looking that I was surprised he was even able to cut and lay down his cards without dropping them. A strange choice of soothsayers.

"Phew, kid, this is adamant stuff. The Ace of Wands is your card. I mean, there are *multiple* wands here." That comment and a few other forgettable earwigs cost five dollars.

There was a combined restaurant/bookstore nearby where we ate. After the meal, we went into the store to browse a while, each going in his own direction. About fifteen minutes later I looked up and by coincidence saw Lily outside talking with Lincoln's stoned fortune teller. Still sitting, he pointed to something on the table in front of him. I couldn't make out what but assumed it was one of his cards. Lily paid close attention and wrote hurriedly in a small note-book she often carried. He'd speak, tap the card, gesture, and she'd scribble scribble scribble. I watched until they finished. She took out money and gave it to him. They shook hands and she started back toward the store. I lowered my head to the book in hand. Don't ask me what the title was. I couldn't say. She came in and right over to me, smiling and friendly.

"What do you say, lover? About ready to go?"

"Give me another five minutes. I want to check one other thing."

She went to find Lincoln while I asked the woman at the counter for the section on tarot cards. There were two books. The first said, "Wands. This suit indicates animation and enterprise, en-ergy and growth. The wands depicted in the cards are always in leaf, suggesting the constant renewal of life and growth. The associations are with the world of ideas, also with creation in all its forms." The second said, "It is the suit of beginnings, of formless fire energy. It requires clear goals and plans, it requires a firm foundation for the energy not to burn itself out. Notice that the knight rides through a desert, devoid of houses and people as well as trees and water. With-out something to carry that energy to a purpose, the desert will not open up to life."

The way I usually do "Paper Clip" is to draw the two figures and their surroundings first, then write the caption. Normally I know how I want it to look and sound, but there are times when the drawing completely changes the final words.

A line I came up with, driving back from Venice, was: "Truth is like oxygen—get too much of it and it makes you sick." I envisioned my two characters with fishing poles in hand, their lines going into the screen behind them. One of these guys has hooked a fish so enormous that the only detail we see of it is the beginning of a mouth and a colossal eye. Where did the idea come from? I hadn't found out anything real "bad" about Lily, no terrible new truth. Yet. Still, way down deep in my bones I felt something big and surely bad was coming. Heavy intuition. The sound of devils whispering . . .

I drew my two guys fishing, drew their fish, wrote the words "Truth is like . . ." at the bottom of the page, and stopped.

Take out a new sheet of paper. The two are running away from gigantic images of themselves on the screen. I wrote, "Honesty is the Scariest Policy."

New sheet of paper.

I did four different variations on the idea and would have done a fifth if Lily hadn't come into the room and asked me to come to bed. As was her way, she put a hand on my shoulder and looked at what I had on the drawing board. My stomach tensed. What would she say? Could she know why I'd done this?

"Gee, Max, these are cynical. They're not like you. Or are you in a bad mood? Do you really believe this?"

"I believe truth isn't all it's cracked up to be."

"Really? You told me you're not a big liar."

I wanted to say this, I wanted to say that. To turn around and look her in the eye, demand, "Are *you* a big liar? Because you got me running scared, Lily. The more I pursue this, the more my imagination's going bad. What's going on? Tell me your secrets. Tell me the truth. No, tell a lie. Say everything's fine. Even if I don't believe you for a minute."

When she left I started another drawing. The two face the reader. Rising out of the screen behind them is a big hairy monster's arm. It's clear in the next second it'll snatch them up and eat them for dinner. Oblivious to what's coming, one says, "Believe me, Paranoia's the only sure growth industry in the nineties."

"Mr. Fischer? This is Tony Goff."

"Excuse me?"

"Tony Goff, of the Known/Unknown Agency."

"Oh yes, of course. Excuse me."

"I gathered a dossier for you. Whenever it's convenient, I'd like to arrange a meeting."

"Is there a lot?"

"Yes, it's quite substantial. I have, oh, almost a hundred pages of material."

"A *hundred* pages?"

"Yes, well, in a federal case there's invariably a great deal of paperwork."

"Federal? Oh Christ, okay. Can we meet today?"

"I'm at your disposal."

"My God, they're *both* so beautiful!" I looked up quickly to see how Goff reacted to my gush. But it was impossible not to exclaim when you saw the Meiers for the first time. He'd shown me three pictures. You can be fooled by photographs, tricked by light or angle into believing someone is more or less than they really are. But line up three and you get a good idea of what's true. Anwen and Gregory Meier were beautiful. They belonged at gala openings, in glossy magazine ads for tanning oil or skimpy underwear. See a couple like this on the street and you love and hate them in equal measure. The lucky ones. Golden People. Without knowing a thing about them you assume they're rich, successful, have a fabulous sex life, a wonderful life generally.

"Wait till you see this last one." He found a sheet in his thick folder and slid it across the desk to me. "A little different, huh?"

"That's not the same woman!"

"It is."

"Unbelievable. She looks fifty years old and dying of cancer."

"She's only thirty-three now, and that shot was taken several years ago. I tell you, though, I've seen the life sucked out of people for a lot less reason than the one she had. Would you like a cup of coffee?"

"No, thanks. Tell me the story, Mr. Goff."

He rubbed the back of his head and stared at me a long few moments. "Are you a journalist, Mr. Fischer?"

"No. Why do you ask?"

"Because of this." He pointed at the folder. "I know those nonfiction crime books are very popular these days. You know Michael Mewshaw's? He's my favorite. The one about the boy who murdered his parents? Outstanding."

"What does this have to do with the Meiers?"

He didn't appear to be in any hurry. Pushing his chair back from the desk, he locked his hands behind his head, elbows out, and looked at the ceiling. "A million kids a year disappear in America now. One million. That's the newest finding. No big thing anymore. In my opinion, it started going out of control back in the sixties when they began vanishing and turning up on communes. Drugs were suddenly for celebrities and not just weird things beatniks took. And Free Love! Since being a virgin didn't matter anymore, kids could do what they wanted with their bodies and feel grownup the minute they reached puberty. What can my parents tell me I don't already know? Instant independence. Now, to make it worse, there's a fifty-percent divorce rate, which means every other kid comes from a broken home. The real statistics are coming out on child abuse *in* the home. *And* these new, cheap killer drugs . . . Ah, don't get me started. I'm not even talking about teenagers here. Kid fifteen or sixteen runs away, they're old enough. Maybe not enough to know better, but they can fend for themselves.

"The Meiers' baby was kidnapped. Two months old. They were living in Garamond, Pennsylvania, at the time. Gregory Meier was a banker in Philadelphia. He went to Haverford College, his wife to Bryn Mawr, which is right next door. Both of them came from New Jersey. High school romance, from what I can make out. They'd been married two years when the baby was born. A boy. His name was Brendan. Brendan Wade Meier."

"A boy. This was how long ago?"

Goff looked through his papers. "Nine years. Nine years and . . . three months."

"Go on."

He didn't. He stared at me instead. "You don't know any of this, do you?"

"No, nothing."

"You don't know these people?"

"No."

"That's funny, because I would have sworn you did. Just by the way you talked to me about them the first day. Gave me their name and said look into it . . . As if you expected me to know who they were too.

"Anyway, Mrs. Meier went to the Garamond Shopping Plaza one afternoon. Her husband liked French bread, so she'd gone to buy a loaf at a special bakery there. According to her testimony, she left the baby carriage in front of the store, but only because there was a big plate-glass window that allowed her to see it clearly from inside. Said she'd done it many times before. There was no one else in there, so the exchange took no more than two, three minutes. She left the place, stuck the bread into a bag hanging off the side of the carriage, and wheeled it away. Now comes a very key point. She said when she left the store, she did *not* look into the carriage. Only slid the bread into the bag and walked to her next errand. At the door to this next place she looked down to see if the baby was okay and discovered for the first time it was gone."

"What—" I stopped; I had to clear my throat. "What happened after that?"

"What happened? It's all in the folder, but basically another small face went onto the milk cartons: 'Have you seen this child?' The boy's been missing nine years, Mr. Fischer.

"The Meiers did everything they possibly could but turned up nothing. My sources told me they're still spending a great amount trying to find him.

"But, you know, a lot of the time with a tragedy like this, almost worse is what happens to the parents. What I gathered was Mr. Meier suffered some sort of breakdown. Then they moved from Garamond to Missouri—"

"Fowler, Missouri?"

He looked a while through the file. "Yes—Fowler, Missouri. That's right."

"Where she had a car accident?"

Goff nodded, still scanning his file. "I'm not on any kind of firm ground when I say this, but *I* don't think it was an accident. There's a real feeling here she was trying to kill herself."

"Why do you say that?"

"A hunch."

"Can't you be more specific?"

"Look at that last picture of her. It was taken right before they left Missouri. That's a very tortured person. And the only description I found of her car accident makes me just as suspect."

"I read the same article."

"Think about it." He put up a hand and started counting off the details on his fingers. "She admitted she was going too fast. She lost control of the car on a dead-flat interstate, although the weather was good—"

"How do you know that?"

"I checked the weather bureau's records. Lost control of the car just when she *happened* to come up on one of those seven-foot-round reinforced concrete pillars that hold up an overpass? No, it's too fishy."

"You think she tried to do it because of the loss of her child?"

"Yes, and other reasons. A happy young woman marries her high school boyfriend, goes to a good college, graduates into safety and affluence. Has a baby fast and sets up house in the suburbs. Her husband lands a good job at the bank. It's all a little dull, but very pleasant too in its way.

"One day this fairy-tale princess, so pretty and so safe, hops into the station wagon with her new baby and toodles down to the store to buy her man's favorite bread. Sounds like Little Red Riding Hood going to Grandma's house." Goff stood up and, turning his back to me, touched the face of one of the fish mounted on the wall. "Then within what?—thirty seconds?—her entire life became incomprehensible. Like an unknown foreign language. Every word she once knew and relied on suddenly had a completely different definition. Imagine waking up one morning and discovering every word you knew yesterday has a new meaning. 'Child' doesn't mean child anymore, it means terror, loss, dread. You speak yesterday's words and phrases the way you always did, but no one understands today. Not even you, finally. 'Where is my baby?' now means 'Death's here' or 'God died today.'

"Most of us had trouble with foreign languages in school. What happens when *in one second* our own becomes Russian or Farsi? And after that second, it never ever goes back to the way we knew it before.

"Anwen Meier had had a gentle, protected life. She had no preparation for what hit, not that anyone ever does. Her baby was stolen, her husband broke down, neither of them could ever get over the loss . . . I can understand damned well why she'd try to kill herself."

"From Missouri they went back to New Jersey?"

"Right. Bought an old chicken farm in the town of Somerset. That's near New Brunswick, where Rutgers University is. They run a dog kennel out of their farm. Raise French bulldogs. Ugly little things. Ever see one? They look like potatoes. Potatoes with bug eyes."

I sat there hungry for more, yet already overfilled at the same time. Who were these people with their beauty and tragedy? What were they doing three times in the bottom drawers and hidden corners of Lily Aaron's life?

"Mr. Fischer? Are you okay?"

"Yes, I was just thinking about what you said."

"I thought so. I want to tell you something I tell every client at this point in an investigation. It's only a piece of advice but I feel compelled to tell it to you. How we proceed afterward is your decision.

"I've been doing this work twenty-two years. People ask me to look into things . . . whatever their reasons. Although it may sound contradictory, I'm not a curious man. The work interests me because it's logical and clear-cut: gather facts, present them, let a client decide what to do with the information. Sometimes I feel like a librarian—you tell me what subject, I'll go back into the stacks and pull out all the things we have on it.

"But now I give my little talk, free of charge.

"What I want to tell you is—stop now. I can guarantee the further you pursue this, the more it'll upset you no matter how important you think it is. Chances are, you're upset already. Most people are. It gets worse. People are curious, so they hire me. But once I give them a first bunch of stuff it begins to chew them up. Cheating wives, dishonest parents . . . there's many good reasons to hire an investigator. But finish it now, I'm telling you. Unless it's absolutely imperative, or doing it'll save someone's life, stop now. Pay me, walk out the door, and forget it. That may sound strange coming from me, but I tell ya, I've seen *so* much pain in this job . . . I don't get a charge out of seeing people dissolve. I lose some customers, but there's never any lack of them in this business."

"You're probably right."

"I know I am. In fact I'm so right, I'll bet I know exactly what you're thinking this minute. You're thinking: He's right and I *will* stop—after I ask him to look into only one more thing. But that's the killer. The 'one more thing' usually ends up breaking your soul. What a client usually has now is their first whiff of smoke. It makes them suspicious, if not downright paranoid. 'What do you mean, you saw my wife leaving Bill's Bar? She doesn't drink!' Things like that. So please listen to me, take your suspicion and try to work through it. Go back to your life as it was and leave this alone—"

I don't know where it came from, but I was instantly furious with this man. Where did he get off condescending to me, saying in so many words he knew what was best and I should go home like a good little fella . . .

"Thank you for the advice, Mr. Goff. But I'll make my own decisions. If I do choose to pursue this, and it's too difficult for you to handle—"

"One more piece of 'advice,' Mr. Fischer. Don't be an asshole when someone who knows what they're talking about gives you a worthwhile tip. Number one—I know how to 'handle' this. I'm only telling you I've seen a thousand people walk right off the gangplank with information they *asked* me to gather. Number two—I don't care what it does to you. I don't care if it makes you happy or sad or shocked. I'm the librarian, remember. I only bring the books. You read them and most of the time they *do* change your life. Guaranteed. I'm only saying: be careful with these books because too often—"

"I *get* your point."

Pursing his lips, he crooked his head a few inches to the side. "Maybe you do."

I have a very good memory. Often too good. People talk so much that sooner or later something's not true. They have good reasons: they want to impress, or be loved or funny. You are not expected to remember their exaggerations, the small lies, the big ones added to the recipe of a terrific story that needed that tasty distortion to make it sound perfect in the telling. But I do remember. Naturally with Lily I was more aware than ever. Two days before my meeting with Goff, she said something in passing that stopped me then, but made me go forward now.

I'd bought a new shirt and showed it to her. Seeing it was made by a company named Winsted, she gave a small start.

"Winsted! How strange. That's the name of the town where Rick died."

The first time she told the story of Rick Aaron, she said he'd died in Windsor, Connecticut. Now it was Winsted.

I casually asked again, "Where?"

She pointed to the shirt label and looked at me. "Winsted. Why?"

"I used to know a guy from Wallingford. Is that near?"

"Pretty near. Did he go to Choate?"

"Choate. Right!"

If she hadn't known about Wallingford or Connecticut geography, it wouldn't have struck me so hard. If she hadn't said her husband died here one time, and there the next. But she did, so I did too.

"Yes, you're right, there is one more thing. I'd like you to find out everything you can about a man named Rick Aaron. He went to Kenyon College and died in either Windsor or Winsted, Connecticut."

My detective wrote this down on a pad. "Windsor or Win*sted?*"

"I'm not sure. Check both."

He called back three days later. No Rick or Ric or Rich or Ricky or Richard Aaron ever attended Kenyon College. No one by that name had ever died in Windsor, Windsor Locks, Windham, Winchester, *or* Winsted, Connecticut.

So I told my own lie. After a long telephone conversation with my brother, I told Lily he was coming to New York. I wanted to take a break and fly there to be with him. Maybe we'd go see my parents too. That'd be a nice surprise for them, eh?

She said it sure would. When are you going? Day after tomorrow. So soon? Then I guess we'd better make up for the time we're going to lose. She slid into my arms, looking, smelling, feeling lovelier than ever. I realized, though, after she grunted the second or third time that it wasn't her lust for me but that I was hugging her too tightly. Holding on for dear life, squeezing as hard as I could in hopes I'd find a real Lily in there somewhere behind or beneath skin and bones. A real Lily with a real child and true history of her own. How can you trust someone's love when you can't trust them? I remembered Mary's story about the people who thought they owned a dog but it turned out to be a giant rat. Her other story too, the one about the naked woman tied to the bed while her husband lay on the floor in his Batman suit. Dogs that are rats, love so complicated one needs bondage and Batman to make it work. Perhaps without knowing it, Mary was telling me at the beginning of my relationship with the Aarons the same thing as the detective: Stop now. Stop before you realize what you've brought home, before you start making the ridiculous or terrible changes necessary to fit this situation into your life.

"I particularly like the comment one critic made about Beethoven: 'We feel he knew what can be known.' Wouldn't it be wonderful if someone said that about us?"

"Fuck you, Herb!" Reaching forward, I snapped off the car radio with a vicious flick. Fall in love and everyone everywhere, everything, every other word's suddenly "love." Lose someone and the same applies. Since leaving California, I'd been hearing nothing but references to full knowledge, insight, clarity, understanding. Even an introduction to a Beethoven symphony on the radio reminded me of my feared task. On the plane, a terminally obnoxious woman behind me with a voice like a musical handsaw spoke for five loud hours about a woman named Cullen James whose autobiography had changed this woman's life. According to the acolyte, Cullen had somehow left her body and traveled to another land where (as usual) she went through all sorts of hair-raising adventures. But by golly she persevered, learned THE TRUTH, and returned home a Whole Person. I'd seen this book in stores but one glance at the summary on the dust jacket made me put it down fast. Beethoven is one thing. It seems possible that via their gifts, geniuses might be able to find their way through life's maze. However, deranged housewives, aging movie stars, or Retro 1960s gurus who announce unashamedly they hear God or ten-thousand-year-old warriors telling them the secrets of the universe . . . give me pause. I know if God contacted *me,* I'd at least be a bit humble. The way these nuttos describe it, they're all on a first-name basis with Him. Besides, little daily truths are hard enough to bear. Told THE TRUTH by one who *knows* would, if we survived, surely scorch us inside and out like a blown fuse. It did me.

Driving down the New Jersey Turnpike toward Somerset, I tried to imagine the worst-case scenarios so that I'd be at least partially prepared for whatever guillotine blade was about to drop across my life. I had called the Meiers from L.A. and made an appointment, ostensibly to look at their dogs. I talked to Gregory, who had a pleasant but nondescript voice. In the background was the sweet static of yipping puppies.

I got off at the New Brunswick exit and followed his directions to their farm. What was I expecting? Probably something small and lovely, like a spread in *House & Garden* or *Casa Vogue*. You know— one black Bauhaus chair to a room, exquisitely rustic beams and brass hinges, a swimming pool in back. Or nothing. A house for two broken people who were limping through the rest of their lives, having given up on the idea of anything beyond breathing and a sufficient roof overhead.

What greeted me was far worse.

As I drove down a long and remote country road, the flat, single-story houses leading to the Meiers' address all ran together in my mind's eye. The kinds of places and surrounding human geography one would expect out in the middle of a semi-nowhere. Rusted mailboxes, cars up on blocks in the yard, women staring suspiciously at you as they hung droopy-looking laundry on gray lines.

Whoa! I did an exaggerated double take when I saw the house. I also said, "What the hellll!" because it was so strange-looking and so utterly, utterly out of place there. The colors struck me first— blood-red, black, and anthracite-blue stone. Then you saw, realized, the dazzling every-which-way angles at which they were set. Metal piping slithered up and along the sides of the structure like stripes of silvery toothpaste. What *was* this thing? Who would build such an interesting provocation in the middle of that undeserving country-side?

As I closed in on it, my next thought was it's a downed UFO! They always fall in distant cornfields where only indifferent cows or farmers look on. I'd recently read a columnist in the L.A. *Times* who'd specifically addressed that question. If there are creatures from other planets snooping around Earth, how come they never land in New York or Moscow, where both the leaders and the action are? Why are they always sited outside places like North Platte, Nebraska? After a gander at this steel-and-stone whatever thirty yards ahead, I thought maybe *I'm* about to have a close encounter.

Better to wave the flag of one's stupidity than try hiding it. What I was seeing was one of the early versions of the now re-nowned Brendan House.

Anwen Meier studied architecture in college and spent sum-mers working in the offices of Harry Radcliffe, the famous architect. Although she didn't continue her studies after graduation, the sub-ject remained a hobby. She was content to marry Gregory and set up house. After the child was kidnapped, her husband broke down, and she had her car "accident," she decided the only thing in the world that would save them would be to start life over again doing only the things that truly mattered to them. Her father had died and left her a small inheritance. Along with that they sold everything they could, including the stocks and bonds Gregory had been buying since he was fifteen years old. In the end they had a little under seventy thousand dollars. Anwen wisely decided to split it in half—thirty-five thousand would go to the continued search for their son, the rest toward their new life in New Jersey.

She loved architecture, Gregory loved dogs. In their early thir-ties they did what most people feel they can do only after they retire —live the life they want. Dessert at the end of the meal. In the case of the Meiers, it was not dessert. It was the only nourishment either of them could digest. They would buy something simple and sturdy way out in farm country where land was cheap. Over the years she would make it theirs. He would raise his beloved French bulldogs. If they were clever and hardworking they would make it. Neither used the word "luck" anymore. Luck is the poor man's God. Both stopped believing in *Him* the day their child disappeared.

It gives me such pain to write this.

I pulled up in front of their remarkable home three thousand days after they lost the boy. I needed to look some more and collect my thoughts before ringing their bell. What would I say? Could I pull off looking them over, asking certain questions that had nothing to do with dogs, and still get away without their becoming suspicious? Do you people know a Lily Aaron? Do you know why she would know you? Have you ever been to Los Angeles or Cleveland or Gambier, Ohio? How about a man named Rick Aaron? Although I have a strong hunch he doesn't exist—

"Hi! Are you Mr. Datlow?"

Unaccustomed to my made-up name, I still turned so quickly in the seat it must have looked odd. I'd been staring blindly at the road while thinking and hadn't heard her come up from behind, although the driveway was gravel and her boots made loud crunches when she walked, as I heard later following her back to the house.

Whether it was the years of suffering, a hard and active life lived outside much of the time, or simply premature aging, Anwen's face was beauty ruined. Deep sunken eyes and too thin all over; her cheekbones were as prominent as ledges. Still there was so much loveliness left in the face that you wished her head was a balloon you could pump more air in. Fill it up and shape it back out to what it must have once been.

"We've been waiting for you. Gregory's back in the barn. Come on, we'll go find him. Or would you rather have a cup of tea first?"

"Some tea would be great." I thought it better to talk to her alone first, rather than take them both on at once.

"Fine, let's go in the house. Do you mind if I ask how you heard about us? Did you see the ad in *Dog World?*"

I got out of the car and stood near. She was taller than I'd first thought. Five eight or nine, some of it from the boots she wore, most her natural height.

"Yes, I saw the ad, but I also heard about you from Raymond Gill."

"Gill? I'm afraid I don't know the name."

Neither did I, having made it up a second before. "He's a well-known breeder in the West."

She smiled, and oh man, the beauty she once was was very plain to see.

"People know of us out there? That's reassuring. Greg will be so glad to hear it."

I followed her across the driveway to a thick wooden door which had a great number of different patterns running across it like an intricate parquet floor.

"That's quite a door. It's quite a *house!*"

She turned and smiled again. "Yes, you either love it or hate it. No one's ever wishy-washy when it comes to our house. What do *you* think?"

"Too early to tell. First I thought it was a spacecraft from another planet, but now I'm getting used to it. Is it kooky inside too?"

"Not as much. But it *ain't* down-to-earth either! Come in, see for yourself."

We were in the living room when she mentioned the boy for the first time. Until then, her voice and persona had been that of a friendly tour guide. She was clearly used to showing either bewildered or astonished people around her house and had thus created an appropriate self for the role. The room was crowned by a giant cathedral ceiling, parts of which—like patchwork panels—were stained-glass windows through which different colors of light streamed down and carpeted the floor.

"Amazing. I don't know what to say about your house, Mrs. Meier."

"Anwen."

"Anwen. One minute it's enthralling. The next, or the next room we go into, I think I've had too much to drink. This room is extraordinary. The way you've combined the stone and metal and wood, the windows up there . . . It *is* a UFO. Otherworldly!"

"But the other rooms? Where you felt drunk?"

I shrugged. "You can't win 'em all."

"I'm glad you're honest. I'll tell you why it's like this. My husband and I have a little boy. He was kidnapped nine years ago. Until we find him, this house will be both Brendan *and* everything we want to give him in his life with us."

There was no remorse or self-pity or stoicism in the way she said it. These were the facts of her life. She was telling them to me but asking for nothing.

"I'm very sorry. And you have no other children?"

"No. Neither of us can conceive of another child until Brendan comes home. So my husband raises dogs and I work on the house. One day our son will come back and we'll have lots to show him."

Right there, at the end of her sentence in those last four or five words, I heard the smallest hitch of pain in her voice.

"When we bought the place it was only an ugly old chicken farm. My original idea was to create something Brendan would like. Childlike but not childish, you know? A place with moods and colors and tantrums."

"Tantrums. That's a lovely idea."

She surveyed the room with hands on hips. "Yes, but it changed after we'd taken away most of what was originally here. First I wanted it to be for him. Then I realized until he came home it had to be for us too. So I made more changes. More and more and more. I was studying to be an architect before we got married, just so you don't think I'm completely nuts!"

She told a little of their history, leaving out the parts about her husband's breakdown and her car crash. The way her version went, they'd lost the child, changed jobs a few times, finally got a strong urge to return to their home state and live life the way they wanted. I asked no questions. Her lies were gentle things; lies to a stranger who needn't know more about their ongoing pain. I don't think she wanted my pity so much as my understanding of why their house was so different. It was both her child and her art, for the time being. Like some kind of impossible and heartbreaking golem, she was trying to bring it to life with her care, love, and imagination. When the boy returned she would direct it back to him. Until then, all of the energy and emotion she had for her child would go into trying to make this inanimate thing animate.

Every room of their house was a different world. They had cut through some of the walls and ceilings so as to build bridges linking one to the next like surreal dream sequences. One bedroom was only crooked objects at cockeyed angles. Pictures in free-form frames and the only mirror were all mounted on the ceiling. A hole had literally been punched through the wall at foot level and filled with glass. It took a moment to realize it was a window. Another, called the Fall Room, contained only soft objects in two colors.

There are eccentrics who build houses out of Coca-Cola bottles or Wyoming license plates. Architects who design churches to look like melting candles or airports like manta rays. But the most singular and frankly exhausting thing about the Meier house was the raw obsession at work. Anwen said nothing about it, but it was plain she knew that if her mind sat down for a time to rest, it would realize the deadly hopeless truth of her situation and destroy her. So she never really sat down. She planned and built and tinkered with the only link she felt she still had to her lost child.

A little black dog waddled into the room and over to my leg. I bent over and petted it.

"That's Henry Hank. My husband names all the puppies after old boxers. We know the customers change the names when they get them home, so Greg gets a kick out of having a whole stable of fighters around him for a few weeks."

Another one came in and was introduced as Gil Diaz.

"Hello!"

At first I thought her husband looked fine. Much more robust and healthy than Anwen. Very tan and filled out. Those were the impressions that crossed my mind when I stood up to meet him. As we were moving toward each other, one of the dogs started barking and Gregory looked down to see what the hubbub was. Seeing him up close, I realized his skin was tanned the unnatural brown-orange that come from tans in a bottle. When I was a boy and that junk had just been developed, a guy in town bought some Man-Tan and slathered himself with it. For weeks he looked like he was wearing a kind of dreadful burnt-siena lipstick, badly layered, all over his unfortunate body. I suppose they have improved the product since then, but not much, by the looks of Gregory Meier.

He shook hands oddly too—a much too big and powerful burst when we first touched and squeezed, then nothing. His hand went completely flaccid. I remembered he had had a breakdown. The longer I watched him, the more signs of his fragility and eccentricity were evident. In the end I had the feeling they might have "retired" to the country from their previous life because the pressure had been too much for this man, and would be for a long time.

"Darling, he says a famous breeder in the West recommended us. A man named Raymond Gill?"

"Raymond! Sure, I know Raymond. Nice man. What does he raise again?"

"Pugs."

"Pugs, that's right. Nice man."

He cleared his throat much too often. He paid such dramatic, overly close attention to what others said, even when it was trivial lighter-than-air chitchat, that it was disconcerting. He tried so hard and that's what made it so fucking sad. He wanted you to think you were a very important person to him, despite having met only minutes before. He wasn't a sycophant or a glad-hander either. He probably did like me, because I was nice and pleasant while there, but the pathos was in his rictus smile, a handshake that died after too much first squeeze, the scary-adoring way he looked at his wife. By comparison, she was the strongest person on earth.

The most embarrassing moment came in the middle of a discussion about the merits of the French bulldog over other breeds. Gregory broke off what he was saying and grinned. "Do you know what H. L. Mencken called Calvin Coolidge? 'A dreadful little cad.' The tongue should never show in these dogs, as I'm sure you know."

The change from dogs to Mencken to dog tongues came so fast it took several seconds to register. I'm sure I overreacted, because when I turned to Anwen, she was frowning and puckering her lips at me as if to say, "Sssh! Don't show him you heard." This wild skid from one side of his mind to another happened again twice while Gregory spoke but I pretended not to notice.

So what was worse, his brittleness? The way the Meiers lavished their ghostly love on each other and those gargoyle dogs? Or simply the power of their house? The house/monument/golem they'd needed and built to replace their lost child.

It was quiet torture remaining there that long, sad afternoon. I needed more than anything to get away and think. To sit in a bar or a hotel room, a corner anywhere alone where I could talk to myself about what to do next.

I was ninety-five percent certain Lincoln Aaron was their son. But there remained things to do to make sure. I did them in New York by contacting yet another detective agency and having them check out Lily's "parents," Joe and Frances Margolin, in Cleveland. No one by either name had lived in that city for thirty years. The same was true about a child named Lincoln Aaron, purportedly born in Cleveland eight or nine or ten years before. No hospital or governmental bureau there had any record.

Why am I getting ahead of myself here and telling the most important part of the story before it happened? Because I already knew the truth that day sitting in the Meiers' living room. Sitting on a soft couch with a cup of aromatic tea, I knew the woman I loved more than any person on earth was a criminal and a monster. Kidnapping is monstrous. Like murder and rape, it undermines the only real givens we have in life: my life, my sexuality, the issue of my blood are my own.

Lincoln once made up a story about crows with blue eyes. It wasn't good or interesting, but his image of those inky birds with azure eyes haunted me long after. Crows are smart, sneaks, loudmouths. I like them very much for what they are. If I saw one sitting on a branch smoking a cigar I'd laugh and think yes, that's right. But blue eyes belong to babies, angels, Swedes; put them in a crow and the funny goes away. The imp becomes perverse. Several phone calls away from knowing my love was a nightmare, I couldn't rid my mind of the boy's image. A crow with blue eyes. His mother, my friend and love, the very worst kind of human being. Crows with blue eyes. Lily Aaron, kidnapper.

When the visit was over, after I'd seen the house and all the dogs and we'd talked until the three of us were in a late-afternoon stupor of too much information and too many words, they walked me to my rental car. I thanked them for their time. To get out of having to buy a dog, I told them what I really wanted was a gray one, which they didn't have. One of their females was due to give birth in a few weeks and I'd call to find out if a gray was among the litter. When Anwen asked for my address and telephone number in Portland (where I supposedly lived), I made them up.

As I was turning the key in the ignition, Gregory touched my arm and asked me to wait a second. He reached into his back pocket and pulled out a sheet of white paper. While he carefully unfolded it, I glanced at Anwen, who looked uncomfortable and embarrassed for the first time that day.

"I'm sure you haven't, but I ask everyone we meet. I know it's crazy, but I'm sure you'll understand. Anwen told you what happened to our son. This is what they think he'd look like today. The police have these machines that can draw a face in a kind of long-term projection. Take someone who's five years old, press the button, and you get an idea of what they'd look like at twenty. It's really amazing, but they say with a baby it's very hard." Gregory's face wavered, fell, rose, tried to smile, couldn't. "The bones are so soft when they're that young. They don't have much distinctiveness in their faces then. You've never seen a boy out there in Portland who looks anything like this, have you?"

Cold, cold, such cold poured across my heart and froze me. Taking his bent sheet of paper, I forced myself to look. But for long seconds I honestly couldn't *focus* on what was there. My life was in my hands and that is the final danger.

When the anxiety settled some and I saw the drawing, it was with the most horrid relief that I realized it wasn't my boy! The eyes were wrong, the round cheeks, a chin that was soft when it should have been unusually prominent. This wasn't Lincoln. For a moment I felt absolved. There's no way Brendan Meier is Lincoln Aaron. Hooray! Thank God. Amen. Then came the most perverse synapse, for I felt a terrible urge to say, "He doesn't look like this. The eyes are much deeper. He has Lily's wide mouth. His hair—" And I didn't know if I was meaning their boy or our boy or the same boy. My heart was the first to know. This was the moment to tell the truth, but my heart went both secret and dead to them. I was almost sure of Lily's crime against this couple but could almost physically feel my whole self, starting with my heart, turning away. There's a proverb that says a person has a chance at the splendor of God twice in his life—once in early adolescence and again when he is forty-five or fifty. Conversely, I could literally feel myself embracing evil then. Perhaps I would come back later and tell them the truth, or go to Lily and confront her, but now I handed their picture back, made a small apologetic smile, and said no, sorry. What was worse, seeing the pain on Gregory's face as he took it and looked at the drawing for the millionth time or Anwen's glance of pity at her husband? Or was it even the drawing itself, this bad counterfeit of a boy's face that was so much handsomer and full of character in real life.

Driving away, I watched them in the rearview mirror until I passed over a small crest and they were gone. Only then did I become aware of the pressure in my bladder. It felt like I'd explode if I didn't piss immediately. There were no houses around or cars coming down the road, so I stopped, jumped out, undid my pants, and barely wrestled it free in time before the stuff blew out of me in a fury.

Despite all of the terrible matters flying around in my head, it was bliss to pee. All the complicated, perverse, and dangerous things that had happened and were sure to come, none was more important than this dumb little function I did ten times a day.

"Winner and still champeen, the cock!" I announced to the New Jersey countryside. Which reminded me of Lily's sweet curiosity about my penis. One of the first times we went to bed, afterward she held it in her hand and inspected, jiggled, poked it until I raised my head from the pillow and asked if she was conducting a science project. No, she'd just never had the nerve to look at one so closely.

"Never? You didn't even look at Rick's?"

"Naa, I was always too shy. I always felt self-conscious, you know?" She looked up from her position across my thighs and beamed. Partners in crime. Such a happy, comfortable moment. So adult and childlike at once, like playing Doctor. It was around that time I began thinking how deeply I loved this woman.

I had two options—fight or flight. I doubt if many people ever seriously consider running away from their lives altogether. It is either childish or desperate, and luckily few of us behave like that or experience such dark extremes. I knew one woman who was beaten very badly by her husband. An hour after he left the house for work, she packed a small bag and took a taxi to the airport. Charging a ticket to New York on his credit card (wanting him to think she'd gone there), she paid cash for a ticket to London. The ploy worked, and by the time he found her months later, she was safe and well protected.

In comparison, that seemed so cut-and-dried. Her life was threatened and she ran. My situation, "my danger," was more complex and tricky. Yet in this era of quick relationships, when people go from A to Z at the speed of light and then separate, I *could* have gotten away with saying to Lily: I'm sorry, but this isn't going to work, bye-bye. The easy, despicable way out, but given the alternative . . . Plus what *was* the alternative? I'm sorry, sweetheart, but I have to tell the police about you.

Sometimes the solution to a problem comes so quickly and resolutely that it leaves no trace of doubt about what must be done.

While I was driving back up the turnpike toward New York, my mind was fidgeting wildly about what to do. Traffic was busy but not enough to heed. The radio was on loud, tuned to a rock station; my companion for the trip.

There were so damned many Lilys in this. The Lily I knew. The Lily I thought I knew. Lily the kidnapper. Lily—

"Hey!"

In a far part of my mind I had heard the sound of a very loud car rattling up behind on the left. But turnpikes are full of clanging clunkers you ignore and just hope they don't strangle you with their exhaust.

"Hey, fuckhead!"

In the middle of my muddle I looked quickly toward the shout. Right out my window, a man was pointing a gun at me. He wore a huge grin and every few seconds kept yelling, "Hey! Hey! Hey!" Then he laughed a screech and, before I could move, pulled the trigger and the gun exploded.

I pitched the car to the right. Because I was in the slow lane, I hit no one. Screech and his driver both howled with delight and, clanking louder, their car sped up and away.

Braking, I pulled further over onto the shoulder of the road. Why wasn't I dead? He must have fired a blank. Why would he do that? Why hadn't I panicked and crashed? Luck. Or blessed. Why had he shot at me? Because. Life gives no explanations or excuses. We're the ones who think them up.

Sitting there trembling and cursing, thanking God Almighty for this break, I felt the moment slowly unwind and pass. Adrenaline stopped pumping terror and relief through me and shakily my own life with its present and future returned.

Lily returned too, and what filled my mind once the scared-to-death feeling passed was immense love for her. Love no matter what. Death one moment, Lily Aaron the next. I had survived and, returning to life, thought first of her. It was clear she was all that mattered. Cars rammed and rummed by on the left, night was purpling the sky. I would go back to her. I *had* to find a way to bring our love and a new life together through this wall, this *world,* of fire we now faced.

. . . . .

I rang the doorbell but no one answered. After waiting a while longer I used my key. It was three in the afternoon. Lincoln would still be in school, Lily at the restaurant. Dropping my bag on the floor, I smelled the familiar bouquet of home—scented candles, dog, cigarette smoke, Lily's Grey Flannel cologne. As I walked slowly through the place, it struck me as a kind of museum now—a museum of our life as it *had* been. Everything the same, everything different. This is where we played Scrabble together, that is where I spilled chili sauce on the carpet. A comic book of Lincoln's was on the table. I picked it up and riffled through the pages.

Lincoln. This new world centered on him now, and the contradiction, if that was the word, was that he was one terrific kid. Smart and well adjusted, he often had a sense of humor and insight that made him a real pleasure to live with. Who knows how much we're born with and how much is a result of upbringing and education. From living with the Aarons and watching the way the two interacted, I believed Lily was a great mother and had had a profoundly positive effect on the boy. That was part of the problem: she was so good for him.

Cobb was lying on his big bed in the kitchen. When he saw me, his long tail whacked the floor a couple of times. I waved hello and that was enough for him. He groaned contentedly and closed his eyes.

For want of something to do, I opened the refrigerator. In among the bottles and bags was a white clay figure of what looked vaguely like one of the characters in my "Paper Clip." Why it was in the fridge was a mystery, but such enigmas are common when you live with a ten-year-old. Taking it carefully off the metal shelf, I turned it slowly in my hand. Was the artist ten years old, or nine as the Meiers had said? I thought constantly about that sad fragile couple, their house and the scarred life they led. How thrilled they would be if they were shown this figure and told who'd made it. How much joy it would give them to know it was by their son, who was well and happy. Like filling their lungs with air all the way instead of shallow breaths.

"Max! You're back!"

Lost in thought, I hadn't heard the door close. Turning, I felt small arms grab me from behind and hold tight.

"Max, where have you been? I missed you so much! Did you see my "Paper Clip" statue? I made it for you. You know who it is? You like it?"

I took him in my arms and closed my eyes as tight as I could. That way the world stayed outside a moment. Besides, I had begun to cry as soon as I knew it was him. There was no way to stop it.

"I like it very much, Linc. It's the perfect welcome-home present. I'm really happy to be back."

"Me too! We didn't do anything while you were gone. But we talked about *you* a lot."

"Really? That's great."

He pulled away and looked up at me. "You're crying?"

"Yup, 'cause I'm so glad to see you."

He grabbed me again and hugged harder. "You'll stay home now, won't you?"

I nodded, holding him to me, rocking us back and forth. "Yes, I'm here now."

"Max, I've got a lot to tell you. Remember that kid Kenneth Spilke I told you about? The kid who threw the chalk at me?"

Through a fog of jet lag, love, and concern about how I would react when I saw his mother, I listened as Lincoln unrolled the carpet of his life since I had been gone. So much had happened! A pitched playground battle with Kenneth Spilke over a girl, a telephone conversation with that same girl about kids they both hated, and a test in school on the digestive system, then two lousy meals Lily had cooked one right after the other when he had specifically *told* her he didn't want broccoli again . . . It was great to hear him toot on about these matters. I watched and listened to him with full attention. If only life forever could be these minutes, full of fifth-grade news and expectancy about when his mother would be home. Ironically, other times I would have listened with only half an ear to this wrap-up, the other half for an opening door. Now he had it all because he was the only normal left in my life.

"And what's up with your mama?"

"I told you, she cooked these two gross meals—"

"No, I mean what *else?* What's she been doing?"

He shrugged and licked his tongue back and forth over his teeth. "I don't know. Working, I guess."

I would've taken that as sufficient if I had not happened to look up and see the expression on his face. Lincoln wasn't good at hiding things. He was too open and friendly; wanted you to know what was going on in his life.

"What, Linc? What is it?"

He glanced at me, couldn't keep his eyes there, looked away. It made me frown. "What's the matter?"

"I didn't know if you'd come back."

"What? What do you mean?"

"I don't know. I thought maybe you were leaving us for good." His voice got much louder. "I mean, why should you stay around? Maybe you don't like us anymore or something."

"Lincoln, why are you saying this? Where did you get the idea—"

"I don't know. It was just kinda surprising when you went away like that. Zippo and you were gone. How was I supposed to know?"

"Because I would *never* do that to you. I would never just walk out on you. I'm your friend. Friends don't do that to each other."

I gestured for him to come and sit on my lap. We talked some more but I could barely follow what he was saying because my mind was working so fast.

"Max?"

"Yeah?"

"Did you bring me anything from New York?"

"Sure! Sure I did. How could I forget? Come on." I went to my suitcase and got out the T-shirt and basketball sneakers I'd bought him in New Jersey.

"You got 'em, Max! They're exactly what I wanted. Oh, you're great! Thank you!"

It's so easy to win a kid's heart with presents. He'd been wanting the trendy shirt and shoes a long time but Lily refused to buy them because they were ridiculously expensive.

"Do you want to see them? Should I put them on?"

"Of course! Are you kidding? You have to wear them for the rest of your life."

He held the shoes in one hand, the shirt in the other. Looking at me, he dropped them and hugged me again. "You're the best, Max. Just the *best.*"

While he worked to put them on, I tried as best I could to grill him in a subtle way. Had anything happened while I was gone? Anything special or different? How had Lily acted? He was much more interested in the new shoes—I got mostly "I dunno" and "I guess" in answer to my questions.

A car door slammed outside, followed by the sound of a key turning in the lock. "Anybody home?"

"Here we are, Mom. Max's back!"

"Thank God."

Suddenly there were flurries of sound in the kitchen—Cobb's tail hitting the floor, Lily talking to him, something being placed heavily on a counter, some chatter from her that was too far away to be understood. Then there she was. It felt to me like we were meeting for the first time. My heart beat hard.

"You didn't answer. How's your brother?" She sailed into the room on a cloud of love and self-confidence. I was home, we were a family again. She didn't know what I knew. I was afraid of what she hadn't told me. How much different could our hearts have been at that shared moment in our lives?

My *brother?* What did he have to do with this? At the last second I luckily remembered I'd gone to New York ostensibly to see Saul.

"He's okay. Naughty as usual. Making lots of money."

She strode over and gave me a big long kiss. "We missed you. Lincoln said I talked about you too much." She looked like a great meal; you didn't know where to start first. Sirens were going off in my head and heart, love bats swooping and lifting, men on pogo sticks bouncing around wooden floors. How was I supposed to feel about this? Or deal with it? I adored this woman. Lusted after her every spent breath. She terrified me.

"Well, bucko, tell the truth, are you glad to be home with us?"

Before I could answer, Lincoln picked up a leg and stuck it in her face. "Ma, check out the sneaks! Air Jordans. He got 'em for me in New York."

"You bought those things? Are you out of your mind?"

"I guess so."

"I guess so too, but it's a nice mind. We're extremely glad to have it back."

When Lincoln left to show his shoes to a friend in the neighborhood, Lily and I stayed in the living room.

"Why are we suddenly so quiet? Have we already run out of things to tell each other? How was New York?"

"Someone shot at me."

"What do you mean?"

"A guy shot at me while I was driving." Grateful for a story to tell so I could stay away from the important subject, I dragged it out, exaggerating here and there, making it even worse than it was. Not so that I would appear heroic or more levelheaded, but because telling a woman a story is one of the greatest pleasures in life. Holding their attention, seeing their reaction, making them laugh or rear back in shock or wonder . . . The woman you love is the true listener, the supreme audience. Even when she is dangerous and you are afraid of her.

Lily heard me out. When I was finished, she put her head down on her lap and mumbled.

"What?"

She looked up. "I don't know what I would have done."

"I was very spooked."

"I'm not talking about spooked, I'm talking about *life.* If I'd answered the telephone and heard some state trooper in New York calling to say you were dead, I don't know what I would've done." She closed her eyes. "I might have gone mad. Yeah, I think I'd have gone crazy. I thought about you *un*endingly when you were gone, Max. Like I was sixteen again and in love for the first time. I passed a flower store and wanted to go in and get you some for your desk, those white tulips you like so much. Even though you weren't here. I bought stupid little presents and hid them under your pillow. I couldn't wait to hear what you'd say. But so what, that's love, right? Remember I told you when I masturbate, my fantasy is always a faceless man who makes love to me? Even that changed. When I did it this time it was *you* there, and the more I could remember about you, your voice or the way your hands touch me, the hotter I got. I masturbated all the time, Max. You and I fucked and fucked and couldn't get enough. We never got tired. We did it on beaches, in cars, other people's beds, everywhere. One time I imagined us doing it on Ibrahim's desk in the back of the restaurant. It was so strong. I couldn't stop thinking about it. I wanted you so much." She stood up. "Come on, let's do it now while Lincoln's out."

"Lily—"

"No, I don't want to talk anymore. I don't want to think about dying or you being away. It was hard enough for that short time. I want to make love now and smell you. I want that great smell all around me. I just want more right now, Max. Okay? Tell me your other stuff later. Come on." She took my hand and pulled me toward the bedroom. More erotic than anything was the way she held my hand. She kept squeezing it and letting it go slack, as if her hand itself had its own pulse, or a way of hurried breathing. Squeeze, stop, squeeze, stop.

She wore purple socks. White sneakers and purple socks. She sat on the bed and flipped her shoes off but kept the socks on. The silver belt buckle on her jeans was jerked open, then the *sttttttrrrrruttttt* when the pants buttons came undone one fast after the other.

"Hurry. Hurry hurry hurry." She pulled the sweater over her

head and she wore no bra. Her breasts dropped heavily out of the soft wool. She sat in bikini panties, arms stretched behind her, and watched while I wrestled out of my clothes. When my slacks were off, she reached into my underpants and touched my cock. Her hands were freezing cold. I almost jumped back. She wouldn't let go. Pulling me gently toward her, she took it in her mouth and the cold-to-warm was so sharp and quick that I felt my knees almost go. Lily didn't like sucking cock because it made her feel cheap and whorey. Knowing that, I never asked her to do it. What good is sex when it's not wanted? So was this a one-of-a-kind welcome-home gift, or did she genuinely desire to do it? Unsure, I eased myself out of her mouth and knelt down so we were face to face. "Don't. You don't have to—"

"I *want* to."

"No. The other's enough." Pushing her back on the bed, I pinned her arms above her head and ran my tongue up the long course of her neck. Her throat worked up and down and I thought she was trying to swallow. But then she began crying, gasping. I got off her. She lay on her back, arms above as if still held down. Eyes open, tears rolled down the sides of her face in a steady stream.

"I missed you so much. I got scared, I missed you so god-damned much. It's not right to be like that; it's not healthy. I'm not a weak person. I'm *not,* but look at how I was acting. You weren't even gone that long." She lifted her head off the bed and looked at me. "Maybe I shouldn't be telling you this. You could kill me with it if you wanted. You could twist me in half."

Walking in an hour before, I was resolved to have it out. Face her with what I knew and demand an explanation. But my resolve began slipping with Lincoln's happy greetings and many kisses. Now this.

Staring her in the eye, I said the truth but she naturally misunderstood. "I know you."

"You know me better than anyone. Better than anyone ever has."

"I *know* you."

"Yes. Fuck me."

"All these things you haven't"—I entered her hard—"told me!"

"Yes." Her legs wrapped around my waist. I felt the socks on my back. Her arms tightened around my neck. "Secrets. Crybaby. Secrets."

"I hate them."

She stopped moving.

"I hate your secrets."

The fear on her face turned into a smile. "Take them. Take them all. Fuck me now. You can have them all."

I pushed as hard as I could. She closed her eyes, chuckled.

"I want them. Promise me—"

"Just do this now. Yes, that. Whatever you want. Whatever you want. You . . ."

It was so good. And when it was over, the boy would come home and we three would sit at the kitchen table and be a family again.

Lily came quickly, which was not like her, but then kept pumping and moving, keeping it going as long as she could. "Max, I love you. Oh, Max." She rose and fell. Her eyes were shut above a huge smile. I watched. Half of me swam in her like a sea, the other half watched. Watched her from as far away as the moon.

"Absence makes the heart lose weight."

Gus Duveen looked at Ibrahim like he was a bad smell. "What does *that* mean?"

"This is a saying in Saru. It is what Lily felt when Max was not here. I had an uncle who married a woman who turned into paper. This is not uncommon, but he did not know it until it was almost too late."

Squeezing my knee under the table, Lily leaned over and whispered, "I love Ibrahim's stories."

"My uncle went on a business trip to Umm Hujul and met a

woman there. They fell madly in love and he asked to marry her. This was all right and everything went according to plan. After the wedding, they returned to Saru and he created a household for her. Then he is a businessman, so he must go out and return to work. He is a traveling salesman all over the Middle East but no big worry. He told his new wife he would be coming back every week to see her. Now, the first time he returned, she was happy to see him but was much, much lighter. When he picks her up in bed, she almost floats out of his arms. 'You must eat something!' he says, but they are so glad to see each other nothing more is said about it. The next time he returns to his house, she is fifteen times lighter. She can walk on water now, but no one is impressed because she is not holy, only skinny. My uncle thinks this is not love, but blackmail: this is her way of making him stay at home. So he tells her he did not marry a balloon, and if she wants to lift off the earth, he will not be interested in her anymore. Desperate, she says, 'Take me with you and I will do anything.' 'Are you crazy? Women do not go with men to their business.' But she is very stubborn and says, 'Well then, unless I can be near you always, I will lose the rest of my weight and disappear. I cannot help it. My body loves you too and has its own mind. I don't want to die, but if *it* wants to it will, husband.' "

Lily caressed the inside of my thigh. Since returning from New York, I'd experienced a completely new side of her: hungry, worried, agitated. We made love more than ever before, but her body stayed tight as a strung bow and never seemed to relax. Even when we'd finished and lay there in the calm dark, I felt her tension. Too soon she would want to start again and I had to catch up to her desire. Out of the bedroom, she was overly bright and peppy. There were few quiet moments anymore; out of the bedroom everything had to be either in motion or in the planning stage. I had the feeling she instinctively knew what I'd discovered and wanted to steer our lives away from that moment of truth, that moment of impact. As long as she kept moving, talking, planning . . . the disastrous facts could be avoided. Yet how could she know what I'd found? I knew about women's eerie sense of intuition, but did it go this far? Were they that clairvoyant?

On my part, I simply hadn't had the courage to confront her. I justified this cowardice by figuring I wanted to observe her a while with my new knowledge in hand. Scrutinize someone from a different position and you see new things. Look at them with X-ray eyes and their beauty becomes bones and blood, curves, dips, cells, cause and effect.

"But God does not let us love someone only a little while." Ibrahim reached over and touched Gus on the arm. His grumpy lover smiled back at him and nodded. "My uncle was a man first and a businessman second. He loved his wife and did not want to see her turn into air. What could he do? One day right before he was to leave again, they were playing together. You know the way lovers play. He had a ballpoint pen, and because the point was not out, he pressed it to his wife's neck and pretended to write something. Now remember how thin she was. He kept on doing it. But you know what happened? She was *so* slender that her blood rose up to the edge of her skin when the pen touched over it, like fish to food in the aquarium. And then there was his name, written in blue blood beneath his poor skinny wife's skin! My uncle was horrified but fascinated too, of course. Once he saw this and showed her, he wrote many other things too and all of them stayed visible on her the longest time. Hours, probably."

"Fucking guy used his wife for a pad, and they lived happily ever after," Gus said, ruining the end of the story.

Ibrahim was delighted. "You're so smart, Gus. That's right. He took his wife to his business meetings now and could explain her presence there when he said he would be taking notes on her during the meeting. If nobody believed him, he would just show them how it worked. She became his paper."

A moment later Ib was called to the phone and got up from the table, leaving the rest of us to look at each other in the wake of this story. Gus spoke first.

"Sometimes I genuinely think he believes them."

Lily waved him off. "Oh, he does not. He's just being entertaining."

"But they all have some kind of point, don't they? They're not just Arabian Nights." Sullivan Band spoke. "What was that one about?" She was due to go on duty in a few minutes. "Sometimes I use his stories in our drama group. As exercises. The only thing I got from this was women are weak and'll do anything to be by their men. Sex-ist!"

"It's not about weak women, it's about transformation. What happens to us, or what we are willing to do for the people we love."

"That's right, Max."

"I agree."

Sullivan held up both hands. "I think you're wrong, but *c'est la vie*. I have to go be a waitress." She stood and walked to the kitchen, passing Ibrahim on the way. They spoke for a moment, then continued in their different directions. When he got to the table, he grinned at me.

"You think my uncle's story's about love, Max?"

"Whatever it's about, I liked it. Would you mind if I used some of it in 'Paper Clip'?"

"No, that would be an honor. Does everybody have enough to eat? Yes? Because I'm sorry but Gus, Lily, and I have to go and talk to a man about salmon. Come, partners, the salmon man is waiting."

The three of them walked out together, leaving Alberta Band and me at the table. Lunch for employees at Crowds and Power was a full-blown affair, starting around eleven and continuing for the most part until they were done and not when the doors opened for the day to the public. I loved eating with them, listening to their stories, offering some of my own. The restaurant was a United Nations, a hotel lobby of comings and goings, greetings and goodbyes. The food was good, the people who prepared and presented it intriguing.

"Max, can I ask a favor?"

"Sure."

"I never told you, but I'm a really big fan of your comic strip. Could you draw me a little sketch of the two guys in it? Nothing elaborate or involved. I'd love to frame it and put it on the wall of my apartment."

"Alberta, I'd love to. Do you want it drawn on something special?"

"No, anything would be great."

"I've got a nice sketchpad in the car. Let me go get it and I'll do one in there. But stick around—I've got an idea and need you here to do it."

When I returned, she had combed her hair and freshened her lipstick.

"Okay, sit right where you are. I need you for about ten minutes."

Alberta is a good-looking woman, so it was a pleasure to use her as a model.

"What're you doing?"

"Keep your pants on. You'll see when I'm finished. Turn your head a little to the left. Yeah! Like that. Stay still."

We chatted while I drew and she gave up trying to guess what I was doing.

"Alberta, tell me about Lily. Whatever comes to your mind. I always like to hear what other people have to say about her."

Rather than ask what I meant, she folded her hands in her lap and looked into the near distance.

"She was the one who hired us, you know. Sullivan and I'd been working at this dreary deli up on the Strip. The boss pinched our asses too many times, so we hauled freight out of there. Not many places hire two people at a time, and you'd be surprised at how biased they are against hiring sisters. Like the two of you're in cahoots and'll steal 'em blind. Anyway, we heard there might be something here and we came down for an interview. First thing I saw when I came in the door was Mabdean, who'd just cut off all his hair and looked like a big black genie in a bottle. I turned to my sister and said, 'I'll wash floors for this place if *he* works here.' Gus came around but wouldn't deign to talk to us, Ibrahim was out, and we waited around till finally Lily asked if she could help us. We thought she owned the place, judging by the way people kowtowed to her. I don't think we talked ten minutes before she gave us both jobs and then a week later Mabdean and I moved in together.

"What do I think of her, aside from the fact the woman turned my life around so I was finally happy for the first time in years? I think she's solid and really caring. But I'll tell you something. The moment you asked me that question, this one funny thing came to me immediately. You know how she likes biographies? Always reading about someone's life, but it's never really one kind of person or another. Composers, businessmen, Hitler . . . I guess she just likes knowing how other people lived, huh? Anyway, once she was reading the autobiography of John Huston, the director. I asked if I could borrow it when she was done. When she gave it to me, there was one thing marked. Love her as I do, I think she's extremely anal retentive about her books, because every one I've borrowed is in perfect condition, no matter if they're hardcover or paperback. All my books are very well lived in, you could say. But she lent me this Huston autobiography and inside there was a passage tipped with one of those orange markers kids use in school. I was so shocked to see it. That's all—just that one the whole three or four hundred pages, but I remember it because I'd never seen it done in any of her books. It said, 'I've had nine lives so far, and I regret every one of them.' "

I had to will my head to stay down and my hand to keep drawing. "What was it again?"

" 'I've had nine lives so far, and I regret every one of them.' I mean, that does *not* sound like Lily Aaron to me. To tell you the truth, I think she can be a little screechy sometimes, and a bit tight-lipped, but in toto she has it together. A hell of a lot more than me, that's for sure. I mean, a nice son, a semi-famous boyfriend . . . Hey, am I ever going to get to see your picture?"

I turned the pad around and handed it to her. Across the top

was written: "Alberta and the Band." I'd drawn her and my characters holding hands, taking a bow, as if after a performance.

"Max, that's fabulous! Thank you."

She pulled it carefully off the pad and kissed my cheek. "I know
exactly where I'm going to put it. I'll tell you one last thing about
Lily. A few months before she met you, there were a couple of actors
in here one night making trouble. They were drunk and got ugly-
rowdy. Mabdean usually takes care of things like that, but it was his
day off. First Ib, then Gus tried to talk them down, but these ass-
holes were out of control. This was their party and they were goin' to
do it their way, fuck you very much. Things started getting out of
hand and someone said maybe we should call the cops. But Lily said
no. She reached into her purse, pulled out this little black gadget
that looked like a light meter, and went over to them. Without saying
a word, she touched one, then the other on the arm and these guys
flipped off their barstools onto the floor like they'd been shot. Neither moved, and the whole place got real quiet real fast. Lily stood
there like Madame Gunslinger and put the black thing back in her
bag. The only comment she made was: 'They'll come around in a few
minutes.' She had one of those totally illegal cattle prod things you
use against muggers. The kind that shoot out five trillion volts into
whoever's trying to jump you. ZAP and ZAP—on the floor like dead
meat. That took balls! I don't know if I'd have the nerve to use one.
I've heard they can cause some serious permanent damage if you do
it wrong or touch a guy in the wrong place. But your girlfriend
didn't hesitate a second. These guys crossed the line and she zapped
them. ZZZZZ. You should have heard the sound. Like this high
cracking. Phew. It still gives me the shivers."

"What happened to the men?"

"Nothing. We carted them into the kitchen until they came to
and then they took off. No one ever told them what happened either.
They had absolutely no idea what hit 'em."

"Where'd Lily get the zapper?"

"Wouldn't say. Even when I said I wanted to get one, she

wouldn't tell. What nerve, huh? Walk up to a stranger and stick 'em with that. Something else too—I was looking at her face when she did it. Max, it was *real* cool. Not scared or nervous, like you'd expect. Tough. I would not make that woman pissed off if I were you.

"Time to go. Thanks a million for the drawing. I can't wait to show Mabdean."

I sat at the empty table finishing my meal and my drawing. I started by sketching a little boy and a giant dog standing side by side. Guess who? In the next frame, a baseball comes flying in from the side. Next frame, ball hits boy on the head. Next frame he goes down. The drawing became almost automatic. I wasn't really sure what was up, so I let my hand continue. The kid lies motionless. His dog watches for a frame, then picks him up in its mouth and carries him to a house. It's obviously not the boy's home, because when the people open the door and see what's there, both throw up their hands and scream. The dog is scared into dropping his bundle and running away. They pick up the still-unconscious boy and bring him inside. I stopped there and checked my watch. I'd been working almost two hours but something was definitely up—my brain hatching an idea in this, its vocabulary for the day. I went on. At first, Alberta and Sullivan kept coming round asking if I wanted anything, but after I said no, thanks enough times they left me alone. The restaurant filled with the lunch crowd and the women were busy enough with their customers.

The couple bring the boy into the bedroom and lay him down on their bed. Until now there'd been no dialogue in the story, no captions, no words. I decided to keep it that way. The man and woman look at each other and smile foxily. He runs out of the room and comes back in the next picture with a giant tool and paint boxes. Bending over the unconscious child, the two of them go to work on him. Sawing, painting, hammering, things fly up in the air—clothes, bones, a sneaker. Arms and legs, tools and flurries of wild work. The woman runs out of the room and returns with a bizarre, forbidding tool. Holding it in front of her, she literally dives back into the high dust cloud that's risen above the bed. The two step out of it a moment for a rest, but magically the melee of flying objects and dust continues without them. They leap back in. The cloud disappears, but all we see are their two backs and many working arms over the bed/operating table.

In the next frame the boy is sitting up, but looks completely different. He is obviously still dazed from the smack on the head and the transforming operation. Holding up a mirror, he looks at his reflection with no recognition. Next, the three of them are at a table eating a big turkey dinner. The little guy's plate is full and he's smiling. There's someone at the door. Close-up of a hand going BANG BANG BANG. Close-up of "parents" exchanging worried looks. Mom answers. Outside, two sad-faced adults stand next to the big dog who brought the kid here. There's a discussion. Close-up of four mouths talking at each other simultaneously. But it's plain the new parents lie to the real: Are you crazy? He's our boy. Look at him, does he look like either of you? Not at all. Not one speck. The real parents and dog leave together, brokenhearted. The dog looks back over its shoulder as the three of them walk away into a sad sunset. In the meantime back at the dinner table, something else terrible is happening—the boy's body and face are coming apart and beginning to melt.

"Cooool, Max. Definitely gross!" Lincoln dropped his school bag on the chair next to mine and, leaning on my shoulder, bent over for a better look. He was holding a sandwich they'd probably made for him in the kitchen. "Elvis, you gotta see this."

Elvis Packard, Lincoln's best friend, came over and condescended to look while devouring one of the restaurant's fat éclairs. I felt like snatching it out of his hand. I disliked Elvis so much that anytime he came within radar range, my tongue turned dry in my throat and I could barely greet the little shit. The son of two movie agents, he had the manners of a hungry jackal and generally behaved like a spoiled brat gone nuclear. Worse, he was only ten but already capable of seriously nasty things. Even worse, Lincoln was fascinated by him and the two were inseparable.

"Hi, Linc. Elvis, how are you?" He chewed. He stared at me. He said nothing. "Are you speaking today, El-Void? How about 'Hi, Max, nice to see you'?" Both Lincoln and I looked at him to see if there'd be a response. There wasn't. "Elvis, granted we don't like each other. But I don't like you for good reasons—you're rude and sneaky. You don't like me because you don't like anything, and because I'm probably the only person who ever talked to you like this. Therefore, let's work out a deal: we're allowed to dislike each other, but we must remain civil. Know what that means? We say hello, goodbye, please, and thank you. That's all. Those are the rules from now on. If you fail to follow them, I have the right to squeeze your eyeballs into your sockets until you become civil again."

Lincoln was giggling but Elvis was not.

"Why are you always mean to me?"

"Because you threw a hamster against a wall. Because you hit my son on the head with a flashlight. Because you step on our dog's tail whenever you don't think anyone's watching. Because of two hundred other reasons. However, Lincoln likes you, so I will endure you. But behave around me, sweetie pie. I'm bigger than you."

We dueled with our eyes a moment until the little poltroon looked away. I'm sure he was planning some later outrage against me, but for the moment I'd won and victory was sweet.

"So, Lincoln, what's up?"

"Nothin'. What are you drawing? Can I see the whole thing?"

Sliding the book closer to me, I slowly closed the cover. "Not yet. Maybe if it comes to something. You know how I am—I don't like people looking till something's finished."

He turned and translated for his friend. "Max's weird about his cartoons. He won't show them till he thinks they're ready. You should see some of the great stuff he threw out!"

"My father doesn't think your cartoons are funny."

"Tell him that's a compliment, coming from the father of Elvis Packard."

"Huh?"

"Hey, Max, you wanna do something?"

"Like what?"

"I dunno. Elvis has to go home and I thought we could hang around. You know."

"Okay. What do you want to do?"

"Where's Mom?"

"At a meeting with Ibrahim and Gus."

"You think we could go to the movies? Remember we wanted to see the robot one?"

"Right. Sure. Let's do that."

He threw a beaming look at Elvis that said, "Isn't my dad great?" and made me feel bulletproof. He was such a nice fellow. Generally it was so easy to please him. Looking at the two boys, I couldn't imagine what it would be like to live with Elvis Packard. If he didn't whine, he snuck. He lied outrageously, but when caught, he denied ever saying any such thing. I am making him out to be a dreadful human being but that's only because he was. I'm sure most parents know an Elvis P. Usually these Children from Hell live next door (i.e., conveniently nearby for endlessly frequent visits) and for some inexplicable reason are the favorites of your own normally sane, well-balanced offspring. You ask yourself a hundred times what do they *see* in these weasels, these snide whippersnappers who enter your house every time like minor criminals casing the joint or snobs vastly amused by what they see.

Luckily Elvis took off after finishing his éclair. He said "See ya" to Lincoln but nothing to me till I put a thumb on my eye and demonstrated what I'd do if he wasn't civil. The "Bye" he offered could only have been picked up with a hearing device.

"You hate him, huh, Max?"

"Well, there are other people I like more. Come on, let's catch a flick."

Both of us liked going to a four o'clock show. Theaters are empty then and the whole place is yours.

Despite Lily's oft-repeated warning about ruining our appetites, I bought a super-jumbo tub of popcorn with extra butter and we hunkered down to watch the latest High-Tech/Robot/Space Opera extravaganza where the machines had all the best lines while the humans spent their time running down corridors or shooting at each other. Besides his monsters, Lincoln was also going through a phase where he loved robots. His walls were covered with photos of Robocops 1 & 2, R2D2, Robot Jox, etc. He practiced walking and eating like one, drew pictures of them, the works. When I was a boy I had my passions too, which included comic books and autographs, among other things, so I fully understood how these obsessions worked. As a result, I was the one who usually went to these god-awful films with Lincoln as well as anything else that had to do with them.

Walking out of the theater into a warm early evening, we discussed whether it was better to build a killer robot with Gatling guns for hands or only your regular crushing pincers.

"Lincoln, I've got a question. It may sound a little funny, but answer it anyway."

"Okay. Is it about robots?"

"No, about you. I want you to tell me your earliest memories. The things you remember from when you were a little, little kid. But don't make it up. Don't tell any stories, okay? Only truth."

"I don't know. I don't think your memory is alive when you're that little."

"Sure it is. Try."

"Okay. I remember climbing out of my crib and walking into the TV room. Mom was watching TV and eating oatmeal. She took me on her lap and gave me some. She was really surprised I got out. That was funny. I remember the oatmeal."

"Great. What else?" We walked slowly down the street. He took my hand and held it in his soft one.

"I'm thinking. How come you want to know?"

"Because I'm interested in you. Don't you think it's interesting to know a person's first memories? Like the *first* thing they ever remember about the world?"

"I guess. What was *yours?*"

"Riding in my father's taxicab and smelling his cigarettes. The ceiling of the car was a kind of gray upholstery. I remember the color very well."

That appeared to satisfy him. "I remember the oatmeal thing. Also when we got Cobb. I remember being very small and this big giant dog came into the house and scared me. Mom kept saying it was okay, he was nice, but I wouldn't go up to him. But you know what's funny is he was scareder than me. You know how he doesn't like to be touched or anything. That's because the guy who had him before beat him up and made him scared. Mom said when we got him, he would go out a door but not come in. He'd go down the stairs but not up them.

"Oh yeah, and I remember my dad once."

"That's not possible, Linc. You never saw your father."

"Did too! I know I saw him once when I was a baby. I remember his face and I remember he put his finger on my nose like this. Once." He tapped his nose with his index finger. "Really, Max, I swear."

"I believe you. It's just different from the story your mother told. She said you never saw your father. And he died when you were only a year old."

But what if he'd seen his *real* father? What if the man who'd touched his nose was Gregory Meier, not the all too mysterious Rick Aaron, who was turning more and more ectoplasmic as time went by? It made sense.

"Tell me about it."

"I remember Mom holding me in her arms and this big man's face like a balloon coming down on me. Then he touched my nose like I told you. That's all, but I knew it was my dad."

"Did he say anything?"

"I don't know. I don't think so. Max, can I talk to you seriously now?" He stopped walking and turned to face me. I stopped too.

"Sure."

"Elvis had this newspaper that said there was a woman in Europe who had sex with two hundred men in one night. Is that possible? He said it was, but I think it's bull."

"Where does he get these magazines? Was it *The Truth* again? Where does he buy that rag? Who sells it to a ten-year-old boy?"

"He *says* he steals it from the drugstore. I don't know where he gets the others. He's always showing me stuff with naked girls or things that say a guy cooked and ate his whole family. No, but really, is that one true? Nobody can do it that much. Can you have sex that much?"

"No! Come on, you know those newspapers are goofy and full of baloney. We talked about it already. Most people are happy to have sex once or twice a week."

His mouth tightened and I could see he was biting the inside of his lip. "I never asked anyone questions like this, Max. Not Mom or anyone. You're the first, like, adult I know I can talk to who doesn't get ticked off or upset or something."

"Your mom's a good egg. She'd answer you."

"Unh-unh! She gets really angry at me sometimes when I ask questions. You don't know, because you're not always there. You're different. You're like my friend *and* my father at the same time. I know I had a dad, but you take his place in every way."

"Thank you very much, Lincoln. That makes me feel wonderful inside."

He sounded indignant. "It's true! Living with Mom was okay, but you know how we don't get along. She doesn't see things the way I do. Sometimes I don't ask her things or tell her what I feel in my heart 'cause she'll flip out or something. You're different. You and I talk about everything 'cause I know you won't dump on me or yell 'cause I asked something sexy or maybe stupid . . . I don't know. Ohh, I've just got to have a hug from you!" Startling me, he grabbed me around the waist and hugged really hard. People walking by us on the street looked and smiled. A man and his boy and their love for each other filling every corner of the world.

On the ride home, we had a pinballing discussion about robots, sex, Elvis, Lily, me. Lincoln continued his endless list of "best/ worst" questions in the usual rapid-fire delivery: What was the name of my best friend when I was ten? What was the grossest car acci-

dent I ever saw? List my qualities for the greatest-looking woman in
the world. Was Lily the best kisser I'd ever kissed? When he did this,
and it was often, I imagined him compiling a never-ending personality profile of me for his inner files. Once after a particularly long and
grueling session—with Lily off in a corner of the room smiling—I
drew her a picture of the back of a small boy sitting at a giant desk
with a giant quill pen in hand surrounded by ceiling-high piles of
folders and messy papers. I titled the drawing "Reviewing Max
Fischer."

When we pulled into the driveway, he'd just finished asking if I
thought God might be a plant.

Pulling up the hand brake, I stared ahead through the windshield. "A *plant?* What makes you think that?"

"I don't know. It's possible, isn't it?"

"Yes, I guess so."

"Max, remember the time you said if God was so powerful,
could He make a rock even He couldn't pick up? That's the coolest
idea!"

"It is, but I didn't think it up."

"You *didn't?* I told Elvis you did. Know what he said?"

"What?"

"That you're weird. Max, I gotta ask you one more thing. I
haven't told Mom about this yet because I wanted us to talk about it
first. Since you can't be my real father, you wanna be blood brothers?"

I was touched yet horrified. Sure, I'd become his blood brother;
then as "family" I could tell him not only is Lily *not* your mother but
she's going to have to go to jail too. What would happen when he
heard the truth about her? Understood what she had done to him? I
wanted to be his father, wanted to marry his false mother and live
happily ever after with both of them. But none of it was possible
now. I had to do something about the predicament; I couldn't ignore
the appalling truth any longer. If nothing else, I had to confront her
and ask: What are we going to do? What are we going to do with our
love and perfect life now that we're doomed no matter how we slice

it? I'd smiled on realizing that if she weren't the cause of it, then logical, clever Mrs. Aaron would have been the perfect person to go to for help with this monstrous problem. Excuse me, Lily, could you step out of your body a moment and help me with this trouble I'm having with you?

"What do you think?"

"About being blood brothers? I think it's a great idea. When would you want to do it?"

"Now! I'll go get a knife."

"Whoa, horsey! A *knife?* Are you nuts? A little pin'll do just fine."

"Yeah, but a knife—"

"A *pin,* Linc. I'll give you my blood, but not my arm."

He raced off, thrilled. We were about to go on an adventure together, just us two. His mother and the rest of life would have to wait outside while we did it—it was only ours and that's how he wanted it.

I did too. Tonight we'd prick our fingers, press them together, and vow eternal brotherhood. A ceremony old as human friendship. We'd smear our shared red over the lens and blot out the imminent rest for a moment. So long as I didn't know what to do next, being happy with the boy an evening more was as good as things could be then.

Our house had been cleaned the day before. The wooden floors shone, pillows still lay plumped and in line on the couch, a sweet lingering smell of soap or furniture polish was in the air, despite Cobb's own ripe perfume. It would take three or four days of living in these rooms to make things wrinkled and ours again. I liked both —the clean order followed by the clutter and jumble that came from three people's full speed ahead across the same space.

"Max, do you think this'll do?" He came running full tilt into the room, a long sewing needle held in front of him.

"Don't run! I've told you not to run with something sharp in your hand. It's really dangerous!"

"Yeah, but I—"

"But nothing, Lincoln! Think about it a minute and see how dangerous it is. You trip, you fall on it, and maybe it goes in your eye. Or into your *neck*—"

"Okay. I believe you."

"No, you don't. You've got that look that says I'm being a drag. But look here and my expression says you're a total dope, running around with something sharp like that in your hand."

"A dope, huh?" Dropping the pin, he came at me in his usual bent-over attack position for wrestling. He went for my knees, but I grabbed him on either side of his waist and, picking him up, turned him upside down—a move that never failed to make him shout his delight.

"Cheater! No fair! You're stronger. Let me down!"

"Damn right I'm stronger, dopo."

"Dopo?! All right, you're dead!" Upside down, he grabbed me around the waist and shook me side to side as best he could. Off balance, I stumbled with him in my arms across the floor. We were both laughing. He bit me on the leg, not hard but hard enough.

"Hey!"

"Attack!"

I loosened my hold just enough to make him think I was going to drop him. He squeezed harder. "No!"

Wobbling us over to the couch, I dropped him there after making sure he'd fall on a soft target. Lying on his back, he puffed and wiggled his fingers at me like tentacles. When I dropped down next to him, he grabbed my head. We went at it on the couch, the floor, the couch again. I let him put a full nelson on me, then slipped out of it and put one on him. You have to be careful, though, because kids are sensitive about wrestling. Some want to win every time, others lose. It's a diplomatic act which, if you do it wrong, can end up a big insult. Lincoln liked it fifty-fifty. He liked being overwhelmed, held in the air by his feet so he could wail and thrash, but never too long. Next, he wanted you in his power a while—a long headlock or sitting on your chest and twisting your nose usually sufficed. The most endearing thing about wrestling with him was when he had you in a hold, he never tried to hurt. One grunt or yelp and he'd let go immediately and apologize like mad. In contrast, I'd once been foolish enough to wrestle with Elvis, at his insistence. The little germ circus punched me square in the balls. "Accidentally," of course.

"I got you now!" Holding on tight, Lincoln rode the back of my leg as I elephant-clomped around the living room, trumpeting like I imagined a wounded elephant would sound. Vocal effects were an integral part of our wrestling.

"Death to all Bee Hees!" He spanked me hard on the ass.

"What's a Bee Hee?"

"You!"

"Bee Hees forever!" I turned and, bending down to peel him off, banged my head a real whack on a hanging lamp. It hit, I went to grab my head, the lamp swung out and back and hit me again. "Christ!"

"Max, are you okay?" His voice was stricken.

"Yeah, yeah, I'm okay. Did you see that? It hit me twice! Undoubtedly one of the dumbest things I've done in a long time—twice by the same lamp. You have to be very talented to do that!"

"Let me see. It's bleeding, Max!"

I turned to a wall mirror and saw a thick lip of blood above one of my eyebrows. Gaudy, but nothing serious. "It's okay. Would you go to the bathroom and get me a wet tissue and a couple of Band-Aids?"

"Sure you don't want to go to the hospital or something?"

"No, it's not that bad. Just get me those things, would you?"

He left and I checked myself in the mirror again. The perils of wrestling a ten-year-old. An idea arrived. I called out, "Lincoln, where'd you put that pin? The one we were going to use before."

"I think it's on the table there." He returned with a dripping washcloth and a handful of Band-Aids. "Why?"

"Because this, compadre, is my half of blood brothers! All you've gotta do now is prick your finger and touch my head."

"Touch your *cut?* That's disgusting, Max!"

"Hey, I'm ready with my blood, *brother.* You think I'm going to cut myself somewhere else? This is good, and there's certainly enough of it. Come on, find the pin and let's do the deed." I took the things from him and touched my head with the cloth.

"I found it."

"Good. Poke yourself in the finger *carefully.* We don't need two emergency cases."

"Will you do it for me? I'm a little nervous."

"Linc, we don't *have* to do this."

"No, no, I want to! I just don't want to do my finger myself, you know?"

"Okay, come here. Give it to me. Put your hand out."

"Is it going to hurt?" Through tightly squinted eyes, he watched me take the pin.

"No, it'll be one—"

"Ow! You didn't say you were going to do it so fast! Let me see. Whoa! Look at that blood! Hea-vy!"

"Look at my head! Want to compare who's worse?"

"Do you really think I should touch you there? It's a pretty bad cut."

"I don't think you're diseased. Come on, let's do it. What should we say? 'With this blood, I thee wed'?"

"Very funny, Max. You're a real loser."

"Thank you." I dabbed my head. "What about 'Blood on blood, *Brothers in Arms*'?"

"That's the name of the Dire Straits album. Wait a minute, I got it! What about 'Bee Hees forever'? Just that alone."

"You don't think it sounds too much like the Bee Gees?"

"No, Bee *Hees.* Like I called you when we were wrestling."

"If you like it, let's go with it."

He licked his lips and slowly moved his hand toward my head. "Okay. We say, 'Bee Hees forever' at exactly the same time. Right? I'll count to three, and as soon as I touch you, we say it together. Okay? Okay, one-two-three." He touched his open finger to my open head.

Blood to blood.

" 'Bee Hees forever!' Hey, Max, say it. Come on!"

She had shipped Lincoln off for the weekend to Elvis's house. She'd taken the night off from work to cook us an elaborately exotic dinner. She wore a new dress. Afterward, she made love stormily and with delightful originality. Not long after we'd finished and were lying on our backs in the dark, only our fingers touching, she began to cry. That had happened a couple of times before with her after sex, so I lay still and stroked a finger up and down her thumb.

"I have to tell you something, Max. It's bad and I'm very scared, but I know I have to tell you." She turned and slid closer to me. I think she was facing me but it was so dark in the room that I had no idea what she was doing. It felt like she was having a long close moment of me either to give her strength or to burn something into her memory in case what she was about to say destroyed us. Saying nothing, she remained like that. I kept silent and didn't move. Finally groaning deep and sad, she mumbled, "God," and slid away. She took my arm with her, pulling it across her flattened breasts. Kissing my hand, she pressed it to the side of her face and kissed it again. "I love you more than any man I've ever known. I love you so much that I have to tell you these things even though—" She undid my hand from hers and pressed it to her lips. She kissed the palm, the fingers. She curled it into a fist and pushed it against her face. There was a strong and frighteningly fast pulse beating in her throat beneath one of my fingers. "I've done terrible things. If you were anyone else in the world I would never, ever tell. You have to know that. It's very important to me because I believe there has to be truth between people who want to spend the rest of their lives together. Even when it's something as bad as this. It's such a contradiction—I love you so much that now I have to tell you the thing that can kill me."

I didn't turn to her and show her an expressionless calm face which, if she could have seen it in the dark, would have told her I knew already. Instead, her confessor, I spoke quietly toward the ceiling. "What would kill you?"

She sat up suddenly. The movement made a small breeze that swept the smell of sexy funk and her cologne past me. "A crime. I committed one of the worst crimes on earth. Me, Lily Aaron. I cannot believe I'm telling you this. You have to have the history right from the beginning. Maybe that'll make it easier to understand. Probably not. There's no way to understand this.

"When you were a kid, was there one thing you wanted more than anything in the world? I mean, so much that your hunger for it tore you apart?"

"I guess being a cartoonist came closest. I wanted that pretty bad."

"I wanted a baby. I wanted to be a mother. My earliest memories are of playing with dolls. But I never saw them as adults, as other girls do. I never had tea parties for them or talked to them like I was a woman and we were all grownups. The only kind of dolls I wanted were babies. If someone gave me an adult doll or even a Barbie, I'd throw it in the back of the closet. I could never understand why someone would want Barbie. A teenager? Who would want to play with a teenage doll? I wanted babies. I wanted my own."

"Why?"

"I don't know. It was always in my blood from the beginning. When I'd see a baby carriage on the street I'd race up and look into it like I was looking at God. Didn't matter if the kid was black or yellow or white. It was a baby and that was enough. If I was lucky, the woman would see my love and let me hold it a few moments. I remember being so terrified. What if I dropped it, or it didn't like me and cried, or I did something else wrong? But holding it made me so happy, Max. It was the greatest feeling I knew on earth.

"When I was twelve, my mother allowed me to babysit in our neighborhood. I used the mimeograph machine in my father's office, printed up an advertisement for myself and stuck it up on every telephone pole on our block. The younger the child, the better. You know how most sitters watch TV or talk on the telephone to their friends once the parents have gone out? I never did. I'd play with the kid till it was dead tired, give it a bath whether it needed one or not, then put it in bed and watch till it fell asleep. Lots of times I'd bring my homework into their bedroom and do it by the crib while they slept. I was your ultimate dream babysitter; totally trustworthy and in love with every kid I sat for.

"This is boring, isn't it? I'm boring you, but believe me, it's all important. Anyway, it's time to undo my first lies. My family name isn't Margolin, it's Vincent. And I come from Glenside, Pennsylvania, not Cleveland."

"Why did you tell me those other things?"

"Because I've been Lily Aaron from Cleveland for almost ten years. I became her so well that now I have to remind myself of the name Vincent. It's not me anymore, I'm the Lily you know."

"Sounds like I don't know Lily."

"Yes, you do! You know me better than anyone. You just don't know this part because no one has ever known it. No one ever could. Please let me go on and don't interrupt. I'm afraid if I don't tell it all to you now, I'll start lying again and I don't want that. It's taken me this long to get up the courage to do it, and the more I've grown to love you, the more difficult it's become. I guess it's like having a baby—once it starts coming, you just want to get it out." As she spoke the last part of the sentence, she began crying again and this time it went on and on. I asked if there was anything I could do but she said no, just stay here, don't go away.

I was so calm I was . . . interested. Interested to hear the details of her story and how she would phrase saying she had stolen her son. Weeks before, I would have been sweating and shaking too at this point in her tale, waiting for her to admit her secret sin. Then I probably would've grabbed and shaken her, screamed *I know it! I know you did that!* Not now.

The weeping ended and she tried to speak through those gasping hitches of breath that come after you've cried hard and your body is trying to bring itself back from the brink.

"But wh-wh-when I got to be a teenager it all changed. I-I-I didn't ca-care about kids anymore. I lost all interest i-in them. There were boys now, and being popular in school was so important. All my interests changed. I hung around with girls who thought if you died and went to heaven, you got to be a cheerleader and had your own Princess telephone.

"And sex. Before, that wasn't really connected to babies: it was like one day you'll have a husband and somehow the two of you together will make children appear. But in eighth and ninth grade, the hormones began singing and boys you once hated started looking wonderful. Remember that? Everything's suddenly about sex and being noticed. Not actually having sex, but all the things buzzing around it. Brassieres, flirting, who's going with who, who's rumored to be doing what . . .

"I wasn't noticed at first because I wasn't beautiful like Alexa Harrison or Kim Marcus, but I was adventurous and willing to try things other girls wouldn't. I was the first in our crowd to French-kiss and word got around fast about *that.* I liked it from the very beginning. I liked kissing and being touched, although I'd never let anybody touch me in *the* places because that just wasn't done. But I rolled around a lot! By tenth grade, a few friends of mine were making love pretty regularly, but I wasn't. Funny thing was, I had the reputation for being fast and loose, while these 'bad' girls were seen as Little Bopeeps. They could have done the whole football team but no one would've described them as being naughty. Only me."

"Did that bother you?"

"Not as much as you might think. It wasn't true and I knew it. If someone believed I was a slut, they weren't my friends anyway. The people who mattered knew the truth; they knew who I was.

"So I did as I pleased and didn't lose my virginity till I was eighteen. A senior in high school, which was pretty old in those days.

"The tricky part began in college. I didn't go to Kenyon, as I told you. I went to NYU. I'd always wanted to live in New York, and at the time, I wanted to be an actress. But it didn't work out that way. My sophomore year, I met a guy named Bryce who hung around with the most interesting bunch of people I had ever met. Students mostly, but there were some writers and musicians, and actors sprinkled in there too. One of them had even been in an Andy Warhol film. You can imagine how I fell for them. Miss Glenside, Pennsylvania, meets the Lower East Side. Everybody did drugs and slept with everybody else. After a couple of months I did too. It was no big deal. Besides, these people considered you liberated if you slept around, not a slut like they had at home. And dope made it nicer, smoother, or sometimes if you did have worries, it made them go away, so it got to be my all-purpose cure-all. Little Lily Vincent makes the scene. The problem was, none of us was very talented, although we talked a good game. We knew all the correct words to use to make it sound like we were up to big things.

"Right before summer vacation that year, I started bleeding badly and having terrible cramps. I'm very regular and this scared the hell out of me because I had never had any kind of trouble down there. I had an IUD by then, so I thought it had something to do with that. I went to the university hospital and they kept giving me tests. At the end they told me I had something called pelvic inflammatory disease, PID, and it had dangerously infected all through my insides—the spleen, uterus, liver . . . They didn't know whether it came from one of the men I'd slept with or the IUD itself. It was a horrendous experience. I was in the hospital three weeks. When it was over, my tubes were so badly scarred that it left me infertile."

She said the last line unemotionally. The word at the end was the most important in her life, the one that eventually razed everything, but she put no special emphasis on it. No verbal underlining or topspin.

"I'm not good with these terms, Lily. I'm sorry. Does that mean you could never have children?"

"I'm not sterile, no, but the doctors said with the kind of extensive scarring I have on my fallopian tubes, the chances of me ever conceiving are almost none."

There was a silence thick as blood.

"Lincoln."

"Lincoln."

"And Rick."

"There is no Rick. What I told you about Rick Aaron is based mostly on this guy Bryce I knew. He was in and out of my life for a long time. Do you want to ask questions now or can I go on? I'd prefer to tell you the whole thing first. I don't think you'll be confused after."

"Go ahead. But I'd like to turn on the light. I want to see your face."

"Please no! I can't do this if we see each other. I'm afraid of your face. But your voice is so calm. How can you be so calm hearing this? That frightens me too."

"Go on, Lily."

"Okay. They told me in the hospital I was lucky to be alive. My parents drove up to get me and my mother started crying the moment she walked in the room and saw me."

"Who are your parents? Their name is Vincent?"

"Laurie and Alan. My mother's dead. She had Alzheimer's disease and died not recognizing anyone. My father still works for a Ford dealership near Philadelphia. We have very little contact. I told Lincoln both of them were dead."

"Does your father know about Lincoln?"

From blood to stone. Hot, alive, and tactile before, her silence now was cold and dead. It held. She snorted once, as if I'd made a small joke not worth a full laugh. Her answer was superb.

"The only people who know about Lincoln are the people who know Lily Aaron."

"And Lily Vincent?"

"She was eaten by Lily Aaron in their one and only trip together across the U.S. I can still remember checking into a motel in Illinois and, without thinking, signing the register 'Lily V.' Then I stopped, put a period next to the V, like it was my middle initial, and wrote 'Aaron' after it. It's easy to become another person. You only have to be willing to leave who you were at the door and walk away."

"Was Lincoln with you on that trip?"

"Yes."

"Go back and tell it from where you got sick in college."

"I came out of the hospital and spent the summer at home recuperating. That was the year my mom started showing signs of Alzheimer's. My father ignored both of us. He doesn't like sickness and only came up to get me in New York that time because she insisted. The two of us sickies sat on the porch and watched Mom's portable TV.

"One day when I was very down and blue, Bryce pulled up at our door and said everybody in New York missed me, so when was I coming back? It was such a compliment. I was so touched. In the end he turned out to be a King Shit, but Bryce also had a real, dangerous talent for knowing when and how to make *the* perfect gesture. Like driving all the way to Pennsylvania to see how I was. Do you know anyone like that? They'll do ten terrible things, but know exactly when to do one nice one that'll erase the others from your mind. It's a nasty, interesting talent. But there's something else I've thought about with that. A person can do ten bad things, then one good one and it'll get you back into the hearts of people. But if you do the *opposite*—ten good things followed by one bad—you're no longer trusted. If you're bad, they remember the good. If you're good, they remember the bad. Each man makes his own shipwreck, eh?

"Clever old Bryce joined Mom and me on the porch and even went down to the showroom the next day with Dad to check out the new models. What a laugh. Bryce didn't give a damn about cars. He didn't give a damn about anything but himself. I'd been a willing and convenient partner for him. I later found out he let one of his friends fuck me so long as they supplied him with dope. Nice boyfriend, huh? But most of it was my fault. At that point I should have told him to leave, then either transferred to some college nearby like Temple or dropped out altogether and changed my life.

"But I didn't. I barely waited another week, threw my things in the car, and went back to New York to be with him. That was sophomore year. The only good things about junior year were my language classes and starting to work in a restaurant in the Village. I immediately realized how much more I liked that than acting. The smells of good food and seeing people happy . . . Sure, there are drunks and idiots sometimes, but rarely. People come to restaurants to relax and do things they never do at home. I love the way they dawdle over their liqueurs or have another cup of espresso even though it's bad for them and will keep them awake half the night. How women go to the bathroom and come back all fresh and made-up again, ready for another few hours. How they go in there and chatter like teenage girls at a prom. I love that laughter. There's so much laughter. Real ha-ha, or sexy, or totally surprised. I love men showing off for their women and the women letting them do it. People holding hands and people you'd never expect picking up the check. When they leave, men hold coats for their ladies and you know so many of them'll go home and make love and talk or hold each other cozily after. That great cloud of good feeling that comes with a good meal and new perfume and a couple too many drinks. *I love that.*"

"Talk about yourself. Don't tell me about restaurants."

"I'm almost finished with college. Junior year was nothing but what I told you. Senior year I really thought I was getting myself together. Bryce and I split after I found out about his pimping me to his friend. I was way down on the drug intake too. Usually just some grass and a little coke if it was around, but nothing else. The people I'd thought for so long were fascinating and going places started sounding like old records I'd heard a thousand times before. It was then that I realized these guys spent all their energy talking and planning, but never doing. They were so petrified of failing that they didn't dare take chances because they might flop and embarrass themselves. Since they were all like that, though, they were safe. But I'd reached the point where I wasn't interested anymore in getting into the La Mamma troupe or Paul Morrissey's new film, so their yakking turned me off. I spent more and more time at the restaurant learning whatever they'd teach me. It was like that great moment in life when you're young but suddenly get an idea of what you want to do with the next forty years of your time. That was me; I'd sighted land. Know what I mean? Then the raisins came."

"What do you mean?"

"That's a famous line from Lincoln. We were watching a documentary on TV once and the announcer said in a very deep, impressive voice, 'And then the rains came!' Lincoln was four, I think. He turned to me and in as deep a voice as he could find, said very proudly, 'Then the raisins came!' He said so many great things like that when he was little. I wrote some of them down.

"Anyway, one fine day in March my father called to say Mom was dead and already buried. He hadn't thought I'd want to make the trip down just for that. 'Just for that' was the exact phrase he used, the mean-spirited drunk. The truth was, he didn't want to be bothered any more than he already had. That ended my relationship with my father. Never in a million years could I forgive him for doing that. I got there as soon as I could and stood at her grave apologizing for having let her down. I went back to the house and told my father he was a selfish, evil prick and the greatest last blessing Mom had had was to die from a disease that let her forget all the lousy things he'd done to her for thirty years.

"The upshot was he threw me out of the house and cut me off financially. My mother left some money but I didn't get that till a long time later. But fine, I'd finish college on my own. Scared as I was, it pleased me tremendously to know I would never have to come and see him again. Know what my last words to him were? 'When you're old and dying, Dad, know there is not one single person on earth who loves you.' And then I walked out.

"I left the old dumpy car he'd given me in the driveway and took a bus back to New York, feeling right and strong but so sad about Mom.

"I got to the Port Authority terminal, the bus stopped, and I had one of those unbearable panic attacks where you freeze in the middle of life without a fucking clue as to what to do. I sat on a bench for an hour and shook. The only thing that entered my mind was Bryce's phone number. I thought that must mean something important; an omen or a sign through all my confusion. I staggered to a phone and called him. He sounded so happy to hear from me. Started off by saying I was completely right—all the old gang were a bunch of failed phonies and I'd been the first to see that. How perceptive of me. I told him what was happening and he told me to come right over.

"I've never been able to figure out whether he was so nice to me that next week because he saw how needy I was or because he was only setting me up again for one of his sucker punches. Whatever, he couldn't have been kinder. We talked about what mattered to me and he said smart, helpful things. He took me to dinner and the movies. Didn't touch me till one night I went to him and said please. He was my knight in shining armor and by the end of that week I was hooked on him again. Only now I had so little confidence, so much pain and confusion, that he could have told me to walk out the window and, if he'd been nice about it, I'd've done it. He said I should take it easy and do whatever I thought would help get me strong again.

"I didn't do anything. Didn't go to classes, didn't go back to work at the restaurant, didn't see anyone besides him. When I needed money, I took a job for a couple of weeks at Kentucky Fried Chicken or another quick-food place where they hire anybody off the street who doesn't look like a total zombie.

"One evening my knight brought home some opium and we smoked it up. I was a goner. About the time I was supposed to graduate, Bryce said it was pretty expensive living these days, implying what with dope and food and all, I was a mighty stone around his neck. Which was total bullshit because I never took money from him and I paid for the groceries. He was also selling dope at a steady clip, which he failed to tell me, and had fat, fat pockets. But all those veiled complaints were only a smoke screen for what he had in mind for me.

"In view of all the nice, self-sacrificing things he'd done recently, would I do him a big favor? It was real simple. He had a friend coming into town for the weekend, but since he'd already committed to something else, would I be willing to go out with this guy and show him around?

"Max, we looked at each other, knowing exactly what he was asking me to do, and you know what? We smiled at each other. Smiled like sure, it's only the last of my honor and dignity and probably my sanity but take it, babe. Sure, I'll let your stranger fuck me."

"Why didn't you leave?"

"Because I was frightened. Of everything. I couldn't go out the door of the apartment without checking my pocket three or four times to make sure I had the key. The key to that door was the most important thing in the world those days. It was my talisman. As long as I had it and could get back into that dark, musty place I could function. Walk out on the street, do some errands, maybe go to work and cook chicken for a few hours, just so long as the key was there and I could run my finger over it in my pocket and feel its hard outline. My world had shrunk down to a two-room apartment with kitchen, and even that was too big for me sometimes, too much to handle. I had no strength and no desire to think clearly about my situation or decide. Those things take real, serious energy but there was none. Plus I was thrown a real curve: the weekend came, this friend showed up, and surprise surprise—we hit it off like we'd been pals a hundred years. I had such fun! We went to dinner, took a Circle Line cruise around Manhattan, and ended up drinking champagne in bed in his room at the Biltmore Hotel. I felt like a queen and he treated me so sweetly. I'll tell you, I can understand why some women like being call girls. Given the right kind of men, you're treated well and with respect, and if you're not particular about who you have sex with, there are worse ways to make money."

"Lily, you're *very* particular about who you have sex with."

"Exactly. That's why it left such a scar. I think I would have slept with this man anyway because I liked him so much, but when it happened, I didn't know if I was doing it 'cause I wanted to or because it'd been arranged and was expected of me.

"The next morning I left before he got up and thought okay, that's that. I've learned something and it wasn't *so* bad. But it was. In the pit of my stomach I knew it was.

"Luckily when I got back to Bryce's he wasn't there. I've never been a snoop, but for some reason that morning I felt this overpowering desire to go through our whole place top to bottom. I'm not sure why. Maybe telepathy. Or maybe it was a strange way of getting back at my roommate: due to him, someone had looked in all *my* private places last night, so it was fair I got to look in Bryce's. In his shaving kit were twenty-two dime bags of heroin. He was dealing smack! If we had been busted, I would've been booked as an accessory, at least, and the son of a bitch never told me what he was doing. Heroin! Never gave me the chance to decide whether *I* wanted to live in a powder keg while he played Mr. Smooth Operator. And next it hit me: did that mean I'd slept with one of his *customers* last night? More than likely. He'd already used me like that once. I was fully aware of Bryce's way of bartering for the things he wanted in life. But then again, I'd had such a nice time, why should it make a difference? Because it did. No matter how nice the guy had been, the only reason my old friend and *protector* had put us together was to offer me as mattress-meat bonus to one of his good customers.

"I walked around the apartment saying 'Fuck you—fuck you—fuck you' under my breath and snooping like a dog on a scent. Thank God for it, because way in the back of the closet, stuck in a pair of hiking boots he never used, was a jumbo wad of hundred-dollar bills. Without any hesitation whatsoever, I took ten of them, threw some things in a duffel bag, and left. I wanted out of there, out of that life, that city, *tutti*.

"I got on a subway and rode to one of the last stops in the Bronx, staring at the floor the whole way. One of the first things I saw climbing up the steps of the station was a used-car lot filled with

the biggest automobiles I'd ever seen. Oldsmobiles, Pontiacs, Buick
Rivieras. My memory is that they were all gold and purple and sea-
foam green, like rides at an amusement park. Maybe I was totally out
of it, but these cars seemed *gigantic.* I guess my perspective on things
was so off-kilter . . . Anyway, I went over in wonder, just to have a
look before setting out wherever I was going. But the moment I got
there, this wonderful black man in a sharkskin suit and yellow tie
came out of a little office to the side of the lot like a magical character. He said, 'I *know* I got what you're looking for!' I put down my
bag and said, 'Maybe so, but what've you got for me under five
hundred dollars?' He clapped his hands together and looked at the
sky like deliverance had arrived. 'Lady, I'll answer that question with
a statement: I got cars here you could drive *to, through,* and *back*
from World War Three in.' I laughed and wanted to hug him and
buy any car he had to sell. Instead, I said I'd been going through the
worst period of my entire life and was at the end end end. If I
bought a car now, I needed it to take me a million miles from New
York and not break down, because I didn't have any more to spend
on it. He gestured for me to follow and we walked way to the back
of the lot. Wedged behind all those big balloon cars like the runt of
the litter was a tooth-colored Opel Kadett station wagon. He said
he'd sell it to me for three hundred and fifty dollars even though it
was worth twice that. He'd checked it out personally, and far as he
could see, it was sound. I asked if that meant it was good and he
said, 'It's tinny, but it'll take you out of hell.' There was no one left
to trust and he'd made me smile when I needed it, so I pulled out my
money and the deal was done in half an hour.

"I drove a few blocks down the street but pulled over when I
came to a sign for the entrance to the turnpike out of town. Where
was I going? How about north to Boston? New Orleans? Chicago?
But if I was going to follow that kind of spontaneous yellow brick
road, I wanted to start from the real beginning, which was back in
old Glenside. Besides, even though I no longer had my mother,
much less a home, if I really was going to leave this part of the
country for good, I wanted to see the old stomping grounds one last

time. Our house, the places where I used to hang out, my high school. So I made up my first destination of that trip—Glenside, Pennsylvania.

"You can get there from New York in a few hours, even driving slowly. I was in no hurry. I didn't know what I was going to do when I got there. Take a last look, smell the air a little, get my bearings back . . . whatever. There was a radio in the car and I sang along with it the whole way down. Things felt good. There really is a lot to be said for traveling light. Dropping whatever you have in your hands and movin' out. One of the games I played while driving was trying to remember what I'd actually packed in the bag. There wasn't much."

"You're the second woman I've known who's run away from her man. The other said when she opened her bag later most of what was in there was underwear."

"Underwear, exactly! The same with me. What does that say about girls on the run? With me it's not hard to figure out—being clean again. Taking a shower, then putting on fresh underpants and a bra is always a total psychic lift. Sounds silly, but it never fails to make me feel new again. And I definitely needed to feel new after what'd been going on those last weeks.

"I drove into Glenside about nine that night. First thing I did was cruise by our house, but no lights were on and no car was in the driveway. It brought me way down. If only the place had been lit up like it was when I was young. Walking home in the winter after volleyball practice when you were tired and cold, you'd come over the hill at Teresa Schueller's house and there was your home, lit up and warm-looking, the yellow porch lights on in front, maybe smoke coming out of the chimney. Mom would be in the living room read- ing her book till you came in, we'd kiss, and she'd go to the kitchen to finish cooking dinner now that everyone was home . . .

"She was dead and my father was probably down at the Ma- sonic Hall with his buddies or with a dull woman who was as sad and stupid as him. Driving there, I thought I'd had no expectations other than to see the place and then move on to wherever the rest of my life would happen. But there was our house and it was dark, smaller than I remembered, and the bushes in front had been cut down so low they had no more shape. Those stumpy bushes started me crying, and I peeled out of there like a kid in a drag race.

"I drove to a bar in town and was there about fifteen minutes when a guy named Mark Elsen came up and said hi. Mark was one of those sweet guys from high school who are kind of drippy but have a crush on you. Most of them go into the Army after graduation, but eventually end up back in town afterward running the family appliance store. In school I knew he liked me and would come over to talk whenever he got up the nerve. He was actually rather good-looking and nice, but dull as an empty cardboard box.

"On the other hand, who was I to talk? There I was at the bar, ladies and gentlemen, Miss Lily Vincent, half a day away from a marvelous life as a burnt-out, doped-up loser who'd spent last night in a stranger's bed as baksheesh for a drug deal, most likely.

"Mark was probably both the best and the worst person I could have bumped into that night on the face of the earth. He was so delighted to see me, so happy I'd come home and we'd bumped into each other. I felt *adored.*"

"Wasn't that good for your ego?"

"Yes, for about an hour, but then reality came back, and no matter what he thought, I knew who I was and how close the demons were.

"To make matters worse, I did the most pathetic thing and could not stop myself. He kept asking what I was up to in 'the Big Apple.' He kept referring to it like that, like he was hip too 'cause he knew the nickname. Which only made him more heartbreaking. 'So what's going on with you up in the Big Apple? Acting school, huh? Got a Hollywood contract yet?' Not an ounce of cynicism in the way he said it. He assumed I was already a great success and would be out in L.A. knocking 'em dead in no time. Know what I did? Started lying. Told him the most outrageous whoppers and fantasies. Like I was in this elite acting class at NYU taught by Dustin Hoffman. I was going to be in an Andy Warhol film soon, and I hung around the

Factory with Lou Reed . . . It embarrasses me even now to think
about it. Later he admitted he didn't know half the people I'd mentioned, but it sounded tremendous. That was his word: tremendous.
Whatever I said, he'd say, 'Tremendous, Lily. That's tremendous.'
He bought me drinks and a steak sandwich while I slung the bullshit. He kept shaking his head and saying 'tremendous,' like he
couldn't get over my magnificence. Such a nice guy. I didn't have to
do that. He thought I was great without any fluff. I could just as
easily have cried on his shoulder and told him what was really happening. He would've been sympathetic."

"You said those lies for yourself, not him. You wanted life to be
the way you described it. It was a performance. For him, you *were*
the actor in the Warhol film, the girl who knocked them dead in
New York. Nothing wrong with that."

"No, nothing wrong. Sad. End-of-the-line sad. It got so bad
that he was asking me what Warren Beatty was like. I sat there with a
cigarette in my hand, looking off into deep space like I was seriously
considering his question, and said, 'I like him, but I know people
who don't.' "

That made me laugh. Lily joined in and it was as if a wave of
relief flooded over us both in the dark nervous bedroom. I knew
what was coming, knew we were moving toward it like the top of a
long staircase, but this laughter now let us stop and catch our breath
before the last push.

"It *is* funny, isn't it? We talked for another couple of hours and
got a little drunk. Not much, but enough to make him more impressed and me more daring. I was the one who suggested we go out
and take a drive somewhere. Out in the parking lot, he asked if I'd
like to go in his car. When I said yes, he pointed to a brand-new
Camaro Z-28. A really beautiful, souped-up thing that sounded like
a jet plane when he started it. I remember 'Z-28' because it sounded
so technical and dangerous, like a weapon, but when I asked Mark
what it meant, he didn't know.

"We drove around and he told me more about what'd been
going on in town since I'd left: who married who, who moved away,

what stores had changed, small-town news. You think you don't care about that once you've left and are out in the big world, but when you hear it you're fascinated.

"We ended up at Dairy Queen eating banana splits. Mark kept asking about different famous people he was sure I knew. Oh, the tales I told! How he ate them up. You're right, it *was* a performance and I loved it. I remember him listening so intently that he held a spoonful of ice cream in front of his face for minutes, not eating it because he was too enthralled with what I was saying. That handsome face, his mouth hanging open like a kid's, chocolate sauce dripping onto the table." She went silent, sighed, cleared her throat. "I put my hand over his and said I wanted to fuck him."

"You didn't! *That's* bad."

"Sssh. Let me talk. I thought: What the hell, I'm going to act this out to its total end both for me and for him. We got back in his car and I told him to drive to the parking lot behind the high school. There were famous town rumors and jokes about people doing it back there, but you knew none of them were true, because it was too dangerous; the police patrolled the area about five times a night. They followed no fixed schedule, so no one ever knew when they'd come next. Mark knew what I was getting at and got scared. He didn't want to go, but I said either there or no place, deal's off. If he'd said no, and was more scared of the cops than hot to have me, it would've been the crowning blow to my ego. As it was, he hesitated a long time before turning the car around and going back. But that was the whole point of telling him to go there! It *had* to be dangerous, there had to be risk involved. Who'd remember just another fuck at the end of a dark country road? I wanted it to be a solid-gold memory. One that'd make him chuckle and shake his head when he was fifty-eight and sitting on a porch with arthritis and not much else. How many of those do we have?"

"I've noticed something. You keep using the word 'fuck.' That's not a 'you' word. Plus, you make it sound like you're trying to club something with it. 'Who'd remember just another fuck—' Why are you talking like that?"

"Because that's what this was—fucking. Fuck—hard, fast, get to the point and then get off. Men like to fuck. Fuck and come. That's what I wanted to do with Mark—fuck him like he'd never had it before, and then disappear in a puff of smoke. A dream come true and gone a moment later before any of its glitter fell. Let him remember me that way. This one night in the back seat of his new car behind the school when he finally got to fuck Lily Vincent and she was a firecracker deluxe."

"Were you a firecracker?"

"More! As soon as we got there, I straddled him and took my clothes off as sexily as I knew how. When he reached out to touch me, I wouldn't let him, because I wanted him like corn in hot oil. Know how it sizzles and dances around in the pan right before it explodes into popcorn? I wanted him scrinching around in the seat and going crazy with sex for me. *I wanted someone to want me!* And he did."

"Were you wonderful?"

"I was."

"Were you turned on?"

"A little toward the end. But no, not much. It was too much like gymnastics. I was working too hard to make him hot and think he was driving me crazy."

"I'm jealous."

I heard her turn. Her voice was high and excited when she spoke. "Really? Why? It was so long ago and I was faking the whole thing."

"Because jealousy is greed. I want it all and don't want to share any of it ever. Sometimes when I think about it, I'm jealous of the men in your past and what they did with you. I'd like to go back and take all of the kisses and fucks away from them and keep them for myself."

"That's nice, Max. I never thought of it that way."

"I do. Go on, firecracker."

"Well, we did it a couple of times and I think I was satisfying. You asked before if it was good and I said a little, but that's untrue.

It *was* good because I threw myself into it totally. I licked him and kissed him and hugged and groaned. At first, I was thinking: What else will make him hot, what else'll make him howl at the moon? But you get caught up in it, even when it's a performance. I liked it and it *was* good.

"When we were totally exhausted and done, we got dressed and sat there not speaking. After counting slowly to a hundred, I said I wanted him to go now and leave me here. I wanted to walk back through town alone to my car. He was flabbergasted. Go away? How could I say such a thing after what had happened? I started growing impatient, wanting to be out of his car and alone again. He said he loved me, and besides, how could I have done it so wonderfully if I didn't feel anything for him? I didn't answer, but began to resent him although the whole spiel had been my doing. He got desperate and asked, was it a time thing? It had happened so quickly and spontaneously, was it just that I needed some time alone to sort out what'd happened? Luckily he supplied that excuse to escape, because I was in no mood or shape to cook one up. Yes, you're right, Mark, I am confused and want to be alone to think. That calmed him. Ever since then I've wondered what would have happened if he had said no. Just been strong and absolutely insisted I stay with him the rest of the night. But old sweetie Mark Elson didn't do it. Instead, he got out of the car and raced around to open my door. We kissed goodbye. He pulled me close and out in the middle of that big empty parking lot whispered, 'What's going on, Lily?' Which was a bull's-eye question, because I hadn't the slightest idea, and had come today hoping to find a way home. Or else I *did* know what was going on: me breaking apart, faster than the speed of light. I pushed him away and started running in the opposite direction. He called me, but when I didn't stop, he yelled out, 'I'll be at the store tomorrow, if you need me!' I needed him, all right. I needed everyone in the whole world holding one of those giant firemen's nets people fall into when they jump from a burning building. But it was too late."

"Why? Why was it too late?"

"Because by then I was so far gone, I was jumping from every corner of the building, not just one. They wouldn't have had enough nets to catch me.

"Running felt good. As I moved, for half an instant I considered going home and asking Dad to let me spend the night. What a laugh! Home, Sweet, Dark Home.

"I could feel Mark's warm sperm begin to run down the inside of my leg. I thought of babies. All those Mark-babies that would never be. No babies would ever come out of me. The sickness and the scars had put an end to that. Another possibility down, how many more to go? It had been so long since I'd thought of children. This was the town where I'd been a child, but I was running from it now, running from my life, running *out* of life, and knowing there was nothing to run to. I would never be able to create life. It hit me *so hard* then.

"I ran and ran. It was about three miles from school back to the bar but I got there fast. Gasping, I hopped into the car and started it up. It bucked backward into a retaining wall because I'd forgotten to take it out of gear when I turned it off. That lurch scared me into clearness a little. I put my hands on my face and rubbed up and down till it got hot. Then I started the motor again and drove slowly out of the lot.

"It was still dark when I left, but morning birds were singing. I started crying as I passed by different places in town. I said goodbye to them. Bye, library, Beaver College, Marilyn Zodda's house. Some were important, others only part of my life's map. They were all about to disappear forever. I knew I'd never go back there, so this was it. Bye-bye, Howard Johnson's. I actually rolled down the window and waved at that stupid restaurant! Bye, fried clams and cigarettes after school there with Marilyn and Lynda Jones in our favorite booth. Bones Jones. Goodbye goodbye goodbye. Boom—end of Glenside days. I rolled out on that highway and *drove.*

"Until the car died an hour later. Smoke began pouring out from under the hood and, poof, it stopped. I was calm, rolled it onto the shoulder and turned it off. It was a beautiful morning. I got out and stood beside the car while the sun came up over those hazy blue fields. Not many cars drove by but that was okay because I didn't feel like flagging one down yet. I assumed the Opel was a goner, which meant I'd have to start out again some other way. The idea left me blank.

"A truck driver pulled over and took me to the next town. I got a mechanic at a gas station to come back and look. Amazingly, it was only a broken fan belt, a nine-dollar repair. Plus, the man had the part with him in his van. I should've been ecstatic, but when he told me, I had nothing to say. He must have thought I was a zombie. A zombie who was suddenly hungry. While he worked on the car, I asked if there was a good place to get breakfast in town. He recommended the Garamond Grill."

"Garamond? Garamond, Pennsylvania?" This was it: Brendan Wade Meier was kidnapped there.

"Do you know the town?"

"No, but I know what you did there."

"What do you mean?"

"I mean Garamond. I mean Anwen and Gregory Meier and their son Brendan, age about nine and a half now. Last seen in a baby carriage outside a store at the Garamond Shopping Plaza. *I know what you did, Lily, I know you kidnapped him.*" I turned on the light next to the bed and lay back down. Closing my eyes, I told her how I'd gone through the house after her bizarre and suspicious behavior when Lincoln was in the hospital. How I'd found her newspaper clippings about the Meiers and hired the detective to investigate. Then about my trip East, meeting the desolate couple, being shot at on the New Jersey Turnpike.

It was my turn to talk. I didn't care about backseat fucks, Marilyn Zodda, or twenty-one-year-olds having nervous breakdowns. They were momentous to Lily, the stars making up the constellation of her life. Telling me was her way of positioning them, ordering their past chaos so they would make sense for both of us.

But I didn't care, because I knew things now that she didn't. In the end, it came down to a fundamental fact: She *had* kidnapped her son. Torn open the fabric of sanity and reached deep into the darkness behind it for an act she thought would save her from falling into that dark altogether. The horrors we're capable of doing to save ourselves.

In itself, it made everything else in life, much less her story, supremely unimportant.

Later in passing, in anecdotes, in late-night confessions and midday conversations, I heard the rest of the story. She fled with the infant across Pennsylvania, often with it on her lap, the hum and bumping of the car over the roads a natural rockabye-baby that kept it quiet or gurgling happily. It liked to shake its hands or take her little finger in its mouth and suck noisily. It, *he* (it was a while before she thought of the child as a boy) enjoyed music and often jiggled frantically when rock and roll was on the radio.

She "christened" him Lincoln after a week on the road. To pass the time while driving, she thought for hours about different men's names. Twice when the weather got nasty she stopped at a cheap motel and spent a contented evening scanning local phone books and newspapers for names, then saying interesting ones aloud to herself and the child nearby on the bed. But "Lincoln Vincent" didn't sound good. Since she had to change her last name now, she decided to find one that fit well with "Lincoln." "Aaron" came to her somewhere near Pepper Pike, Ohio.

At first she had driven west as fast as possible without breaking the speed limit. However, once across the border into Ohio, she moseyed around the back roads of the state, each morning poring over a map and then aiming toward towns whose names interested her: Mingo Junction, Tipp City, Wyoming.

After buying the car, Lily began the trip with a little over six hundred dollars. She tried to spend it carefully, but there was gas and food and so many things to buy for Lincoln that her money was gone in three weeks. She stopped in Gambier, Ohio, and took a job at a combined occult bookstore/head shop that catered to Kenyon College students. She told the hippie who owned the place she was running from a junkie husband back East who beat her. The boss said only, "Bummer," and allowed her to bring the child to work. She rented a tiny apartment near campus and, when not working, learned how to take care of a baby.

From the beginning, people were kind and accommodating. She didn't know if that was because her luck had changed or because they saw how happy she was with her radiant, chuckling child. Joy brings you quickly into the hearts of others. She knew what she'd done was monstrous, but she'd never been so happy. Her life had two exclusive purposes now which, miraculously, played against each other wonderfully and excitingly: she was a new mother, she was a criminal.

Lincoln and Lily Aaron lived in Gambier almost two years. The small college town was the perfect place for them. It was rural but stimulating, liberal and diverse enough so that a pretty young single mother and her toddler didn't raise eyebrows. Of course, she was careful about what she said. If pressed, only with the greatest reluctance would she tell the story of husband Rick back in New York who'd caused them to flee in the first place.

When the bookstore went broke after a year, she began working as day manager and hostess at a steak house in town. That meant putting Lincoln in a day-care center, but the one in Gambier was a lovely light-filled place, full of teachers overflowing with a leftover 1960s-ish enthusiasm for the care and education of young children. At the same time, Lily was able to learn more about a business she had really grown to love. She made friends and for a short time had a boyfriend who was an exchange student from Vietnam. He was gentle and smart and an extraordinarily good lover. When he suggested she go back to New York, divorce Rick Aaron, and return to marry him, she left Ohio instead.

On a hot, quiet Saturday in August when everyone was out of town or inside hiding from the sun, she and her stolen child got into the loaded Opel (which had been checked and tuned for the occasion) and drove away. She told Lincoln they were going on an adventure to someplace new and different, and if they liked it there, they'd stay. That was fine with him, so long as she was around. Whether it came from not knowing his father or an inherently unsure nature, Lincoln did not like to be separated from Lily for long. It was all right at the day-care center because he liked the people there and it was clear they liked him. But his mother was the undisputed center of his universe. It didn't matter if he liked life here: if Mom said it was time to go and it would be fun where they were going, he was the first one in the car. So long as she was there, so long as he knew she was always an arm's length away, it was okay.

They drove north because of a man she had learned about and contacted in Milwaukee who could create false papers and passports for her and the child. Not having been near a big city for two years, she found the clash and clamor of it jarring. Once the forged papers were ready they headed north again, ending up in Appleton, Wisconsin. Lawrence University was there, and although it was a much larger town than Gambier, she liked it and they stayed.

Portland, Oregon, was the last stop before the Aaron family landed in Los Angeles three years ago. Almost immediately after arriving, she saw an ad in the *L.A. Weekly* for a job in a restaurant. It had been placed by Ibrahim Safid.

"Why didn't you tell me you knew?"

"Lily, if you were in my position, what would you have done?"

"Run away long ago. But that's because I've been running for ten years. The slightest blip on the screen and I'm outta there." Naked, she sat in the lotus position facing me. "Have you told anyone?"

"No one. Look at me! Believe that: I've told *no* one."

"All right. What can I say, I *have* to believe it. What are you going to do, Max? I cannot believe this; you *know*. You know about it. What are you going to do?"

I put a hand on her throat and gently pushed her back down. Lifting myself, I climbed on top and, spreading her legs with a knee, slipped very carefully inside her vagina. Her eyes widened but she didn't speak. I pushed until I was as deep as I could go, then moved her arms over her head and covered them with my own. Silently, we lay like that for some time. The moment and the knowledge between us transcended sex, yet I was very hard. Her mouth was to my ear when she spoke barely above a whisper.

"I love you. No matter what you do to us, or me, know I love you more than I've ever loved anyone."

"I do know that."

"It's so tragic. This is all I ever wanted from life: you here, Lincoln sleeping in his room. I was just praying, but stopped because I didn't know what for. Praying you won't tell, praying you'll never stop loving me. It's all mixed up. And who am I to pray? What God do *I* go to for help? People say they want justice, but that's not true. We only want things to work for us and no one else. Even now, a big part of me keeps saying I don't deserve this 'cause I'm a nice person. I do good things for others. Isn't that crazy? Isn't that sick? Oh, Max, what *are* you going to do? Do you know?"

"Yes. I'm going to marry you and try to be a good father to Lincoln."

"Oh God. Oh God." She began breathing oddly, as if she were panting. Our faces were inches away and we stared into each other's eyes. Neither of us smiled, there was no joy in or near us. No matter how much she hoped for it, I don't think she was prepared for what I had said. Keeping her unforgivable secret meant giving up most of what I believed.

"You would do that? You'd do that for me?"

"Yes, Lily. It wasn't a hard decision to make."

She wrapped me in her arms and, rocking us from side to side, started saying, "Oh God. Oh God," again.

PART THREE

BEE HEES FOREVER

"Let us cover, O Silent One, with a sheet of fine linen,
the stiff, dead profile of our imperfection."

—*Fernando Pessôa*

Mary and I watched the three of them cross the front lawn and walk toward the house.

"How old is Lincoln now?"

"He'll be seventeen in a few weeks."

"Good Lord, that's all? He looks a hundred."

"I know."

"Good, clean living will do it every time, huh, Max?"

If it had been anyone else, I would have snapped back something mean, but Mary did not need more meanness. Her husband had died two months before and, tough as she appeared, her core was melting down toward pure hopelessness.

"*What* does his T-shirt say? Am I reading what I think I'm reading?"

" 'Fuck Dancing—Let's Fuck.' It's one of his favorites."

"Oh, Max, you let him walk out of the house in that?"

"No. He walked out of the house wearing something different this morning. Probably had the shirt in his bag and changed at school. We used to fight about these things, but he wised up and does it all different now. Diversionary tactics; the art of the end run.

Never, ever argue, but if you don't like what's said, figure out a detour around that lets you do exactly what you want. Our son is an expert sneak."

"And the leather jacket is Elvis Packard?"

"Right. The girl is Little White."

"Why does that name sound so sinister? She looks like a woodpecker. What does her shirt say?"

" 'Nine Inch Nails.' That's a rock group, in case you don't have their album."

"I thought it was a manicurist."

The door opened and the three clomped in. They all wore oversized black combat boots that laced halfway up their shins. The rest of the uniform consisted of tattered jeans and T-shirts. Although it was cold outside, Elvis was the only one wearing a jacket. It was covered with oversized safety pins, chains, and buttons that said things like "You Disgust Me."

They shadowed through the room, making no eye contact, and would have passed without a word if I hadn't spoken. "Lincoln! Mary's here. Can't you even say hello?"

"Hello, Mary," he said in a monotone, then made an exaggerated face at me as if to say, "Okay, are you satisfied?" As one, the gang smirked and kept going. A few moments later a door slammed at the back of the house.

"What a bunch of criminals! How do you live with it? Are they here every day?"

"Just about. They skulk into his room, lock the door, and turn on Carcass. Have you ever heard of Carcass?"

"I take it that's a rock group too?"

"Yes. Want to hear some of their song titles?" I reached for my wallet and pulled out the small pad I carry to write notes on possible ideas for "Paper Clip." "Here it is. 'Crepitating Bowel Erosion.' 'Reek of Putrefaction'—"

"Delicious. Hey, they're *not* 'Wake Up, Little Susie,' but don't kids always have their own music? We did. What one generation adores, the next thinks is stupid."

"Mary, for Christ's sake, *'Crepitating Bowel Erosion'?*"

"You got a point. What else do you think they do in there? Whose girlfriend is she?"

"Lincoln told me both of them do her, but 'none of us are really into fucking, ya know? So it's just a kinda thing we do in between things, ya know?' "

"Wow, he said that? Times have changed, huh, Max? We spent half our *lives* thinking about sex. You think that's true, or was he only trying to impress you?"

"He doesn't want to impress me. Or anyone. He wants to lie on his bed and listen to Carcass."

"And do drugs."

We looked at each other. I chewed the insides of my cheeks. "What did you find, Mary?"

"Names and places. I found what you expected."

"And?"

"And he does lots of drugs. The girl usually buys them because she's friendly with a guy in an East L.A. gang who deals. By the way, her human being name is Ruth Burdette. She got it because she was the girlfriend of a guy in a gang called the Little Fish. When you've screwed a Fish, you get to be called a Little."

The fact Little White had a real name and history surprised me almost more than the fact my son took drugs.

"As soon as Lily and I got married, we started talking to Lincoln about drugs. He was always so afraid of them. A couple of times I remember he actually had nightmares where bad guys were chasing him around with giant hypodermic needles. What kind of stuff is he doing?"

"Cocaine when they have money, crack when they don't."

"Lily will go mad. She refuses to accept this. She only thinks he's going through his rebellious period."

"You've got to change that. Get her to accept it and work on the problem with you. Otherwise the kid will die. Simple as that. Get some counseling, maybe check him into a drug program—"

"You sound like a public health pamphlet. Believe me, it's not so easy. He *hates* us, Mary. You don't understand. Anything we do, say, or think, he gets a look on his face of pure revulsion. We're the enemy. Us with our clean sheets, paid bills, cable TV . . . We can do nothing right in his eyes. Whatever we give him he assumes is rightfully his, but whatever we tell him he disregards."

"So he's an ungrateful little shit. He's still under age. Stick his ass in a rehab center and too bad if he doesn't like it." She lit a cigarette and flicked the match into the fireplace. "What the hell happened to that boy? He was the most wonderful child. Funny, charming . . . Remember how Frank loved him? You guys did everything right. He was loved, you gave him the right amount of discipline. Read to him, took him places . . . What happened?"

"He grew up. *When* she admits to anything being wrong, Lily thinks it might be partly due to Greer."

"No way! I don't believe that. Why would a little sister turn him into the Creature from the Black Lagoon? Knowing you two, you probably bent over backward to give each kid their share of love. Plus the fact Greer adores him. He likes her, doesn't he?"

"Yes, I think so. He's nice and gentle to her. They actually have whole conversations and once in a while he'll even help with her homework. He seemed to be happy when Lily got pregnant. And you're right—we spent a lot of time making sure each got their share, which wasn't easy in the beginning because Greer was such a handful. You remember."

"I sure do! If you'd asked me then, I'd have picked Greer to grow up and look like that. She was a large pain in the ass."

"Yes, but look at her now. It's like the house is partitioned between Us and *Them*. Aliens and earthlings. Lily, Greer, and I on one side"—I jerked a thumb toward Lincoln's room—"the Three Horsemen of the Apocalypse on the other."

"What do you think they do in there? I mean, besides *not* screwing and listening to Car Crash."

"*Carcass.* They listen to music and watch horror movies. Every once in a while you hear a scream and other goofy sounds from those films."

"Yeah, but what else? Didn't you ever look through the keyhole or . . . you know?"

"I went in there once when Lincoln forgot to lock the door. That's another thing. He put a lock on the door that could keep an elephant out. The only one of us he lets in is Greer."

"What did you see?"

"That's what's strange; the place was spotless. He has no pictures on the walls, the bed was made without one wrinkle, carpets swept . . . It reminded me of a Marine barracks. It was too *cleeean*. Creepy clean."

"That doesn't fit, does it?"

I was about to answer when I saw Greer's school van stop in front of the house. She got out, immediately dropped her school bag, bent over, and patted her fanny with both hands for the benefit of someone inside the van. Then she wiggled it, picked up her bag, and walked toward the house without once turning around to see if her performance had had the desired effect.

She wore red jeans, a white polo shirt, and black sneakers. Her hair went up off her head in two pigtails. The face was more mine than Lily's but there was a lightness that brought it all together, an aura of combined humor and naughtiness that came only from her mother.

Greer was five. Our miracle child. The child born when we thought there was no hope in the world of Lily conceiving. From the day she came into the world, she was trouble. Born premature, she gave the impression she was angry at having been brought in on our schedule rather than hers. She needed blood transfusions, experimental medicines. For a shaky ten days they thought one of her kidneys was bad and might have to come out. In her first weeks we thought and talked of little else. One night I had to tell Lincoln his new little sister might not survive. Perhaps that is when it started with him. He asked repeatedly if she was going to die. As calmly as I could, I told him I didn't know, three different ways.

"Well, why don't you do something about it? You're not just going to let her die, are you?"

"We're doing everything we can. The best doctors in the hospital are working to help her."

"So what? Why don't you get the best doctors in the *world*, Max?" He began to cry, but when I went to hold him, he pushed me away. "What if that happens to me? What if I get sick? Are you guys going to let me die?"

"We're not going to let anyone die. We're doing everything we can." I was tired and frightened, but that was no excuse for what I said next. "I think it'd be better if you thought about Greer now and not yourself. It doesn't look like you're going to die anytime soon."

He was a little boy. Life had grabbed him by the back of the neck and shoved his face into its most vicious truth. He didn't understand. He didn't know how to handle it. Who does? All he wanted was reassurance that we would always love and take care of him, but stupidly I heard it as selfishness and slapped him down with a mean line.

Then again, there is only so much you can do and there are final, unsolvable mysteries. With a clear conscience I can say that for the years we lived together, Lincoln had been my great obsession. Our children *should* be our obsession, but there is a critical distinction. Knowing they are a product of our love, combined genes, and the environment we create from resources, hopes, and effort is one thing. Knowing they are literally us, only in another skin, is the difference between coincidence and fate. No matter how much trouble Greer was, all we could do for her was to give everything we had and then pray to God for the rest.

My parents began staying with us for a month every summer. When he could, Saul would join us. Much of that time was spent reminiscing about our lives and I pumped all three of them for forgotten details, trivial aspects, and explanations about past days and experiences that would give me better insight into who I'd been. What ingredients was I wholly unaware of then that had gone into making me the man I was now? Can we ever really know ourselves without hearing what others think of us?

Sometimes they wanted to know why I was *so* interested in our past. Saul got angry one night when I overdid the questions. What the hell did twenty years ago matter? Why did I persist in trying to dissect or put those days under a microscope? Why not just leave them alone, enjoy the memories of a family that had held together and continued loving one another right up to today? Luckily I had a ready answer which soothed all of them and permitted more questions. I had read about an artist in Europe who'd had a show of paintings she'd done of her own childhood. Pretending it was my idea, I said drawing my history had been a secret dream project for years but I'd only recently gotten up the courage to begin taking notes and do some preliminary sketches. It was something that would take years to complete but, if done successfully, might turn out to be my greatest work. The Fischers were proud of my success as a cartoonist, and once they knew what was going on, they were charmed by the idea. Afterward, they talked and wrote letters or called me long-distance to say they'd just remembered something that might be useful . . .

I listened, read, worried. I worked so hard to learn the exact contents of, then clean up and order, the room that was my life. Not so I could one day draw it as it really was, but to use to help my boy make *his* life into something magnificent.

Mary Poe was correct in saying we had tried to do everything right for our son. But beyond the bedtime talks about God or how thunder wasn't dangerous, the carefully wrapped sandwiches and only two cookies in his lunchbox, the circus, the ball games, vacations, going over multiplication tables together, popcorn, mowing the lawn, talking about the death of the dog so that it became an acceptable part of *life* . . .

Despite knowing what I did, what constantly surprised me was realizing the *only* appropriate way to raise this child was essentially no different from any other good and concerned parent's method.

My history, the secret knowledge, the huge number of books I read and thought about for years all said basically the same thing—love them, teach them humility, balance, and restraint, applaud them, tell them no when it is necessary, admit your mistakes.

Yes, you know these things already and I needn't go on. Maybe I'm only talking to myself now. Like the man who has gone over his checkbook ten times but still cannot find out why he is in debt. I had a hundred dollars. I spent this for this, that for that. I can account for all of it, but why, then, is there less than nothing left? Why had our son turned into a dishonest, sullen, secretive knot of a human being? There should have been something good left over from the years of support, careful guidance, and love. But there wasn't. There was nothing in this "account."

"Hello, Mary Poe."

"Hello, Greer Fischer."

"Did you bring your gun?"

"I did."

"Can I see it?"

"It's just the same old gun you saw the last five times."

"Please?"

Mary looked at me and I nodded okay. She opened her blazer and undid the thing from its shoulder holster. Slipping the bullets out, she held it up for Greer to see.

"Is it heavy?"

I knew what she was moving toward. "Greer, you can't hold it. You know the rules."

"I was just *asking.*"

"I know what you were doing. Look, but no touching."

"Smith and Wesssson. That's the guys who made it?"

"Right."

"Do they make bombs?"

"I don't know."

"Do you have a gun, Daddy?"

"You know I don't. Only police and private investigators like Mary have them."

"Lincoln has a gun."

"What do you mean?"

Greer was very smart but she talked too much. Whenever she was in a room she wanted center stage and would do almost anything to get it, including lie. Looking from me to Mary, she knew she'd struck gold with this piece of information and her expression narrowed down into cunning.

Climbing into my lap, she cuddled up close to my ear and whispered. "Promise you won't tell? Lincoln doesn't know I know. I went into his room and saw it behind the dresser. He has it stuck with tape there."

I nodded as if it was okay. Your brother has a hidden gun in his room? That's okay. I managed to say in an even voice, "I don't know what he needs *that* for. Oh well." As gently as I could, I pushed her down. "Okay, that's all right. Why don't you go in the kitchen, honey, and get a little snack. Mary has to go soon and we have to talk some more. I'll be in in a minute."

Disappointed her secret hadn't made a bigger splash, she put her hands in her pockets and scuffed out of the room.

When she was gone, I told Mary what she'd whispered. She closed her eyes and tightened her lips. "Shit. Okay, Max, stay cool. Don't fly off and get crazy, or you'll blow this. First, you've got to see what kind it is. Maybe it's only an air pistol or something, a pellet gun, he doesn't want you to know he has.

"If not, if it's a real piece, try and get the serial number off it so we can find out if it's hot. You've got to handle this right or we'll be in big trouble."

"I'll take care of it."

"Max—"

"I said I'll take care of it, Mary. I'll do what you told me. There's nothing else *to* do, is there?"

"Not yet. But remember, it could be nothing. Teenage boys love this stuff, but it doesn't mean—"

"I know that, but we also knew Bobby Hanley, didn't we?"

Without making eye contact, she stood and buttoned her jacket. Bobby Hanley was a legendarily violent, frightening kid from our hometown who had ended up dying in a gun battle with the police.

"Bobby Hanley was a criminal. Your son's a messed-up brat, not a criminal."

"He has a fucking *gun,* Mary. How do I know he's not?"

"Because he isn't. Okay? Because he is not. I'm going to go right now and talk to my friend Dominic Scanlan at the LAPD. I'll get him to check out . . . I don't know. I want to feel him out on this. He'll know what direction to take. But we'll find out. You look at that gun and get the numbers off it, if it's the real thing. But don't take it. Don't *touch* it. If Lincoln's done anything wrong and knows you know about his gun, it'll complicate things. I'll call you in a couple hours."

When she was gone, I went to find Greer. She was out on the back patio eating a brownie. I put my arm around her and sat us down on a sun chair.

"Is Mary gone?"

"Uh-huh. Listen, sweetie, I was thinking about what you just told me."

"About Lincoln's gun? I know I shouldn't have gone in his room, Daddy. I know you and Mom said not to. Are you mad?"

"I'm not happy. Plus, I know *you* wouldn't like someone snooping round in your room."

She hung her head. "I'd hate it."

"Okay, then that's that. Let's forget about it. I know how much your brother loves you but he'd probably be really upset and disappointed if he knew you were doing it again. Remember last time? So look, if you don't tell him what you told me, I won't say anything either. It'll be our secret. But you've got to keep the secret, Greer. 'Cause if anyone finds out, you're the one it'll hurt."

"Are you going to tell Mommy?"

"Mom doesn't need to know either."

Hearing that, she knew she was off the hook and could be

mischievous again. "Okay, but sometimes I *can't* keep a secret, Dad. I just have to open my mouth and scream it out 'cause it's like a burp, you know? Like it can't live in my stomach or I'll explode."

"Baby, do what you like, but if you tell Lincoln, he's not going to let you in his room again, because he won't trust you. If you tell Mom, remember what she said last time about snooping where you're not supposed to in the house. I don't think it's a good idea to talk about this with anyone, but the decision is up to you."

"Are you going to tell anyone?"

"No."

"It's bad, huh, Dad? About Lincoln having it."

"I'm not sure yet. I think it's kind of bad because what does he need a gun for?"

"Maybe he wants to protect us!"

"I'll protect us. He knows he doesn't have to worry about that."

"Maybe he wants to show off. Or maybe he's going to shoot someone!"

"I hope no one we know!"

Looking to see if I was serious, her small concerned face relaxed as soon as I smiled and she understood I was joking.

I could trust her not to tell only for a little while because sooner or later Greer spilled any bean she owned. I called Lily at Crowds and Power and said we would be going over there for dinner. She was in a good mood and wanted to know if anything new was happening.

"Nothing much, except I love you."

"That's new? We've been together seven years but only now you're starting to love me?"

"I think we love differently every day. Like the guy who said you can't stand in a river at exactly the same place twice. Today I love you differently than yesterday, or will tomorrow."

"Oh. Uh, Max, are you okay?"

"Is that Mommy on the phone? Can I talk to her?"

I handed the phone to Greer. She took it with two hands and pressed it tight up against her face.

"Mom? Ms. Zuckerbrot says I have to bring two thousand pea-nut butter cookies to class Thursday for our party."

I heard Lily squawk, "Two thousand!?" Greer giggled into her hand and grinned at me. "Just *kidddding*. But I do have to have a lot of cookies for the party. Will you help me make them?"

We worked on her homework together and then played Chinese checkers for another hour.

"Max, I'm going out."

I turned and saw Little White making a flirty face at Elvis. He grabbed her by the jaw and apparently squeezed too hard, because she squealed like a pig and slapped his hand away. "You always *hurt* me, assho—" Seeing us, she caught herself and gave a lame smile. Lincoln ignored them.

"Be back by seven, huh? We're going to the restaurant for din-ner."

"I'm not hungry."

"Lincoln, be home at seven o'clock tonight. I don't care if you're hungry."

Elvis whistled and shook his hand slowly back and forth at my "show of might." The girl rubbed her jaw.

"Whaddya want me to do there, sit at the table with an empty plate and listen to all the fags?"

"If you want to be sarcastic, tiger, you gotta be witty too. You almost have the tone now, but you ain't got the funny yet."

Little White thought this was hilarious. She clapped her hands delightedly. Elvis put a finger out, touched him on the arm, and, pretending to be burned, made a hissing sound and whipped his hand back fast.

"Guess he burned your ass, Linco."

"I guess you better kiss my ass, *Elvo*. Come on, we're outta here."

They trooped out in their seven-league Gestapo boots and I'd guess it was my son who slammed the door and then gave it a loud kick for good measure.

"How come you and Lincoln always fight, Daddy?"

"Because I think he should do certain things but he thinks he shouldn't. Come on, it's your move."

Seven o'clock rolled around with no sign of him. I waited another half hour before going to dinner. I tried to be as calm and good-natured as I could with Greer, while at the same time figuring out what to do with her brother. Getting into his room was no problem—a week after he put the lock on his door, I had a locksmith come in and make me a copy of the key. What I'd told Mary was true—I had been in his room only once since the lock was installed, but I'd also stopped trusting our son long ago and felt the secret key necessary. No one knew I had it, not even Lily.

Crowds and Power was packed with pretties when we arrived. In the years since Lily and I met, it had become one of the "power" spots in Los Angeles for people to meet and be seen. Articles were written about it in trendy magazines, the parking lot was invariably full of the appropriate German, English, and Italian cars with license plates that said things like "L.A. Gent," and getting a table reservation was tough if you were not important. Ibrahim and Gus were still together despite their never-ending bickers, yet I liked them less because of how they had changed with their success. On the one hand, they worked too hard to be cool. On the other, both were overtly sycophantic. This showed in the way they dealt with their increasingly famous clientele. If you were someone, a table was always ready. If you weren't, you might be allowed to sit in the back near the kitchen. The no-man's-land Gus called "Table Hell." There was little of the original warmth and happy frenzy that had been such a precious trademark of the place when I'd first known it. A few years back there had been a palace revolt because of this elemental change of heart. The Band sisters and Mabdean Kessack quit because none of them liked how elitist and false their bosses had become. In a move that troubled Lily because it erased most of what was left of the original "feel" of the restaurant, Ibrahim replaced the women with a gay couple named Ace and Berndt who were both very swish and snobbish but efficient.

"Hi, guys. Where's Lincoln?" Lily had an armful of menus, and her hair, which had grown much longer, was sticking out in all directions. We kissed, then she bent over and traded big ones with Greer.

"He's with his friends. He might show up later."

She gave me her "Is this what I think?" look and I nodded. She grimaced and sighed. "He used to love coming here so much, remember? We had fun. Remember how Mabdean used to make him that special pizza?"

"And his birthday party with the snakes?"

"Golden days at Crowds and Power. How I wish it was like that now. Are you hungry?"

One of the waiters came up and, with the slightest head tip of recognition to us, started talking to Lily in an urgent whisper.

"Just tell her it's not on the menu, Berndt. I don't understand the problem."

Offended, he looked at her as if she'd asked if he had farted. "The problem is, I *did* tell her that, but she insisted we make it for her because we served it before."

"Too bad. She can eat what's on the menu, like everyone else."

"Gus might be upset if he hears you said no. He loves this woman's show."

"I'll worry about that. Please do as I told you."

Flashing a bitchy little smile, he walked off. Lily scratched her chin. "I miss Sullivan and Alberta at least ten times a day, every day. Things used to be so much more merry around here. Once upon a time, we would have made that actress what she wants because we'd have been so excited to have her here. Not no more."

"Mom, can we eat now?"

"Yes, love. Let's find a table." Leading us through the packed room, Lily turned and asked, "Where *is* His Majesty?"

"Last I saw, he was shuffling off to places unknown with Mickey and Minnie. We had a face-off at the door and I told him to stop being such a wise guy."

"I'm sure he loved that. Here, let's sit here. Did you embarrass him in front of his friends? You know how he hates that."

"He hates most things. That's the problem."

"Sometimes he hates *you,* Daddy."

"I know, but that can happen when you have two guys butting heads like we do. You know the way we disagree about things."

"What did you tell him to set him off?"

"To be home at a specific time so we could go to dinner. He said he wasn't hungry, I said *be home.* That was the extent of our discussion. Looks like he decided not to join us after all."

"Mom, Lincoln had his 'fuck' shirt on."

"Thank you for telling me, Greer, but you know the only reason you told me was so you could say the word. Don't think you're tricking me."

"Lil, I had a couple of ideas for the strip coming over. I'd like to leave right after dinner to go back and work on them. You've got early shift tonight, right? Can Miss Muffet go home with you?"

"Sure. We'll have to stop at the market first, but you don't mind staying up past your bedtime a little, do you?"

Sounding out words on the menu to herself, Greer shook her head.

"You look great tonight. That long hair really suits you."

"Oh, Max, does it? Thanks. I think I look like a hundred years old today."

"No, you look great. You're one of those people who get better-looking as they grow older. I'm very lucky to have you, know that?"

We often complimented each other. I didn't know a happier couple. Neither how she had stolen Lincoln nor what had become of him could affect the fact that we loved each other more and more as the years passed.

"Thank you. You're a good guy to say it."

"It's the truth. What are we having for dinner?"

Although it was a good family meal with lots of talk, gestures, and laughing, both Lily and I kept scanning the room to see if the boy had arrived. Sometimes our looks crossed and one or the other would raise an eyebrow as if to say, "What can we do? The kid isn't coming."

But he surprised us.

"Max, I was trying to tell someone today how many newspapers run 'Paper Clip.' Isn't it around three hundred?"

"Yes, a few more, but that's good enough."

"Hi, *Mom.*"

"Lincoln! Hi! Come, sit down."

"Hi, Lincoln. Wanna sit next to me?"

"Hi, Grrrr-eer. Naah, I want to sit next to *Dad.* Right in the heart of the old fam."

The chair to my right slid out noisily. Sitting down, he slapped me on the shoulder. "How're you doin', Max? How's the old provider hanging?"

"Do you want something to eat?"

"I said before I wasn't hungry. I only came by to see you guys." Patting out a beat on the table, he started singing a song about "raising my fam-uh-ly." We watched and waited but he didn't stop. He sang louder. People at other tables started staring and gave him a long once-over. He sang on while we three went back to our dessert.

Greer said she had to go to the toilet and Lily took her.

Lincoln smiled at me. "Hey, Max, what's the difference between a refrigerator and a homosexual?" He said it too loudly, wanting people to hear.

"I guess you're going to tell me."

"A refrigerator doesn't fart when you take your meat out."

A woman at the table next to ours shook her head and said, "Jesus Christ, *crude!*"

I sat forward and put my hand on his forearm. "Lincoln, stop it. What are you trying to prove? You know you shouldn't talk like that here. It's offensive and totally inappropriate."

Instead of answering, he put a thumb in Greer's peach ice cream. Sticking it in his mouth, he sucked the finger. It was so incongruous seeing this mess of a kid sucking his thumb. He closed his eyes in exaggerated delight. I realized it was the first time in all our years together I had seen him make that innocent gesture.

"Lincoln! What are you doing? What is the matter with you?

Why do you make trouble every time you are coming in now?" Ibrahim marched over, seething. He was a kind man but had had enough of the boy's behavior. Our son had caused a number of scenes and near-fights here in the last two years. Cruel comments, jokes as gross and loud as this one, rotten things that he shouted at us about how much he despised the restaurant and all those connected with it. Long ago we had given up asking him to join us, but many times he chose to tag along and then usually wound up making trouble. None of us knew why, other than his very aggressive homophobia. The only reason I'd wanted him along tonight was so I could be sure he was away from the house when I went searching for his gun.

"This is the end. I have had enough of you now. You have no right to treat us like this Lincoln, you are making everyone who loves you crippled. You cut off our legs and then cut out our hearts. Love goes very far, mister, but it is not the universe. Someplace it stops and then that is the end."

"I'll try to remember that."

When Ibrahim was gone, Lincoln asked if we could go outside and talk alone. I agreed and, walking out, asked a waiter to tell Lily we'd be back in a few minutes.

Standing in front of the restaurant, the boy shoved his hands into the back pockets of his jeans. "I *know*, Maxie. I know everything! I found it all out today. Tonight. It's so incredible how in one second your whole life can move from here to way way way over *there*. Unbelievable. A real mind warper. But I know every one of your dirty fucking secrets!" He was so happy. If I hadn't known what was going on, I'd have been shocked by his face of pure joy. "I cannot believe it. I can't believe you didn't tell me anything all these years. Would you have? Would you ever have told me?"

"I don't know."

"Fuck you, Max. Fuck you for the rest of your shit-ass life. Fuck you and Lily and all the lies and everything about you two. You want me to do something for you? You're gonna pay for it. You're going to pay for *everything* now, cocksucker."

"How do you feel?"

He thought a moment. "I feel . . . I feel weird. Like my life, um, has been lived on another planet till now and it just landed here. Something along those lines. I'm sure you can understand what I'm saying, *Dad.*"

"Yes, I understand."

"I bet. Well, good. I wanted to tell you that, Max. But I don't think I want to inform your wife for a while because, um, one 'parent' at a time's enough."

I didn't understand what he meant but had no time to ask. A beautiful silver Mercedes pulled up across the street and stopped. The horn honked. Lincoln waved to it. "Gotta go now. I'll, like, talk to you later, okay?"

"Where are you going?"

"Got some stuff to do with Elvis."

"Elvis? That's him in the car? He doesn't own a Mercedes."

"It's a friend's."

"Lincoln, don't! We have to talk—"

"The fuck we do!" He ran into the street without looking. Yelling over his shoulder, he stopped in the middle of traffic, turned to me, then to the Mercedes, to me. "Now we do things my way, Daddy-o. Now that I know *the big secret.* Just today. It's like my friggin' bar mitzvah! Today I became a *man!*" He threw up both arms, hands in fists, and, waving them at the sky, howled like a wolf. Cars slowed to look. One driver howled back at him. Another sped away from this raving punk. Elvis honked and honked the horn. I stepped into the street but was stopped short when a motorcycle came zooming by. On the other side, Lincoln rounded the Mercedes, ducked, disappeared, and the silver car roared off before I heard the passenger's door close.

Running back into the restaurant, I told Lily I had to go home right now, no explanation why. I had to get to his gun. What might he do on the day he discovered who he was? Maybe go crazy. Or do something crazy. Forget what Mary said. I had to get to that gun before him and put it someplace safe. Then we would talk. Talk and talk until I'd made things as clear as I could to him.

There was a bad accident on Wilshire Boulevard, and the familiar ominous mix of whizzing lights on police cars and ambulances, plus a sputtering orange flare lying on the ground, made the early-evening scene even more neon and ugly. For the first time in years I remembered a day from childhood. On a summer Sunday before Saul was born, my parents took me to Palisades Park in New Jersey. I was about seven and had never been to an amusement park before. The day was a complete success and should have been one of those cherished memories of childhood because I had enough fun and excitement to exhaust ten boys. But fun isn't often as memorable as death.

On the ride home, once across the Tappan Zee Bridge we were immediately stopped by a giant traffic jam. The line went on for miles and was so slow moving that several times my father turned off the engine to keep it from overheating. But there was a baseball game on the radio, my mother had her knitting, and if anyone got hungry there were still a couple of sandwiches left in the picnic basket. We were happy. Dad and I listened to the game for a while, but tired from the day and the sunburn it had given me as a going-away present, I lay down on the wide back seat and fell asleep.

I don't know how long I was out, but I awoke to the sound of Mom's voice. "Just don't make any noise and he won't wake up."

Dad made a long quiet whistle. "I haven't seen one that bad in years."

I opened my eyes, but with a child's intuition knew a moment before she turned that Mom was about to check me. When she did, I pretended to be fast asleep.

"Max's all right. Still snoozing. Oh my God, Stanley! Oh my God!"

I couldn't stand the mystery. What was happening? It probably wouldn't have made any difference if I had sat up and exclaimed too, because both parents were transfixed by the scene outside. I slid across the seat and, peeking through the window, saw a smoking battlefield of wrecked cars, flashing lights, fire engines, people running around. Police blue, firemen yellow, doctors white.

There were bodies. First I saw two together covered by a blanket, their feet sticking meekly out. Next, and most amazing, was the child launched halfway through the windshield of a car. This was in the time before unbreakable safety glass was standard in automobile windows. It was a child; I was sure of that because despite being almost entirely covered by a coating of shiny blood, the visible part of the body was short and thin. The upper torso stuck up through the windshield like it had been shot from the back seat but stopped halfway out. A small arm wearing a wristwatch hung down. I could see the white watch face. That small spot of white in all the streaked, glaring red. A perfect white circle. The rest was blood and crushed, formless chaos. I absorbed it all in seconds. When my mother began turning around again, I zipped back to my sleeping position and wasn't caught. I was too scared to try for another look, and a short while later we were past the wreck and sped up.

"Roll it up, pal." Four decades later, a helmeted policeman held a flashlight and waved it across my face. "You've seen the show. Move on." I accelerated, thinking about my seven-year-old self in a back seat, the dead child through the windshield, and my son.

When I got home there were no cars in the driveway or in front of the house. Good, but that didn't mean anything. He could have been dropped off already and could be inside. I parked on the street and, standing next to the car, took several long, deep breaths before moving. What should I say if he was there?

I started for the house, running questions and answers through my mind, readying myself for whatever he might ask. But would anything give him clarity, or comfort, now that he knew?

I was almost to the door when I saw them. The front of our house is a couple of steps up to a large porch and the front door. There are metal chairs on the porch set back a ways where Lily and I often sat in the evening and chatted when she returned from work.

Two little boys were sitting on these chairs. I stopped, startled to see anyone up there, knowing our family was gone.

"Hi, Mr. Fischer!"

"Hey, Mr. Fischer!"

It was two of the Gillcrist boys from down the street. Nice kids, about nine and ten years old. You always saw them hanging around together.

"Hi, guys. What're you doing up there?"

"Edward dared me to come and sit on your porch."

"What did he dare you?"

"A quarter."

I reached into my pocket, took out one, and handed it to him.

"How come you're paying? Ed lost!"

"Shut up, Bill! If he wants to pay, he can."

"Did anyone come into the house since you two've been here?"

"No, sir. We've been around, I don't know, half an hour?"

"You didn't see Lincoln?"

"Nope."

"Okay. Well, I guess you'd better head on home now. It's getting pretty late."

Edward got up and gave Bill a shove when his brother was slow in rising. Bill poked him back. Edward poked—

"Hey, guys!"

"He's always starting!"

" 'Cause you're stupid!"

"I know you are, but what am I?"

I watched and thought what if they were Lincoln and me? Kids, brothers, two years apart. I blurred my vision and made believe. My brother Lincoln. Little brother Lincoln, who followed me around and was a pain but also was my best friend. Oddly, when I brought my eyes back into focus, the Gillcrists still looked like us. I had to blink and blink to make the picture go away.

Edgy, I unlocked the front door and walked in. Quiet, still, the rooms smelled warm and stale. The normal wonderful comfort one feels walking in the door of your own home was gone. I lived here, but so did he. Everyday objects, the things I knew and normally used without thought, seemed larger and all cocked at strange angles. Like a picture that's been bumped crooked and needs straightening. Our whole house felt crooked and . . . expectant. Was that the right word? As if it were waiting to see what I would do next. A car drove by out on the street. Freezing, I waited to hear if it would stop or pull into our driveway. It didn't. I figured I had about half an hour before Lily returned.

"Lincoln? Are you here?" Walking slowly through the house, turning on lights, I was full of the absurd idea that if he were here, he'd be hiding from me, ready to jump out and pounce when my back was turned. Although that was more Greer's style than his, still I moved cautiously, waiting for him to spring out of wherever. My son the Jack-in-the-Box.

I did a general careful look around before feeling a little more at ease. I smiled at myself for having checked behind the couch in the living room and in a too small closet in the laundry room. But fear comes from noticing the normal has suddenly grown fangs. After today's revelations, that space behind our couch was no longer the innocent place where Greer's tennis ball had fallen.

I got my key to his room from its hiding place taped to the bottom of an unused kitchen drawer. In stockinged feet I walked the long hall to the back of the house. At his door I knocked and again called out his name a few times to see if he was in there. No answer. I had no more time to waste. Opening it, I reached in and switched on the light. Once again the stark white emptiness and order of Lincoln's room was in such sinister contrast to what had probably gone on in there and what was hidden, like the infected peace of an empty prison cell or room at an asylum.

His chest of drawers was five or six inches out from the wall. Squatting down, I tilted my head and slid my hand along the back of the thing. Bingo, there it was. Smooth flat wood for a foot, then a suspect curl of tape peeling up off an edge. Further, the hard angles of a gun.

"Thank God. Thank God." I pulled it off and slid it over. Other than what I've seen in movies, I know nothing about guns, but I did recognize the shape of this one—it was a forty-five. Whether it was real or not was the next question. I knew the Japanese made remarkable full-scale models of guns detailed enough to fool the experts. This one was surprisingly light and either coated or constructed of some kind of rubber or plastic. A plastic gun? How could that be? Engraved on the left side was "Glock 21 Austria 45 AUTO." On the right was the name "Glock" another time, a serial number, the address of the firm in Smyrna, Georgia. It was so light. I've never felt comfortable around guns, but this one was compelling in its simple roughness. I turned it around and around. Carefully, after much figuring and noodling, I managed to release the clip from the bottom. It was full of twelve beautiful gold bullets. It was real. Nothing was more real than that gun.

Before doing anything else, I picked up the phone on his desk and called Mary Poe. While it rang, I held the Glock in my hand and turned it from side to side, sighting down my arm at it from different angles. What an instrument. What a singular piece of machinery. Bang. That's it. That's all it was made to do. Bang—one big hole. Mary wasn't home, but I told her tape I'd found the pistol, that it was very fucking real, and read the serial number off the side. I'd be home for a few more hours in case she wanted to get back to me.

Then I did a queer thing. I put the clip of bullets in my pocket, the pistol in the middle of the floor. Why not just shove the whole thing in my pocket? Because I didn't want it in my pocket. The bullets were bad enough, but as the ugly heart of the gun, without them it could do nothing lying there but suck up all of the light and energy in the room like a black hole in space.

The silence of heavy machinery turned off a moment ago, or of a major highway at three in the morning when no cars have passed for minutes. The quiet of an airplane miles above you trailing its white thread of vapor. There is so much noise in these things that their rare stillness sounds a million times quieter. It is a hush of waiting, not completion. Any minute the noise that *is* the thing will come back with a roar. That was the silence in Lincoln's room after I put the phone down.

Closing my eyes tight, I made fists and lowered my head to my chest. "I hate this. I hate it." Then I began to search.

In one drawer were three packages of condoms. How wonderful! He took precautions! If only it were so tame and simple. I smiled, thinking that in the old days a parent would have had a fit finding rubbers in a son's drawer. Another held a butterfly knife and a Polaroid photograph of Little White, topless. She had lovely small breasts and looked cute with both arms up, in the classic "make a muscle" pose. What was her name? Ruth. Ruth Burnett? Burdette? What would her parents say if they saw this photo?

Here is what else I found. A postcard of a penis and hairy balls with a pair of black eyeglasses over the dick so that the combination looked like a man's face with a thick beard. Written on the back was: "L. You can suck my dick when I'm dead." Another knife and bullet in his desk drawer, two blurry Polaroids of other handguns I assumed belonged to either Lincoln or his friends. Nothing else.

The phone rang. I shuddered and had to lick my lips before answering. "Hello?" They hung up. Whipping it from my ear, I shouted into the receiver, "Fuck you, asshole! *Fuck you!*" People like that should apologize! Say something. Say, "Excuse me, sorry, wrong number." Something at least so I'd know—

"Mine. Oh God, *my* room!" Looking through the house before, I'd ignored my study, taking it for granted Lincoln wouldn't go in there because he never did. Putting the phone down, I looked at my watch, checked around to be sure I'd not disturbed anything so he'd know I was in here. He was so secretive and scheming that I was sure he'd placed hairs across doors or other traps to find out in a minute if anyone had been snooping in his room, but I couldn't worry about it. Things looked good enough. One last eye check around. Drawers closed. Photos back. Closet door closed. Nothing on the desk. Okay, let's go. Whoops, the pistol! I'd forgotten the goddamned gun on the floor and was seconds away from leaving it there and turning out the light.

"Smart, Max. Very smart." Picking the Glock up, I flicked the light and left the room. Outside, I locked the door again and walked down the hall. How dangerous and wrong that must have looked. What's wrong with this picture? Why is Max Fischer charging through his house with a .45 pistol in his hand? Who does he plan on shooting?

Where were Lily and Greer now? At the market. She'd said they were going to stop at the market first and then come home. But I'd been so nuts when I ran in to tell her I had to leave, she might have panicked and would return much sooner than planned. I hoped not. I hoped she'd stay away. I hoped the phone wouldn't ring yet. I hoped my room was still only a room and not a whole new crisis.

The house had grown even bigger since I'd gone through Lincoln's room. A small picture on the wall I'd drawn for Lily loomed, a yellow rug glowed so much on the floor that I stepped over to avoid touching it. You grow smaller. You lose perspective, control. Something is eating you from inside out and there is nothing you can do about it. It's your own fear.

At the door to my room I put a hand on the knob, paused a breath, turned it. Clicked the light on.

Nothing.

Nothing had been touched. The neatness that was my room, that always was the room, was there. Until I noticed the smell. Shit. The place was clean and tidy and reeked vilely of shit. The smell owned the room.

It was on my desk. Two things were on my desk: one of Lily's favorite dinner plates piled with shit, a photograph stuck in the top. Next to it was a green manila folder. I owned only one green folder. Purposely. I kept it in a locked strongbox at the bottom of a locked filing cabinet. In that box was the green file along with copies of my will, insurance policies, and important bank certificates. Lily did not know about the box but our lawyer did. No one but me knew the contents. If I were to die suddenly, he would inform her and give her the extra key. I hadn't told her because I knew she would have objected furiously to the existence of the file. It *was* dangerous and incriminating, but I believed a fundamental artifact of our life and relationship. I envisioned a day when we were older, going through the papers together. I believed experiencing it all again through sixty-year-old eyes and hearts would matter very much to both of us.

The file was thick. It held ninety-three pages of information gathered by the detective about Anwen and Gregory Meier. It also held the diary I'd kept from the day I went to visit the Meiers in New Jersey until the day before Lily confessed to kidnapping her son. Once she had told me the truth, I felt no need to write about what I *thought* was the truth anymore. I felt no need to write about anything at all. It had changed from being what was feared to what *was* from that moment on.

As Lincoln grew older and more untrustworthy, I'd twice moved the box to a safety-deposit box at our bank. But having it there made me extremely uneasy and both times I'd brought it back. To lessen the risk of discovery, I put the "Lily documents" at the bottom and covered them over with stock certificates and other boring papers that had no immediate value or interest to a snooper or a thief.

Even reading through the papers from the detective agency, one would have thought I simply had an inordinate interest in a couple named Meier. People who had tragically gone through one harrowing experience after another and only barely survived to crawl out on the other shore of life. Those Xerox copies alone said nothing.

It was my diary. I could quote specific, damning passages from it here, but what would be the point? You have already heard my questions, alarm, and pain from that time. The diary Lincoln found and read said it all. Except for the one *other* thing I discovered the night of Lily's confession. But seeing the shit and that deadly green folder so neatly side by side on the desk, I did not think of that one other thing. The hideous smell got stronger, closer; it made me want to retch. I walked over and sat down in the chair. Breathing through my mouth, I bent forward and plucked the photograph out of the top of the glistening brown pile. It was of our son squatting on this desk, shitting onto this plate. He was grinning at the camera and giving it the finger. Written in thick black marker across it was: "Look what I found!"

The telephone rang. I glanced at it. It seemed a hundred miles away on the other side of the desk. I didn't have the strength to reach across the few inches for it. It rang again. It rang again.

"Hello?"

"Dad!" His voice sounded so happy. "Now, I *thought* you'd be home. Get my message? It must be pretty ripe by now. What did you tell old Lil to get you home so fast? I bet you hightailed it over to see if I'd be there. Right?"

"Something like that. Lincoln—"

"Shut up. I don't want to hear a word from you. I'll hang up if you start talking. I'm at the airport. I took your extra Visa card and am going to use it for a while. I already got a few hundred out of a money machine with it. Bet you didn't know I knew your code, didja? Do *not* call Visa and stop the card, understand?"

"Yes, use it, but listen—"

His voice grew more confident. "Good, right. I'm catching a plane to New York in ten minutes. Just so you and *Mommy* know, and don't worry. Then I'm going to get a car and drive out to visit Mr. and Mrs. Meier. We need to have a good long talk together."

"Lincoln—"

"Shut the fuck up! I'm going to talk to them and then I'll think about you. Maybe. Maybe I'll come back, maybe not. *Don't* try to follow me. Besides, there isn't another plane to New York for three hours. I checked. Even if you try, it won't do you any good.

"Stay away. You owe me that, asshole. You and Lily owe me a lot more than that. Stay away until I get in touch with you. In the meantime, the only money I'll have will be from your credit card, so do not cancel it."

I had to say just one thing to him. I had to chance it. "Lincoln, the Meiers—"

"Shut up!" The line went dead.

Before doing anything else, I took the plate from the desk, shook what was on it into the toilet, and flushed. Then I rinsed the plate in fresh water until it was clean again. Not good enough. Taking it to the kitchen sink, I poured on liquid bleach and let it sit in that chemical bath a few minutes before cleaning it off with scalding water and soap. Still unsatisfied, I put the plate into the empty dishwasher and turned the machine on. I wonder what Lily thought later, opening the door and seeing only one plate. Strange things afoot that night in the Fischer household.

I didn't want to be around to tell her what had gone on in the last hours. For a short time I considered admitting everything, including Lincoln knowing because he'd read the diary I'd kept hidden from her for years. But that would demand a discussion meant for a night when we had hours to weigh and argue and hopefully come to a peace with each other about my having kept the book around in the first place. There was no time now. Lincoln was about to board a plane to New York and do whatever the hell he planned to do with the Meiers once he got there.

I called flight information at Los Angeles Airport. The boy had told the truth—the plane just now leaving for New York was the last for three hours. No, there were no flights to Newark either. One to Hartford in an hour, another to Philadelphia in two. Both cities were too far away to be of any help. I needed New York or New Jersey but neither was available for one hundred and eighty minutes, plus flight time. For a while I felt hopeful on realizing that even with a valid credit card, an auto rental place won't rent a car to a sixteen-year-old. Right! He'll have to stay in the airport till he can figure a way out, which will buy me badly needed time. Yet this was also the young man who kept a loaded .45 pistol taped to the back of his dresser and had found my most secret of secrets. Which meant, of course, he was enterprising enough to find a way to Somerset, New Jersey, a lot sooner than I would.

Since I had no idea if they still lived there, the next step was to call New Jersey information and ask if Anwen and Gregory Meier still lived in Somerset. They did. Goddamnit, they did. In that strange and spooky house that was supposed to be a replacement for their lost child.

I sat and thought, then hopefully called a couple of different charter airlines listed in the phone book to ask how much they charged to rent a private plane and pilot to fly East. The prices were insane, but I was willing to do it until they said they'd need at least three hours, minimum, to arrange it. I called the airports in Burbank, Sacramento, and San Francisco. Nothing worked. There were flights to New York from these places but not the right connections to get me to them in time.

Seconds after I put the phone down after the last futile call, it rang again. Praying it would be Lincoln so I could tell him the one essential thing he didn't know, I snatched it up. Only to hear Mary Poe's voice.

"Hello?"

"Max, it's Mary. I'm calling from the car phone, so it'll be a bad connection. Lincoln's gun is definitely real, and it's stolen. The serial numbers say it's part of a shipment of guns from a truck that was hijacked in Florida six months ago. It's also a major league weapon, very high-powered shit. Terrorists love Glock guns because they're made mostly out of plastic and can be snuck by airport metal detectors. It's no Saturday night special, Max. It's the kind of piece that gives you the willies even when you carry a gun yourself. But you say it's still there? Then it's all right. Just take it down and hold it in your lap, or stick it in a safe till boyo gets home."

I got off as quickly as I could, after asking her to be sure not to tell Lily about the gun. Having no idea how long I would be in the East, I went into our bedroom and packed a small bag with jeans, a couple of shirts, underwear . . . enough for three or four days. I knew I had to write Lily a note explaining some of this so she wouldn't go mad with worry when she returned and found both of us gone. But what could I say? "I am running after our son, who has discovered he was kidnapped . . ." What *could* be said? There was no time to think about it. I wrote that he had run away, possibly with Elvis and Little White. I was going to try to find him before anything bad happened. That was why I'd run out of the restaurant earlier—because he told me he'd had enough of us and was going to go and live life on his own. It was the kind of lie that left out enough to be almost true. She would go for it and that was all I could hope for at that moment. Lily was stubborn about Lincoln, but not stupid. She knew how angry he was and how unpleasant he could be. Hearing he'd flown the coop would not surprise her. I wrote I would call her the minute I knew anything.

I ran out of the house, locked the door, and unthinkingly looked through the living-room window and saw that I'd left on a number of lights. One memory flicked through my mind of changing a bulb in one of those lamps, calling to Greer to please go to the kitchen and get me a new bulb. "Yes, Daddy." The soft sound of her slippered feet racing down the carpeted floor and in a far part of the house asking her mother for a light for Daddy. What would our lives be like the next time I changed a light bulb in our home? How long would it be before that happened?

In contrast to all the frightening possibilities, the Los Angeles evening was lovely and fragrant. It would have been pleasant to sit out on the back patio, drink a glass of brandy, and talk quietly late into the night. We did that often. Greer would fall asleep in one of our laps as Lincoln had years before. We wouldn't disturb them. It was too nice being there together. When he was still alive, the greyhound would lie on his side near our chairs, his long legs stretched out straight. He was still around when Greer was very young. More than once we'd enter a room and see this tiny girl standing close but never actually touching him.

"Cobb! Oh my God." I remembered something intriguing when I thought of our dog. Lincoln was the only human being the old eccentric let touch him. Until one day the boy ran into the house in tears, wailing that Cobb had just snapped at him. Neither of us could believe it, knowing their special relationship. We reassured him, saying the dog had probably been sleeping and was in the middle of a bad dream or whatever. The three of us went out to find him and see what was up. He was in his favorite place—lying in the sun on the warm stones of the patio. We told Lincoln to go try petting him again. When he bent down to touch the gray giant, Cobb either grumbled or growled. The sound was not friendly. That was the end of an era. From that moment until he died, he didn't want any of us touching him, not even his young pal. He still stuck his tongue out in those long, slow swipes Lily insisted were kisses, but he wouldn't be touched. When was that? Walking to the car, I tried to figure out exactly when the change happened in him. It seemed to have been after Lincoln and I became blood brothers. Or it could very well not have. My mind was racing so fast and trying to tie so many different strings together that it was unhelpful and dangerous. I made up a line that has become a kind of all-purpose prayer for me: "I want calm and not control." As I backed out of the driveway, window down for the cool air needed across my face, a part of me still couldn't believe I was about to fly across country chasing a son who'd found out too much too soon and was doing exactly what he shouldn't.

Turning the steering wheel, I started repeating over and over, "I want calm and not control." Down Wilshire, weaving through the red and yellow taillight traffic, I said it. Down La Cienega Boulevard out to the airport: "I want calm and not control."

The car was almost out of gas. I drove into a station and stopped by a self-service pump. The man in the cashier's booth looked at me through a pair of binoculars. No more than thirty feet away, he used binoculars to see if I was going to rob him. It was a great idea for "Paper Clip," but the life where I did that job now seemed as far away as the Ivory Coast. I went to the booth and slid a twenty-dollar bill beneath a bulletproof-glass window thick enough to stop a Cruise missile. The man held the bill up to the light to see if it was fake. His face was all suspicion. How many times had he been robbed, or simply scared to the bottom of his bones?

"We get a lot of counterfeit twenties."

"I can imagine."

My mother used to say, "You feel black, you see black." The drive to LAX that night was one scene after another of worry or angst or hell, beginning with the man with his binoculars. Was it coincidence that I saw a drunken man standing in the middle of the street screaming, or two police cars screech up in front of a house and the officers jump out going for their guns? Further on, a gang of black kids stood in front of a Fatburger all wearing the same black-and-white Oakland Raiders baseball caps and windbreakers. There must have been fifteen of them in this uniform and they all looked ready for murder. The road widened out and began to rise toward the oil-well-covered hills. Streetlamps dumped their fake orange glare over us. I looked to the side and saw ugly, sinister faces in the cars passing mine. Drivers with narrowed-down heads like weasels, bald rats, and lipless ferrets pointed forward, so eager to get somewhere that even their heads were squeezed down by the G force of anticipation. A young child in the back seat of a Hyundai had its hands and open mouth pressed to the window. A beautiful passenger with long blond hair looked at me with such burnt-out, nothing-interests-me eyes. Was she dead? Was the world I knew suddenly so macabre and threatening because of what had happened tonight with my son? Or had it always been this way and only now was I able to see it with understanding eyes?

I sped up. It was a long time before my plane left but I needed to be at the airport. Needed those clean long boring halls and plastic chairs where you sat looking at nothing, waiting for the time to pass until you could get on a plane and continue looking at nothing for a few more hours.

Before you see L.A. Airport, you see the planes gliding in over the highway to land. They are enormous there, eighty feet above the ground and sinking. Larger even than when they are parked at the terminal. They dwarf everything as they drop slowly in toward earth; you love their size and the fact they're tame, that you can ride in one anytime you want.

I left the car in long-term parking and walked quickly to the terminal. It was an evening in the middle of the week and traffic was light.

So much emotion at the doors of an airport. Hugs and tears, the joy on the faces of those who've just landed and are coming out into the real air after so many hours on the plane. Cars pull up, pull away. Above all else, everything is rushed. A rush to get there, to get out of here. The world on fast forward. Where was Lincoln now? Rushing across the country toward two people—

"Call them! Just call them up!" Whatever is most obvious hides when you're stressed. Two steps into the building, the idea to call and give them some kind of warning came to me. I looked around wildly for a telephone. Over there! I'd taken a load of change when I left the house, which was good because this was going to be one expensive call. I dialed New Jersey information and for the second time that night asked for Gregory Meier's number. Those blessed push-button telephones. How long it took when you were in a hurry but had to twist and twist the wheel of the old machines. Now stab stab stab . . . and you're through. It was ridiculous feeling so pressed for time when Lincoln was still four hours away from landing, but I did. The connection was made and their phone began to ring thirty-five hundred miles away.

"Hi. You've reached the Meiers, but no one's home now. Please leave your name and message and we'll get back to you as soon as we can. Thanks for calling."

There was a peep and the demanding silence that expects you to talk. I couldn't think of what to say. In one minute? If I had told them, "Be careful of a boy who's coming. He thinks you're his parents and could be dangerous," they might have called the police or gotten scared enough to make things even more confusing and difficult. What if someone I didn't know called and told *me* that? I'd think either that it was a bizarre prank or that the speaker was a sadist. I tried calling four more times before taking off, but their machine always answered. What did that mean in terms of Lincoln?

Would they be home by the time he reached them? If not, if they were out of town and not due back for days, how would that affect him? What would he do? Wait? Take his anger and frustration, get back on a plane with it, and fly somewhere else? Knowing our son, he'd wait a short time and then return home. I didn't know which was worse.

Although the plane was half empty, I got stuck next to a woman who began talking the instant I sat down and didn't stop until I got up again, told her I had a great deal of work to do, and changed seats. I wasn't in the mood to be civil. There were only so many hours before New York and I wanted to try to figure out as much as I could. After we landed, there wouldn't be time for thought.

Once we were airborne, the stewardess came round asking for drink orders. I would have killed for a double anything, but bit my tongue and asked for a ginger ale instead. I was exhausted and a drink would put me right to sleep. Sitting by a window, I watched as the plane tipped and banked, then found its way and leveled out over the black and yellow twinkling below. I remembered driving over tonight and seeing planes coming in. How romantic and heart-lifting the sight. Yet how lonesome and small I felt now, climbing up into that same sky.

We passed over a baseball stadium with all its lights still on after a night game. Seeing the field reminded me of an unsettling discussion Lily and I had had a few weeks before.

Like Lincoln, I had always loved baseball. Until I was fifteen or so, the nucleus of every summer *was* the game, whether that meant watching it on television, playing catch with my friends, talking about it with the barber when I went in for a ballplayer's crew cut, trading Topps baseball cards with others . . .

The minute I was old enough to play in Little League, I begged my parents to sign me up. They did, and one of the proudest memories of my young life was walking into the living room after dinner one night wearing for the first time my robin's-egg-blue baseball cap and T-shirt that said the name of our sponsor, "Nick's Shell Station," on the front. My team was named the Yankees, thank God, which made life even better because this was in one of the periodic heydays of the New York Yankees and all of the men who played on that great team were my heroes. Mom put down her crossword puzzle and said I looked "very nice." But Dad paid me the supreme compliment. Giving me a careful once-over, he said I looked just like Moose Skowron, Yankee first baseman and my favorite player.

Our first game was also opening day of the season that year and many people came out to watch. I was assigned to right field, the equivalent of Siberia in Little League because no child ever hits a ball there. However, our coach thought it was a good place for me because I couldn't catch for beans and would do the least damage there. Which didn't bother me a bit because hitting was my dream, not fielding. Nothing felt better than whipping that Louisville Slugger bat around and once in a spectacular while feeling the great "clunk" of wood connecting with the ball. That's what I lived for, not putting a huge leather glove up in the air to stop a ball from sailing by. Batting was heroic, fielding was only necessary.

Our opponents that first game were the Dodgers, a good team, but fearsome too because their star pitcher was none other than Jeffrey Alan Sapsford. His fastball, even then, would have struck out Moose Skowron.

By the fifth inning we were losing nine to nothing. I'd batted twice and struck out both times. Besides that, I'd dropped an easy fly ball and been yelled at by half my team. I knew I deserved their hatred. I was a bum, we were losing, the world was doom. Worse, my parents were there witnessing the debacle. I knew my father had skipped meeting the seven o'clock train (his biggest haul of tired customers) so he could be on hand for my debut. Some debut. I'd failed him, my team, the name Yankees.

The last time I got up to hit, Jeffrey Alan Sapsford looked at me with gleeful disdain. Unforgettably, his second baseman yelled, "Easy out!" and he was talking about me. The whole world had heard. I, the heir to Moose Skowron's throne, was fixed in everyone's mind as an "easy out." Try erasing that kind of mark from your record when you're that age.

Sapsford threw his first pitch and, without thinking, I swung and knocked the ball five hundred and forty miles into deep center field. I hit it so hard and far that the other team froze as one watching the ball soar off into that deep green infinity. The people in the grandstand got up and started applauding before I had even rounded first base. When I came in to home plate, my team stood there waiting for me and cheering as if this were the last game of the World Series and I had saved the day. Pure glory.

We still lost ten to one, but in the car riding home afterward, I was a hundred percent hero and no one could take that away from me, ever.

My parents chattered on about how great it had been, while I sat in the back seat basking in fresh memories and their praise. As we turned the corner of Main Street and Broadway, my father said with a loving chuckle, "And did you know your fly was open the whole way round?"

"What?"

"Your fly was down."

"Oh, Stan, you said you weren't going to tell him that." Mom shook her head and smiled sympathetically at me over her shoulder.

In poleaxed, stunned-still shock, I looked down at my blue jeans. I'd hit a home run in these pants. They were part of the legend's uniform! But there it was—the accusing white slip of my underpants beaming out through my fly. Not much. Not enough to really be seen unless you looked hard or someone drew your attention to it, but *there* nevertheless. The apex of my life—and my zipper was open!

I honestly don't remember if I got over it quickly or if that moment's brain-blasting embarrassment lasted a long time. Until I told the story to Lily, it had been a fond smile from way in my past, the kind of childhood memory you like to tell your partner so they can share a piece of your past few others know. I finished telling her the story with a smile and a shrug. "Max hits a homer."

"That's despicable. Your father is a real asshole sometimes."

"Why?"

"*Why?* Why'd he tell you that? What was the point? You had your home run. It was yours, nothing could take it away from you. But he did—he spoiled it *forever* by telling you about your zipper. Listen to the way you tell it now—like it's only a funny little amusing story. Right? 'Max hits a homer.' You should have heard your voice. It wasn't only that, it was one of the supreme moments of your childhood. A home run! So what if your stupid zipper was down? So what if the whole world knew, so long as you didn't? He's an insensitive jerk."

Call me blind. Or only in love with my father, whatever, I never thought of it like that. I knew the man loved me and wasn't trying to ruin my moment. But like a hammer thrown across four decades, the wrongness of what he did hit me square in the head for the first time.

Looking down from the airplane at the empty, lit baseball stadium, I remembered my wife's indignant voice as she spoke of him.

How many times had we done exactly the same thing with Lincoln? Was that what caused him to turn out so disastrously? Were there hundreds or thousands of things we'd done out of pure love that were nonetheless so flat-out wrong an enemy couldn't have devised a more effective means of destroying our boy?

This is what I thought about while crossing America that night. Pity the man who is not sure of his sins. Beware of the child who is his responsibility.

Halfway through the trip, I thought if only I could stay up here in the air for the rest of my life. As in a children's story, it would have made things so much simpler: Once upon a time there was a man who had made so many mistakes in his life that he decided to leave the earth and never return.

.　　.　　.　　.　　.

It was raining in New York when we landed. Water rolled down the windows in strange patterns as we taxied to the gate. Since it was such a late flight, there wasn't the usual rush of passengers to leave their seats and then the plane itself. People rose slowly and shuffled forward to the exits like tired zombies.

Because I had only a carry-on bag, I walked straight to a telephone and called the Meiers again. It was seven-thirty in the morning. No luck. Next stop was a car rental desk. Within minutes I was behind the wheel of a new-smelling yellow Ford. I figured it would take about two hours to drive from Kennedy Airport to Somerset, New Jersey, but once on the road, morning traffic was beginning. It would take more time.

In the years since we'd met, I had thought very little about the Meiers. The only time I put life aside and concentrated on them was in a dentist's office one morning. Sitting there waiting my turn, I picked up an architecture magazine and started giving it the quick shuffle-through. I passed something, ignored it, and only seconds later did it register. Leafing back fast, I found the large two-page spread on the house I had visited one depressing afternoon in the middle of that first crisis. There it was! Anwen and Gregory Meier's remarkable home. A cockeyed cupola and what looked like a kind of giant bat wing had been added on to the original building, but it was such a memorable place that no matter what, it couldn't be disguised. The text said Anwen Meier's Brendan House, one of the most famous examples of the Corvallis School of architecture, had received yet another prestigious award, this time from a European architectural organization. It spoke of the house as if everyone knew about it and wouldn't be surprised by this latest tribute. I tore the article out and showed it to Lily. Shaking her head, she began to cry. The memory of her face reddening and the glistening tears on her cheeks stayed with me many miles.

Somewhere along those miles was the rest stop where Lincoln bought his supplies. It was the only place he could have gotten them in the middle of the night on the New Jersey Turnpike. He bought big bottles of Coca-Cola. I would guess four of them. Four would do the trick if he was clever and careful about it. Gasoline was no problem. Pull into a station, fill 'er up, and ask the attendant if they sold those jerry cans you keep a couple of gallons of extra gas in for the lawn mower. *Gallons* of gasoline make quite a fire. What did he use for a wick? Probably underpants or a T-shirt. Maybe he took off his "Fuck Dancing—Let's Fuck!" shirt, tore it to pieces, and stuck them into the tops of the bottles. That would have been appropriate: Coke bottles full of golden gasoline and "Fuck" shirt scraps. That's all you need. Anyone who watches television knows how to make a Molotov cocktail, the poor man's hand grenade.

I knew he was bad, capable of things I had never wanted to think about. But even later, after retracing his steps and grasping his motives, I was appalled by what he did that night. If only he had stopped a few minutes to listen, to ask questions and hear the truth, terrible as it was. None of it would have happened. Other things would have, certainly, but not *that* and not to them.

He was a fast driver and had his three-hour head start on me. He also had a great sense of direction and would have no trouble finding the house. When he was young one of his hobbies had been studying maps, particularly exotic ones—Cambodia, Mali, Bhutan— and finding the shortest routes from one heroic or otherworldly-sounding point to another. Timbuktu to Nouakchott. Bu Phlok to Snuol. One birthday we gave him a beautiful brass calipers to measure his distances exactly. He still had those calipers in a desk drawer, along with the bullet and the picture of Little White.

I envisioned him driving eighty miles an hour down the New Jersey Turnpike, stopping only to get gas and the supplies he needed for the job. What went through his head in those hours? At home he always drove with the radio on loud, impatiently turning the dial whenever a song came on he didn't like. Add that to the picture. Add clicking on the overhead light while steering with one hand, looking quickly from his map to road signs approaching, then to the map again to make sure he was going the right way.

Lily had made this same drive sixteen years before, fleeing New York in a car she'd bought with money stolen from a drug dealer/

pimp. She was only five years older than Lincoln was now. All three of us had made this same drive south, all for such different desperate reasons.

I got off at the New Brunswick exit and remembered certain landmarks from my last trip, although the town itself had been cleaned up since then in the typical ways—homogenized, mall-ified. Morning traffic was heavy. Stuck in a long line at a red light, I felt weariness creep up the back of my head and spread. The people around me had had their good night's sleep, hot morning showers, breakfasts to get them up and out and going. Not me. As the light turned green and I was off again, I hated every one of them; resented them their stomachs full of savory coffee, the safe tedium of their jobs. They had children. Their children were not like mine.

New Jersey farm country, the sun only just up. Cows far off in fields, dogs running around free in backyards. Kids standing by the side of the road waiting for the school bus. The closer I got, the tighter the knot in my stomach grew. One last left turn and I was on their road. There's where I pulled over last time because I had to pee so badly. Some of the ticky-tacky houses had been torn down and replaced with attractive, much more expensive-looking places. The invasion of the middle class.

The road dipped, rose, dipped again, and that's when I saw the first fire truck. It was a long hook and ladder coming slowly down toward me. On such a narrow road out in the middle of that no-where, the red truck looked twice as large as it was. Wherever it was going, it was in no hurry to get there. Up in the open cabin, the driver and another man sat with their helmets off, smiling. The pas-senger was smoking a cigarette. We made eye contact and he lifted his cigarette hand in a small half-wave. Another two men stood on the ledge at the back of the truck holding on to silver handles. Both of them were in full uniform and one leaned his head against the truck, looking either exhausted or asleep standing up. I kept driving, only faster now. Why was that truck out here? Where had it been so early in the morning? I saw the smoke about a quarter of a mile further down the road. A police car passed going in the other direction.

Smoke tells the whole story. When it's slow and spirally, aimless, you know a fire has lost its fury or its energy. Without seeing the flame itself, you can be sure its back is broken and will go out soon. If the smoke is hard and fast and billows straight up into the sky, the fire is a bad one, still very alive and dangerous.

A wispy brown pillow of smoke hung unmoving in the pale pink morning sky over the Meiers' house. Some was still rising off the burned part of the building, but it was more an afterthought than anything else. Two fire trucks and a police car were parked on the road in front. Firemen were curling thick gray hoses back into form and generally wrapping up their work before leaving. Three policemen stood close together, comparing notes. People stood around on the street and the edges of the Meiers' lawn watching the goings-on. I parked my car back from the mass of other vehicles and got out slowly. The house was unmistakable except for one thing. Standing there looking at it, I realized the bat wing was gone. The vaguely asymmetrical addition I'd seen pictured in the architecture magazine was no longer there. In its place was a black, scorched, collapsed mess of burnt pieces of things scattered across a wide area, standing, piled, smoking: the metal frame of a butterfly chair, a wooden table that had oddly been burned on only one side, leaving it two legs to stand on, books strewn across the ground. Had the bat wing been their library?

"Tar." An old woman came walking toward me and slowed a few feet away. It was clear she wanted to tell someone what she had heard. "One of the firemen says he thinks it was the tar. They've been working on that kooky roof for *weeks* and he says the gasoline must've hit right on the tar for the whole thing to've gone up so fast. Who on God's green earth would want to burn *their* house down?" She thought her question over and suddenly stared at me with new, suspicious eyes. "You from around here, sir?"

Despite a hole as deep as hell in my heart and growing, I

thought fast and managed to come up with "I'm from the newspaper. They sent me out to see what's going on."

"You're from the *Spectator?* Well, my name is Sandra Hagen, in case you want to use me as your source."

I could tell she loved being able to use that word. "Thank you, Mrs. Hagen. Listen, I just got here. Could you tell me what happened?"

Clearing her throat, she threw back her head as if the television cameras were already rolling. "Anwen wasn't around last night. She had to be up in New York for some thing or other. Brendan was here by himself and was the one who saw the guy who did it."

"Brendan? Excuse me, did you say Brendan?"

"Yes, Brendan Meier, that's her son. Don't you know about *him?* That's a story too! You ought to write that one up first. Do one of those two-part series on them. It's a family that's had more troubles than Job."

"Brendan was kidnapped as a child."

"Right. And they searched till they found him. Rumor has it the Meiers spent a couple hundred thousand dollars looking. Then her husband, Greg, died right after they found the boy."

"I don't believe it! They *found* him? I've never heard of that happening."

"It's amazing. But anyway, Brendan was home last night when this guy threw these bottles full of gas at their house. He heard something outside, which must have been the glass breaking, and ran out. Whoever did it was still standing there on their lawn, watching the whole thing go up. Can you imagine? Nedda Lintschinger, who lives in that house there, the blue one? She woke up at the sound and looked out the window too. Said she saw two men on the lawn and recognized Brendan in his pajamas 'cause he's such a tall boy, you know? Their house was on fire but the strangest thing was, these two guys were just standing there talking! Nedda said it looked like they were having a nice chat.

"Suddenly out of nowhere, the other guy starts screaming,

'What? What? What?' Just like that, then kicked Brendan you-know-where. The poor boy fell down but the other wouldn't stop. Stood right there kicking and kicking him. Now that's what Nedda said. I can only tell you what I heard, but she swears it's what she told the police, so I guess it's true.

"Whatever, the crazy man kept on kicking poor Brendan. Then he lit up another bottle and threw it against the house. *Finally* Nedda ran for the phone to call for help and didn't see what else happened. All we know is the nut was gone by the time she got back to look. Brendan's lying on the ground, not moving. She thought for sure he was dead. Thank God he wasn't. He's in the hospital with some broken ribs and a cut-up face, but they say he'll be all right."

Thanking her for her help and listening while she spelled her name so I'd get it right in print, I left Mrs. Hagen and walked over to the policemen. Luckily I always carry one of those small pocket tape recorders in case an idea comes to me. Introducing myself as a reporter for the *Spectator,* I asked what had happened and held the recorder in front of them. Their story was basically the same. They'd gotten a call reporting the fire and a possible assault in progress. When they sent officers to investigate, they found a burning house and an unconscious teenage boy on the lawn. No sign of the perpetrator. Fire presumably caused by Molotov cocktails igniting buckets of roofing tar which stood near the building. The Meier boy was in satisfactory condition at the hospital and was going to be all right. No idea who the "perp" was. They kept repeating that word—"perpetrator," "perp." Brendan said he'd never seen the other before. It was a boy, however, that much was sure. A teenager dressed like a punk, but the outfit might only have been camouflage, a costume to throw them off the track. Damage to the house was "expensive but not fatal." The cop who said it liked the line so much he repeated it for his friends. If I waited a day or two, I could interview Brendan at the hospital. But I didn't need to, because I already knew exactly what had happened.

Lincoln had read my file on the Meiers and in one dreadful

implosive flash knew we weren't his parents, Lily had kidnapped him.

How could he have remained sane? He did. But he came to the restaurant knowing. He flew East knowing the only thing he wanted to do now, in those first hours of his new life, was see his real parents and punish them. Yes, punish them for not finding him. For not looking hard enough; for not having spent all their time and energy and money to get their son back. Whatever they'd done over the years was not enough. Yes, he read the file and saw what tragic, wrecked lives they'd led since his disappearance, but he didn't care. Whatever they'd suffered, *he* was the one who'd been kidnapped, violated, forced to live a life away from his natural family.

Nor did it matter that we had given him everything we could; we were kidnappers, criminals, monsters. The same words that raged through my head a decade ago when I discovered Lily's secret. And still did. And still did.

It was worse for Lincoln, though, because that secret had been kept and nurtured by people he believed were his parents. Worse, as far as he knew, his real parents had abandoned the search for him.

What he didn't know, what he hadn't given me time to tell him the night before, was the Meiers were not his parents. Lily had not stolen *their* child. The reason she had those newspaper clippings about them and their plight was because she'd once spent an afternoon in Garamond, Pennsylvania. The next day she kidnapped an infant from a car parked at a roadside rest on the turnpike a few hundred miles from Garamond.

That's right, Lincoln. If only you had listened. After her car was repaired, she drove west. Toward evening the next day, her stomach started grumbling and she knew she had to find a bathroom immediately. Luckily there were signs for a rest stop. Speeding up, she got there in the nick of time. Leaping out of the car, she barely noticed a Chevrolet Corvair parked ten feet down the way. No one was inside. No time to think about it. She ran to the bathroom.

Coming out, she saw the car again and would have ignored it

except this time she heard a baby crying inside. Concerned, she started toward it. Way off in the field behind the parking area two people laughed. She looked and barely saw two heads moving up and down just above the grass out there. They were laughing, groaning, wrestling around. They were making love! What nerve! They'd felt like doing it, pulled right off the road, and ran into the nearest field. They were so lucky, whoever they were. She envied them their happiness and their guts. They had everything, she had nothing. Staring into the field unashamed, she wasn't a voyeur; she was looking at happiness. She was drowning in her own life. A drowning woman looking at land for the last time.

But why was the child crying? It had to be theirs. Inside the Corvair on the back seat, a red-faced baby strapped into a powder-blue bassinet howled so savagely that all its features seemed to have congealed in the middle of its face. It certainly needed something—food, a new diaper, a hug—but Mom and Pop were occupied.

Lily looked both ways, saw no one, opened the driver's door, and pushed the seat forward. The child stopped crying a second and glared at her. That meant nothing, but was all she needed. Stepping into the car, she took the baby in her arms and, without once looking back, ran to her Opel and drove off.

One day months later she was in a supermarket and saw that shitty newspaper *The Truth*. The one that talks about alien landings and cancer cures. On the front page was a headline: "The Town Where Babies Disappear." There was a picture of Garamond, which she recognized because right in front was the gas station where they'd fixed her car. She bought the paper and read the article standing outside the market. Two babies in three years had been kidnapped from there, and neither had been found. They gave the names of the families. One was Meier. There were pictures of them and she loved how both of them looked. Wonderful faces. Intelligent in very different ways. They *weren't* Lincoln's parents. She didn't ever want to know who the real ones were, but the same thing had happened to these people so close to where she had taken him. It was too much of a coincidence. After that, she always envisioned them as his parents. So every once in a great while she'd find ways of checking up on them over the years. I saw the clippings. First she called telephone information in Garamond for the address there. When they moved, she got the forwarding address from the post office. A couple of years later she wrote the newspaper in the new town where they lived and asked if there had been anything written about them. She said she was family and was working on a scrapbook for a planned big reunion. She always used a false name when she asked and had stuff sent to a post office box. What difference did it make? Who could connect them to her?

Lincoln could.

If he had torched the Meier house without ever having spoken to them, what would he do to Lily? Now that Lincoln knew Anwen Meier was not his mother, he would leave her alone. But he wouldn't leave Lily alone, that was sure. One way or another, now or later, Lily and me . . . And possibly even—the thought was so horrendous and terrifying my mind almost wouldn't process it: What might he do to his little sister?

I could have stayed and talked to Brendan, but what would it accomplish? Further prove what I already knew? Brendan's story was simply too astonishing *not* to be believed. He had been kidnapped but was found and returned to his parents years later. How maddeningly unfair and ironic that must have been for Lincoln to hear! I pictured the two boys on the Meier front lawn early that morning. Was it light yet? Two boys with histories no human being deserved. One shirtless, in tattered clothes and a porcupine haircut, the other just out of bed in still-warm pajamas (such an endearing image—a teenage boy in his pajamas), talking together on the lawn. What did they say? How had their conversation gone? Walking back to my rented car, I went through half a dozen scenarios of what they'd said to each other in the short period before Lincoln, in an enlightened rage, attacked Brendan and kicked him in the groin. That was his style—kick 'em in the balls, keep a gun behind your dresser, drive off in a stolen Mercedes. Our son. My son.

When he was young and bored, Lincoln would wander into my room with an expectant look on. Checking to see if I was busy, he'd come over and ask, "So, what's going on, Max?"

"Not much, sport. What's up with you?"

"Nothin'. You wanna do something together? Only if you're free, you know. Only if you have time."

I made time; I loved knowing this little boy liked to hang around with me.

I thought about that, racing out of Somerset for the second time in my life. It made me smile. Many of those good memories came during the ride back to New York, making it even more painful. It reminded me of driving away from a funeral. The fine memories of the times you spent with the dead one. All gone.

I had decided what to do by the time I reached the turnpike. At the next rest area I would pull off, find a telephone book, and start calling different airlines. When was their next plane to Los Angeles? What airport did it leave from? I had no doubt Lincoln would go home now. His anger at the Meiers had boomeranged on him in the most shocking, unexpected way. What else could he do but punish Lily a double dose now? First make her tell him who his real parents were so he could try to find *them*. And then . . . But Lily didn't know. I was sure of that. Didn't even remember where on the road she'd kidnapped him. That information could have easily been found by contacting the police in the area, but neither of us did it. Why? Because she didn't want to know and neither did I, having decided to keep her secret all those years ago for my own selfish reasons.

I despaired, thinking of how great a head start he had on me. He was probably at an airport now, if not already on a plane heading home. I'd ask the airlines that too—how long ago did your last flight to L.A. leave? Would it be possible to find out if a certain Lincoln Fischer was on board? Would they tell you that over the phone? No.

I had to call Lily too. Call and warn her to get out of our house, our life, take our baby girl, run as fast as she could from our son, who was coming because he *knew*. And he knew because it was my fault. It was all my fault. Everything bad now I made, I caused. Looking too hard two thousand days ago, I should have left it alone and trusted my love and not my suspicions. My fault. Raising this lovely boy all wrong, not giving him what he needed to grow up a good soul. My fault. Giving him all the wrong directions to the right path. My fault. And taking notes!? Keeping a record of my life as a sinful man? Why? Why had I done these things? You did what you could. You did what you thought was right. No, you did what you thought would save you and Lily and fuck the rest of the world. That was the truth, wasn't it? Fuck the rest of the world. My fault.

Passing trucks and buses, I sped down the fast lane way over the speed limit, thinking how to phrase this impossible phone call to my wife. Lily, he knows. It's my fault. He knows and he's coming to get you. Maybe Greer too. Blame me. No one else but me.

I looked in the rearview mirror and saw an Audi driving up fast behind. Moving over to let him pass, I slid right back into the lane and tagged along behind him a couple of miles. Lily, Lincoln found out about the Meiers and flew to New Jersey. He read my diary— Another car appeared in the rearview. I pulled over again. It pounded by, followed by another right after it. Lily, pack a bag for you and Greer . . . I rolled the window down. Pack bags for you and Greer—

I was phrasing that one out when the sound came up on my left. Did I recognize it? Maybe, maybe some part of me did. A whining and clattering of metal that could only be a car with fatal problems sailing too fast down the road toward blowup land or collapse any minute.

Lily, I kept this diary—

"Hey!" The car was next to me, inches outside my window. "Hey, fuckhead!"

I snapped a look and there was Lincoln at the wheel of the junker, smiling, pointing a gun at me.

"Remember this?" His gun exploded.

I jammed the wheel to the right and braked. My car slewed wildly—too many things to do at once. I tried to correct it, but it wouldn't go. A long overpass loomed. I skidded under it going much too fast. Steering wheel still pulled to the right, I smacked into a cement wall and scraped down along it forever. The evil sound of stone tearing metal on and on. Dark. The dark of a tunnel after the brilliant morning light outside. Scraaaaaaaaaaaape!

I stopped. Finally it stopped. The car was still under the overpass in complete shadow. The smell of damp stone and hot rubber. I was all right. Safe!

Before my head cleared beyond that wonder, Lincoln's face was inches away and yelling. "Get out of the fucking car, Daddy boy!" He must have opened my door because, still confused and terrified by a moment ago, the next thing I knew I felt myself falling out of the car onto the road. My hands hit gravel or glass. Very sharp and painful, it gouged deep. I tried to stand up. The close sound of traffic in a tunnel. Whomp. Whomp. Whoooosh.

"C'mere, you fucking hump!" He took me by the ear and marched me forward toward the light. The morning sun was blinding. Totally disoriented, I didn't try to free myself from his hold even though he was much shorter than me. He kept pinching my ear and, once we'd left the overpass, pushed me off the shoulder of the road to the grass embankment behind. The two of us slid-stumbled down it till the road was high above us and we were crouched among sticks and wet earth. The traffic noise was all up there.

"Lincoln—"

He had the gun in his hand and I recognized it was like the one at home. He had two guns? What was the name? Glock? Grock? I wanted to know the name. It was important to know the name.

He punched me on the temple. Pain and dizziness splashed my face like water. I couldn't believe he'd done it. No one had ever hit anyone in our family. Never.

"Shut up. Remember that day, asshole? Remember that crazy guy driving up next to you and shooting? Remember telling me that story? I *love* that story! I loved when you told it to me! I was your son and it was one of my father's great stories!" He hit himself on the chest with his gun. Thump thump thump. After the last, he punched me on the jaw with his other fist. Pain. The whomp of a big truck going by overhead and then an angry long car horn. Lincoln's face up so close.

Through my panic and pain, I realized something for the first time. "But there *were* bullets in his gun that day, weren't there? And you protected me, didn't you, Lincoln? You stopped it from happening. You were too young to know what was going on, but you still saved me! My God! I never knew till now!"

He laughed in my face, his spit hit my cheek. "You're so scared you're fucking crazy, man! So whacked out . . . Protect you? Save *you,* criminal? Kidnapper! You and that goddamned Lily! *Save* you? Know what I want to do to you both? This, fucker, *this!*" He stuck the gun in the air and shot it three times very fast. The pain in my face was hot and pumping but I had to keep clear because within this moment was the answer. I needed to wipe snot from my nose and chin, but I was afraid he'd take it wrong and think I was trying something. I had to talk to him, tell him what I understood now; understood after seven wrong years.

"Wipe your face, man. Go ahead, do it, for Christ's sake. I don't care. I'm not going to shoot you, yet."

Hands shaking, I tried wiping but couldn't do it right. Disgusted, he jerked my shirt out of my pants and pushed it up across my face. "Come on, come on, get it off." While I did, he started talking again. "Listen to me, and listen really good, because what I'm gonna tell you, you're not gonna forget the rest of your life. Look at me."

"I can't—"

"Look at me, Max!"

I raised my head from the shirt and saw—myself. No Lincoln, myself. This was because I knew now.

"All along you and Lily playing God, thinking: It's okay we

stole him 'cause we're gonna bring him up so wonderfully that he'll be Superman. King of Kings. The champion of the world. *But you were wrong!* You can't take a kid away from his family and think it's going to be okay. There's no way he can be okay. Why didn't you give me back when you knew? When you understood what she'd done!" His voice was a cry.

My face on him changed back to his face, Lincoln's face. Teenage Lincoln's face, so full of hatred for me. I had to tell him what I knew. Had to tell it to him exactly and well so he'd understand and know why it had all happened the way it had. Why Lily took him, why I had gone along with it, why we'd ended up here . . . How it was out of all our hands.

"Lincoln, can I—can I talk?"

"What?"

"Lincoln, you are my Guardian Angel. Do you understand? *That's* why it happened. That's why we're here. Why Lily took you, why I met her in the first place."

"What are you talking about? What the hell are you saying? What do you mean, 'Guardian Angel'?"

"That's what you are! Angels *can* come, but you have to deserve them. But I ruined you by not saying anything to Lily back then. See? I kept you from your real parents because I wanted you and your mother so much. I made you live the lie your whole life. I'm so much worse than her. As soon as I found out what she'd done, I should have fixed it. Taken you back to your real family so you could've lived the life you were supposed to."

His face was dismay and confusion but that line went straight into him. He reared back and stuck the gun in my face. "Yes! You should have taken me home! You should have let me live my real life! Do you know what it was like last night, reading those papers? Suddenly knowing your whole life has been one big fucking fake? Finding about you two and who I really was all those years. All those years you pretended to be my parents? All this—all this stuff at once. Why did I even have to know? Why couldn't I just have lived and not ever found out? My whole life, all you two thought about were yourselves!"

"Lincoln, you're right. Everything you said is right, but listen to me. Let me explain this. It'll help, I swear.

"Even if you and I had never met, you were born my Guardian Angel. Isn't that beautiful? And it's the truth; there really are angels. *If you let them be and don't kill them!* But no, I met Lily and that was my end. Because the moment I discovered what she'd done with you, I was supposed to make it right again. You're right—that was my test, my trial. I had one chance to truly deserve you, but my greed ruined it. Thou shalt not steal. I knew that. Thou shalt not covet. That's why it's all gone bad. It's my fault. I ruined us all. You were such a terrific little boy *before* I found out, but once I did and did nothing . . . That's how you were supposed to be your whole life. But I poisoned you. All the blood's on my hands." He looked at me with lightning bolts of pure energy and hate flashing, black, flashing across his eyes . . . He swung the gun across and hit me on the nose.

"This is no fucking cartoon, Max! I'm not fucking 'Paper Clip'! Stop talking shit! That crazy fucking shit! I'm not your cartoon. I'm not an angel! Why don't you say the truth! Why don't you say the truth for once in my life!"

I think I could have stopped his arm the next time, reached out fast and blocked it, but I didn't. He hit me again on the cheek, on the throat, on the top of the head. I wanted to lift my arms to keep him away, keep him off, but there was no strength. He hit me again and again until I blacked out. The last thing I remember was he kept saying "Daddy" as he beat me with all his might.

"There once was a very great magician who, having grown old, decided to work his greatest magic by turning a mouse into a beautiful woman. After he had finished his masterpiece, he felt that because she was so exquisite, he had to find her the most powerful being in the world for a husband. After much thought, he went to the sun and asked him to marry this woman. The sun was touched by the offer, but said no because 'there is someone stronger than me—the cloud, who covers me when I shine.' The magician thanked him for his honesty and went to the cloud with the same offer. Much to his surprise, the cloud said no too because there was someone even stronger than him—the mountain, whose ragged peaks stop the cloud's movement across the sky. Shaking his head, the magician went next to the mountain but again heard no. 'There's one stronger than even me,' he said. 'It is the mouse, because he can burrow into my side as often as he pleases and I am powerless to stop him.' So at last the magician went home and sadly turned the beautiful young girl back into a mouse so that she could take another mouse for a husband. All things return to their origin."

Finky Linky sang his crazy goodbye song and the show ended. Lincoln turned to me and squinted a disbelieving eye. "A mouse is *not* the greatest thing in the world. It's not greater than the *sun!*"

I could feel a great father-son moral lesson coming on here. I took a deep breath and was about to begin, but when I opened my mouth nothing came out. I could move my jaws and lips but there was no voice in me, not a peep. I cleared my throat but even that made no sound. I tried again. Nothing. Rubbing my neck, I nodded at him. He was waiting for an answer but his quizzical expression asked if I was playing a joke on him. He began to smile. I tried harder to talk but couldn't. My silence began to scare me. I pushed him off my lap and sat up straighter. I tried again. Nothing. Again. Nothing. I began to panic.

I woke up.

The dream was a recurring one I had had over the years and it would have gotten worse as it invariably did if the pain hadn't woken me. I was conscious but there was only pain. My eyes were all right. I opened them and was not surprised to see an unknown white room around me. After a time it made sense that this was a hospital room. My face felt huge and hot. When I put a tentative hand up and touched it, pain barked back at me to stay away, leave it alone or it would really get me. I said okay, okay, I'll be careful. But I had to know how bad the damage was. I had to know what was there. This pain became a dog in my mind, growling in a corner of this big white room, ready to attack the moment I did the wrong thing. As gently as possible, I touched my face and felt a battlefield of cuts, bruises, swelling. Once sure that was all, there was no more, I slid the hand down and over as much of my body as I could reach and prayed thanks when I felt no casts or heavy bandages. He'd done my face. That must have been enough for him.

I saw a buzzer for the nurse and shakily got hold of it. I moved my head too fast and suddenly the pain dog growled loud.

"Well, hello, Mr. Fischer! You're back on earth with us, huh? How're you feeling?"

"Happy to still be around. Can you tell me what happened? But please go slow, I'm not really here yet."

"Sure. The police found your car all banged up and went lookin' for you. They found you down an embankment and you were unconscious. We thought you might have a bad concussion or a skull fracture along with those cuts, but they did a scan and didn't find anything. You're sounding pretty good now. What the heck happened out there?"

I sighed to give myself time, then realized a lie wasn't necessary because most of the truth would do for now. I told her a stranger had forced me off the road and at gunpoint made me go over the embankment with him. Once there, he started hitting me until . . . I couldn't say more and she didn't press it.

"It's so crazy, so scary these days. Sometimes I get scared just going out of the house to buy some milk. My husband told me—" She would have gone on, only a state policeman walked into the room and asked if we might be alone for a while. She took off. Sitting down on the chair next to my bed, he took out a notepad.

I told him the same story, and with a few specific questions here and there, he appeared satisfied. He was particularly interested in what the assailant looked like. I described a man in his early thirties, nondescript, but with a surprisingly deep voice. I thought it best to add one memorable characteristic so this fantasy attacker sounded more real. No, I had never seen him before. No idea why he would want to hurt me. I said who I was, and when asked why I was in New Jersey, I said business. The cop was a nice guy, friendly and sympathetic. He shook his head often, as if he couldn't believe what had happened. When I was finished, he asked me to sign a form and said it wouldn't be necessary to meet again unless I had questions. As he was leaving, I touched his arm and asked how long I had been in the hospital. Checking his watch, he said ten hours. Ten hours! I could barely keep from shouting. Ten hours! What had Lincoln done in that time? All the possibilities were horrible.

Alone again, I eased myself up to the side of the bed and picked up the telephone. It was difficult but I talked the hospital operator into placing a long-distance call to our home in Los Angeles. What time was it there? It didn't matter. The phone rang and rang. Pick it up. Pick up the damned phone!

"Hello?"

"Hello, Lily? Lily, it's Max—"

"Max, Jesus Christ, where are you? It's Mary."

"Who?" I couldn't understand. Why hadn't Lily picked it up?

"Mary. It's me, *Mary Poe.* Max, for God's sake, wherever you are, get home. Lincoln's dead, Max. He hung himself. Lily came in and found him. Max, are you there? Do you hear me? Lincoln is *dead.*"

My clothes were in the closet. There was a mirror on the inside of the closet door with a small lamp over it. I turned it on and looked at myself for the first time in ten hours. My face was as bad as my fingers had said, but I'd seen worse-looking people at bus stops in Los Angeles. The pain dog was bellowing as I slowly dressed. I left three hundred dollars on the table next to the bed, along with a note saying if that wasn't enough to send the bill to me in California.

I opened the door to the room, saw no one in the hall, and walked out. Luckily there was a door that opened onto a large garden. Outside smelled of good fresh things and made me want to cry. It was evening. I walked on cobblestones across the garden and then through some high hedges into the hospital parking lot. A taxi had dropped someone off at the front door and was just pulling away when I flagged it down and got in.

"Hey, you're lucky. I was almost out of here. Where to?" The driver looked in the rearview mirror and his eyes widened. "Holy cow! What happened to you?"

"Car accident. Would you please take me to Newark Airport?"

"You sure you're all right? I mean, it's okay to travel and all?"

"Yes, please just go to the airport."

Hanged himself. It was absolutely the cruelest, most brilliant thing he could have done. What had he said back there? "I'm no cartoon." Did he say that? Yes, something like that. But now this and it was so hideously perfect that nothing in the world could have been more effective. I was certain he had done it somewhere in the house where Lily would have been sure to find him. Lily or Greer.

"Greer. Oh God."

"You say something?"

"No, nothing."

The driver looked at me in the mirror and shook his head. My carry-on bag was next to me on the seat in the dark. I reached into it and felt around for the sketchbook and a pencil. Flipping the cover over, I put the pencil to the paper and began to draw. Except for the streetlights and the occasional car headlights flicking over us, it was utterly dark in the back of the taxi. But I drew and drew, never looking down, only feeling the pencil scratching across paper, doing whatever my hand felt like doing. I drew until we arrived at the airport, where I left the book and pencil on the seat and got out to catch a plane home.

There was a film on the flight. The stewardess gave me a set of earphones but I left them in my lap. It was better to watch without any sound, making up dialogue in my head, guessing the plot as it skittered silently along. Anything to fill my mind.

A very beautiful blond woman has the world in her hip pocket, money, power, a handsome boyfriend who seems to love her as much as the rest of the world does. But she grows tired of it all. One day she meets an enormously fat man who works as a cashier at a supermarket. They talk, she laughs, they talk some more. The next shot is of her waiting for him out in the parking lot after work. He comes out of the store and sees her there, a blond Venus leaning on her red sports car, obviously waiting for him. Cut to his face. His eyes roll up in his head and he faints.

As the film got worse, I became more and more involved. I put on the earphones and turned them way up. The couple must fight the whole world to prove their love is real. Every cliché you could think of was in the film. Her rich parents are outraged, her once nifty boyfriend turns out to be a cad who does whatever he can to break the lovebirds up. They almost part, but true love wins out.

Probably one of the sillier films I'd seen in my life, but I laughed at the lame jokes, sat forward on my seat when things looked bad for them. At the end, when they are off in an idyllic Vermont town running a general store together, I began to cry. There was no stopping it. A middle-aged woman on the other side of the aisle watched me suspiciously. What did she see? A man with a swollen, bruised face crying like a child. At that moment I would have given anything to see that movie again, but the screen went blank, then black. Unconsciously I reached into my bag for the sketchbook, but remembered I'd left it in the taxi. I looked at the staring woman but she had gone back to her magazine. There was nothing left to do but close my eyes and think about my dead boy.

I got the car from the parking lot and drove toward town. I'd been gone a little over twenty-four hours, but the only thing left in the world that was the same for me was this road with the orange lights above and the familiar billboards for airlines, hotels, weekend package trips to Las Vegas and Lake Tahoe. When I passed the gas station where the cashier looked at you through binoculars, I thought of stopping and asking him through all his thick protective glass: Remember me? Forget how I look now; I was the one who offered you a twenty last night and made no trouble. Last night when things were only full of dangerous possibilities. Not like now with my purple split face and dead future.

I passed the hamburger stand where the murderous gang had stood, but it was empty and only full of lonesome yellow light. A few more rights, lefts, two red traffic lights, another right turn, and I was on our street. Welcome home, Daddy. Lincoln rode his bicycle down this street. We had walked the dog together here. "Lincoln, there are some packages on the lawn. Would you give me a hand bringing them in?"

Lily's car was nowhere to be seen, but Mary Poe's black Jeep was parked in our driveway. I pulled up to the curb and turned the motor off.

"I'll count to fifty and go in. Just give me to fifty and I'll go."

The lights were on in the living room and, far away as it was, I tried to see through the window if there was anyone in there besides Mary. No movement, no forms going back and forth. I was counting to fifty in my head as I watched. At fifty I would go. Nothing moved.

Something tapped loudly on my window. I jumped. My mind screamed it's Lincoln, Lincoln's back. He's here, he's dead but he's here . . .

The face at the window was a woman with tan skin and dark hair. Thirty-five or so, she was pretty but there were a great many lines on her face that showed both her age and her experience. I was so spooked by her tapping that I didn't understand when she gestured with a finger for me to roll down the window. I shook my head. She was close enough so that when she spoke I heard through the glass: "Could you put your window down? Please, only a minute."

I rolled it down halfway. Calming down, I realized I knew her face from somewhere. Was she a neighbor? What was she doing out here at this time of night?

"Thank you. Do you know who I am? Do you recognize me?"

"No."

"I'm Little White, Mr. Fischer. Lincoln's friend, Little White."

When I saw her the night before, Little White was sixteen years old with a head of spiky white hair and a face so clown-white/deathly pale you'd have thought she wore special makeup. *This* woman was close to my age, had short dark hair and . . . freckles. Yet the longer I looked, the more that familiar young face came to the surface through this one. The eyes, mouth . . . they were the same. I had seen her so often in the months she'd hung around with Lincoln.

"Can we talk a minute?" She waited. I didn't move. "How about Anwen Meier, Mr. Fischer? How about Lincoln shooting at you on the road?"

I looked again at the house and got out. We stood no more than three feet apart. She was wearing a dark chic dress, a gold bracelet, high heels. I remembered what she had been wearing yesterday: dirty jeans, a T-shirt saying "Nine Inch Nails," combat boots. Now this thirty-something woman, elegant and attractive, her perfume drifting over subtle and flowery, was saying they were one and the same.

"You're not really surprised, are you?" The voice. Yes, it was the girl's voice too, only slightly deeper.

"No."

"I knew you wouldn't be. Lincoln told me what he did to you in New Jersey. He told me why too."

I said nothing.

"I saw him today. Before he did that." She pointed at our house. "He told me he was going to do it, but I couldn't stop him. He called from the plane and asked me to pick him up. Told me to come alone and not tell Elvis. He got very upset and begged me to be there when he landed. That wasn't like him: Lincoln never asked for anything, so I said sure, okay, I'll come.

"I can't tell you how bad he looked when I saw him. In the car at first he didn't say anything, just kept clicking his lighter open and closed till it got on my nerves. I asked him what the hell was going on and he told me. About you and your wife and how she kidnapped him. And about how you told him he was an angel.

"After he was finished telling me his whole story, he asked if I believed him. Know what I said? I'll believe it if you prove it. That's the only way you can ever really know, right? He said, 'Okay, pull over and I'll prove it.' I didn't know what to expect, but I pulled into Loehmann's parking lot and turned off the car.

"He started telling me things about myself no one in the entire world could have known. Things I'd even forgotten, they were so deeply buried.

"I was still shaking from it when he said, 'That's now, that's who you are today. Now I'm going to show you your immediate future.' When it was over and he brought me back, I had no doubt in the world that that was what the next few years of my life were going to be.

"And you know what? They were total shit. First, thanks to Elvis, there were bad drugs which landed me in the hospital twice for long stays. Then a withdrawal clinic. I got out and, to spite my parents, married a painter who decided beating me up was more fun than painting. Worse, he wouldn't let go or give me a divorce until my parents bought him off. And even after that he made trouble for me, the psycho.

"I mean, my life was one big horror story after another. Seeing them unfold like that, I knew they'd happen, because the way I was, they made *sense*. Lincoln showed me every disgusting and pathetic thing that was going to happen to me those next eighteen years. Unbelievable. Eighteen more years of that! I'd be a living disaster area for as long as I'd already been alive till I finally got hold of myself and got it together. Great, huh? Lots to look forward to." She had been speaking nonstop for minutes but paused now and smiled.

"Your angel showed me the ghost of my Christmas Future and it was real, all right.

"Then he brought me back and said, 'That's it. That's what your life is going to be like.' I asked what I could do to stop or change it. Nothing. But there was one thing *he* could do if I wanted: he could make me older. He said when I was thirty-four my whole life would change and begin to be satisfying. He could skip me up there if I wanted, over those gruesome eighteen years, but with my whole history in my head, so I'd end up the same person. It'd just be like going over a bridge, and the water down below was the bad years."

"How do you feel?"

"Better than ever, and it's only been a few hours. The funny thing is, I went home and my parents didn't see any difference."

I knew she wanted to talk more about it, but I couldn't. I needed to ask other questions. "What did Lincoln say at the airport? What did he tell you?"

"He made me promise not to tell. He also said not to tell you what *I* think of you and your wife." She stopped, considered this, went on. "The only thing he asked me to do specifically was give you this." She put her hand in her purse and pulled out a pistol. "He used it on you yesterday."

"What am I supposed to do with it?"

"I don't know. Maybe he thought you'd want to use it on yourself. I have to go now. I did what he asked." Turning away, she walked down the dark street, some of her perfume still in the air.

"Wait! How could he save you if he was so upset? And why *didn't* you stop him from killing himself?"

"Because we were friends and wanted the other to have what they wanted. Because of what you did, Lincoln wanted to die; that was his choice. He was my friend, Mr. Fischer. He'd do anything for me, even at the end. Too bad you didn't know him." She turned again and left. I had no desire to call or follow her. She meant nothing to me, and if her story was true, so what? Lincoln was dead. My fault. My dead angel.

I slid the gun into my jacket pocket and walked across the street to the house.

"Mr. Fischer?" The two Gillcrist boys came up and Bill pointed toward Little White. "Do you know her? Is that why you were talking to her? My mother told us we're never to talk to anyone like her. She's all old and dirty. But you did. Do you know her?"

Before unlocking the door, I rang the bell to alert whoever was inside. I hoped Lily wouldn't be there, because I wanted to see things first and hopefully hear the details. Give me time to think it over before doing anything.

"Who's there?"

"Mary? It's me, Max."

"I thought it was you. What happened to your face? Where have you been?"

"It doesn't matter. Is Lily here?"

The house smelled different. Closing the door behind me, I tried to figure out what it was. Cooking? No. A new perfume? No. Many people. The place smelled of many people being in it all at once.

"No, she and Greer are over with Ib and Gus. The doctor gave her a sedative and it kept her pretty calm, but I wish you'd been here. She found him. He was hanging off the beam in your bedroom."

"Was there a note?"

"Yes. It said, 'This one's for you, Lily. Thanks,' and was signed: 'Not Brendan Meier.' "

"Did the police see the note?"

"Yes. They took it with them. Max, what's going on? What happened to you? Where did Lincoln go yesterday?"

"The police have the note? What did it say again?"

" 'This one's for you, Lily. Thanks.' Signed: 'Not Brendan Meier.' Do you understand it? Does Lily?"

"You said she found the body? Did Greer see it?"

"Not as far as I know. Lily called me last night after you left and asked what was going on. I gave it to her very sketchily, and didn't mention the gun. I said Lincoln had probably gotten into some trouble and you were trying to get him out. She asked me over to spend the night and I came, just in case. Today she was very disturbed because she hadn't heard from either of you. I stuck around as long as I could, then took off for what I thought would only be a few hours. Greer went to school, Lily did her errands, and when she got back in the afternoon, Lincoln was . . . there. She found him when she walked into the bedroom.

"Max, do you know why he did it?"

She was my oldest friend, the person I trusted really more than anyone. "No. I don't understand his note either. Brendan Meier? Who is that?"

"Maybe a friend of his? That's another thing. The police went looking for his friends to question them. Elvis and Little White especially. They found Elvis, but he doesn't know anything. Apparently he started crying when he heard Lincoln was dead.

"Another thing, Max. You've got to go down and identify the body. Lily wasn't up to it and I don't think she should. Before you do anything else, you've got to go down to the morgue and identify him."

"All right. I'll do it now."

"I'd go for you, but they want—"

"I said all right, Mary. I'll go now."

She touched my shoulder, I pulled away. "Will you tell me what happened out there? Was it the gun? Did all this have to do with his gun?"

"No. It had nothing to do with that. I want to look at the bedroom before I go. I want to see where it happened."

"There's nothing there. Nothing left. It's just your bedroom again. Really, there's *nothing left*. Go look, it's just a nicely made bed, a dresser—"

"And a conveniently exposed beam? I want to see it. And I have to go into his room too. I just have to be in both rooms a while. Do you understand?"

She nodded and looked at me with pity. "Okay. Do you want me to take you . . ."

"To the morgue? Is that the word you want, Mary? No. I'll go alone. Just tell me how to get there."

We were standing close to each other. She reached over and embraced me. I held on as long as she did but didn't give back much of a squeeze. We separated. There were tears in her eyes.

"Are you sure you don't want me to drive you?"

"I'm sure. Listen, thanks for what you've done. Thanks for being here last night, and today."

"I'm so glad I was. I wish to God this hadn't happened to you two."

"I once read an article that said only one suicide in six leaves a note. The note rarely tells the survivors what they want to know. At least we have some idea, huh? Lily and I can go around for the rest of our lives knowing . . ."

"Max—"

"Just tell me how to get there."

You think a place is going to rip you apart, even walking through the door will take all your resolve and whatever courage you have. Unlike other words, like "love" or "hate," "morgue" has only one meaning. It is what it is—the place where bodies are brought for a last look. Funeral homes are not the same. If a body is at the morgue, something besides death went wrong, its last breath was suspicious. There it is not dressed in a suit and arranged tastefully, but cut open and examined by someone looking for clues. Unlike that other house of the dead, this is not a last resting place, but rather the last questioning place. The questioners find their answers, not in words, but on the skin and under it.

I thought I would not be able to stand the morgue, but walking through the last door before coming to Lincoln's body, I choked, trying to suppress a big old-fashioned ha-ha! laugh. The doctor leading me to the room looked over sympathetically.

"It's okay. You just look once, say if you recognize him or not, and it's over."

He was way off. I had not laughed from anguish or lunacy, but rather because, putting my hands in my jacket pockets, I discovered I was carrying Lincoln's pistol. A gun at the morgue! Who was there to shoot when everyone was already dead?

"Are you all right?"

"Yes, fine." At another time I would have been very paranoid, but not now. I was in a morgue with a pistol in my pocket, about to be shown my dead son, who'd hanged himself earlier in the day purely because of me and my beloved wife. Thought of like that, a pistol didn't mean much. His gun. My fault. His death. My fault.

"It's here. This one. If you'll just stand back a few feet, please." There were rows of large drawers against the wall and it took an instant before I realized there were bodies in them. In the middle of the room were metal tables with drains at the bottom, but except for one, they were empty. We had stopped at the one.

There was a thin white sheet covering him. Underneath that sheet was our son, our crime, my dead Guardian Angel. The man pulled it down.

I didn't want to see the face first. That would have been too much. As the sheet slipped down, I purposely looked at the middle of the body. He had such a small belly button. When he was young, tickle a finger into that belly button and he'd laugh, laugh, laugh. The arms were thin, the hands delicate. They were not yet a man's hands, but would be soon. I thought of them moving, touching things. Pushing french fries into his mouth, cupping the back of his sister's neck when he'd taught her to swim. My eyes ran up his arms to the narrow shoulders but stopped when they came to the red groove around his neck. The dividing line; a cruel red gash around his neck left by the rope. What was worse, the grayish-white skin on his face, the closed but protruding eyes, or the red cut around his neck?

"Mr. Fischer?"

"Yes? Oh yes, it's my son. That's Lincoln."

"I'm afraid that although the cause is obvious, we'll have to do an autopsy on him because of what we call 'wrongful death.' It's required—"

"I understand." I felt the gun in my pocket. It had grown warm since my hand had been on it. What would this man do if I suddenly pulled it out?

"I'm sorry, but I don't know what your rules are here, Doctor. Would it be possible to be alone with him a few minutes? Is that allowed?"

"Certainly. I'll pull this curtain across too so you'll have privacy."

I hadn't seen the curtain pushed back against the wall, but I was extraordinarily grateful to him for his kindness. He slid it over and quietly said he would be in the next room when I was finished. I thanked him and listened to his footsteps walking away. The door opened and swung shut with a small squeak. Lincoln and I were alone for the last time.

I felt my heart fill with a life full of words I wanted to say to him, all of them apologies, all accepting the blame for this waste and loss. I wanted to bow down to him . . . It became a confused mob of thoughts and emotions, but I didn't want words anymore. I wanted to say goodbye some other way. The worst thing on him was the red gouge around his neck, so I lifted a hand and touched it. Touched the bloody swollen groove with two fingers, ran them slowly down the red line. Thought: I'm sorry. So sorry. I'm so sorry.

Until his head began to move.

Slowly at first, side to side. Was it? Was it really moving? Yes. Oh yes, it very much was moving! Faster, farther and farther side to side.

I looked and now there was nothing on his neck. It was clear, unblemished. No red cut, no death mark. It had disappeared. Just pale skin now. The pale skin of a young man.

When I came into the room he was dead. When I looked directly at him he was dead, his throat cut through by a rope. You know it the moment you see it; one look and there is no question about it. Dead.

Now no mark and he was smiling. Then it sounded like he, this corpse, my son, was clearing his throat. Hmm. Hmm. Ahem. Next there was no mistaking it. A laugh. His head rocked back and forth. Our dead boy laughing. His mouth opened and his tongue, his strangled tongue fat with dead man's blood, burst out dry and obscenely large. His eyes opened. They were bulging.

Side to side. Laughing.

Terrified, I put the gun to his head, to his temple. It moved with his head from side to side. Side to side. His eyes, bloodshot but seeing me, focusing, were laughing too. The red mark was there again on his neck. The death mark. My fault.

He stopped moving. He tried to speak but couldn't with that tongue. He closed his eyes, opened them again. They were normal size. Only the blue-gray skin was the same.

He looked at me. His lips were pale and dry, chapped. "What are you going to do, *Dad,* shoot a dead man?"

I tried to speak but could not. Could not pull the trigger either. My eyes started to blink fast. Tears. I tried to speak but could not.

"Pull the trigger, but it won't work. Or maybe it will if *you* do it. I'm not allowed to. I gotta stay and take care of you."

"Lincoln—"

"I *hate* this! I want to die! It's no trick. I'm not playing any fucking games. I *want to die!* Pull the trigger, please! Maybe it'll work." He smiled again, unable to go on. The smile went away. "I'm so scared! I don't want this. I just want to stop. I just want to go awaaaaay!"

I loved him so. My son. "What can I do?"

"I don't know." Closing his eyes, he rolled his head back and forth, back and forth. The blood-red belt across his neck. "They won't let me go! What else am I supposed to do? *I'm so scared!*"

I slid my arm across his body. He grabbed it with his own and pulled it down to him, hugged it to him. My son. My poor beautiful son. I dropped the gun on the floor and climbed onto the table. I took my son in my arms, pulled him to me. My son. My fault.

"Hug me. Hug me tight."

How long was I there? How long did I hold him, talk to him, try to reassure him I'd do what I could to make it right, to help, before I heard her voice? Lily.

"Max! What are you doing? Get off him! Stop it! Get off him. Oh God!"

Without realizing it, I had my head on his chest and was talking to him, telling him things. I don't remember what things. First I heard her voice, then I understood it was hers, and only then could I lift my head and look at Lily. She was so near. How could I not have heard her come in? She stood so near with the curtain in her hand. Her other hand was on her mouth and she stared at me, disgust, pity, and hatred all together in one look.

"Get off him! Please, Max, get off!"

I was about to answer when I saw the girl over her shoulder. She must have been standing out in the hall and came into the room when she heard Lily yell. Seeing me on top of Lincoln, she raced over and grabbed me by the hair. I read her T-shirt. It said "Nine Inch Nails." The same shirt she'd worn yesterday when Lincoln was alive. The same dirty pants and combat boots. The same white spiky hair and sixteen-year-old face. Little White.

She grabbed my hair and pulled my head back, screaming at me to get off! Get off! In that shrill, furious, sixteen-year-old girl's voice.

I let her pull me. I let her take me off and away from Lincoln. I let her, because seeing her there then as she really was, as she had been all the time, I *knew*. Inside me she had forced a terrible eye to suddenly open and see the truth.

It was only then that I knew, or understood, or whatever the right word is. I knew this girl was sixteen and had always been sixteen. I knew that there were no angels. Knew that short hours ago I had been given one last chance to save my son but had lost it through my madness and excuses.

There was no place left for me.

How lucky Lincoln was to be dead.

And he *was* dead.